NEWBORN DECEIT

How far would you go for the truth?

K T Lyon

ISBN-9798597104805

For
Albert
&
Robert
Loved and missed dearly every day
We will always wake up with you both in our hearts
xx

CONTENTS

Newborn Deceit

Prologue

Cassandra

Hushed whimpers circle around the darkness in my head. I can't open my eyes, but I know they're near me.

He's here. He's here, safe. I hear him, my baby.

All the pain has gone, but the bed is cold and wet. I'm exhausted—my body drained of energy. I struggle to open my eyes. My eyelids are so heavy. I fight with every ounce of my being to open them, to catch just one glimpse of him, my beautiful baby boy. He's finally here. I quickly forget the horrific pain when I hear him, his gentle whimpers reach out to me, he needs his mummy.

I try to lift my arms, to summon him to me but fail, some invisible force weighing me down, pinning me to the bed. Why can't I move, what the hell is wrong with me?

The whimpers break into a cry. Please, I say. Please give him to me, but the words sit on my tongue, too weak to speak. I don't understand; I didn't have any drugs, no pain relief. I refused everything so I wasn't groggy after the birth, to have a clear mind and remember my baby boy being brought into the world.

God, I'm so tired. I'm still lying in darkness—shuffles of feet, heartfelt cries of my baby boy echo over voices in the background. Voices I don't recognise. I try to move, my eyes flicker open and closed, then again long enough for me to catch a blurry vision of a woman at the side of the bed.

'She's coming round.'

I think that's the midwife, I can't remember her voice. Or her being dressed in pink. I can't think clearly. Who was in the delivery room earlier? Where is... Then I feel his hand clutch mine, but I can't reciprocate.

'It's okay, it's okay. Everything's going to be okay,' he says, his voice choked but protective.

'Our baby,' my voice is low, strained, 'Our boy, is he....'

'Shh, everything's going to be okay,' he answers. His other hand is gently running through my hair, calming me.

The noises are fading, I'm falling asleep again, I'm exhausted.

Please, no!

Stay awake, stay awake! Just for one hold, one look at my boy but I can't fight it, I'm forced against my will to let go into silence.

One

Stephanie

Saturday, March 9, 2019

Am I still a dead woman? The question haunts me less than it used to, but my mind still wanders with fear of the unknown.

I feel out of place—uncomfortable. My bones are tense as I sit facing out to the town, studying all those mysterious faces rushing by in the pouring rain. I wish I was one of them; I envy them almost, but instead, I'm sitting here in an unbearably awkward silence.

Everything about me feels off today. My senses tingle, alerting me. But of what? Eliza continues to sit in ignorance across from me, shuffling her paperwork back and forth, scanning every page through her thick-lensed reading glasses. Torturing me, just because she can. She looks that type.

The light bursts of air from swaying paper are hypnotising, I tilt my head back slightly and press my eyes closed. Busily quiet conversations overrun the room, mumbled words being exchanged from one table to the next, but I can still hear *dead woman, dead babies, murders*, clearly in my mind over all the chaotic whispers. I drop my head and open my eyes, trying to shake off the thought.

Eliza's old school mannerisms are intimidating. Her black

outfit screams funeral rather than business lunch. I've probably been to livelier funerals than this. If it weren't for the luminous glow of fairy lights stretched over the restaurant ceiling, I'd be watching the door for the Grim Reaper turning up for lunch reservations. My caramel brown hair pulled tightly into a ponytail, making me feel exposed. My hands fidget nervously with my crisp white table napkin, wrapping it around my fingers over and over like it's my safety blanket, creasing the once perfectly ironed cloth.

Hm, a tiny safety blanket that wouldn't shield us from anything.

Ah, my unwelcome psyche, peering her sarcastic opinion in when it's not wanted.

Piss off.

Charming.

Sorry, piss off, please!

I wouldn't have called the restaurant a classy place. Stretch your arms out and you would violate the next table's personal space. I've had the urge to tell the heavyweight of a man behind me to pull his chair in and give me breathing space since I sat down, but I won't. I've lost the gift of confrontation.

The walls wear shades of scarlet red and pure brilliant white, now pure brilliant dull. Dining tables dressed to perfection in sterile white table linen and sparkling tableware. Kept in beautiful glory by the military like waiting staff with their professional posture and eye for detail, ready to pounce at anyone's command. Floor to ceiling windows connecting to the main entrance projects it's not a place for privacy but still charming.

The lack of conversation kills me, I squirm uneasily in my chair with her hush leaving an opening for me to overthink what she could be thinking, my thoughts wandering into places I try my hardest to avoid.

Screw this.

'How is everything looking, Eliza?' I lean forward, trying to catch her attention with a forced smile, but a grey sparing moustache catches me.

I'm mesmerised by it. The last time I saw that much facial hair draping over a woman's top lip was at my Great-Aunt Annie's funeral when I was sixteen.

'Fine at the moment,' she answers.

She doesn't lift her eyes from the paperwork, I'm thankful because I would talk more at her moustache than directly at her. Not much of a conversationalist, is she?

'Miss Shenton, don't be nervous. You have a solid business plan here.'

Oh, she can speak in full sentences! Instantly I'm relaxed, she's a little less scary when she speaks.

Eliza beams, her eyes skimming every word, her smile growing wider with every new page she turns. 'A very good business plan,' she mutters into herself.

Plans to build a sports centre, with a large, heated swimming pool, a small gym and health room complete with a jacuzzi and sauna. All funded by me and my silent partner, who wishes to remain anonymous.

Your silent partner who is also giving you a massive discount on the building work. I'm slyly reminded.

It's a small plan, but I need Eliza's signature for the building work to start. Her words, not that there were a lot of them, gave me the boost I needed to hear. My psyche finally happy and giving the air a high five with our success, feeling like everything after so long was finally falling into place. I pick up my coffee cup, smiling, happy and slightly smitten with my successful outcome.

'Tell me, Miss Shenton, how long have you been in Valdez?'

'Um, almost six months now, I think.'

Eliza's eyes widen with shock and curiosity. 'Really? I thought you had just moved here. You've done a good job of keeping out of the limelight, so to speak.'

'I like a peaceful life,' I answer quietly, not sure of her line of questioning.

'And what brought you here, of all places?'

'I like cold countries. My daughter and I came for a holiday and never left because we loved it so much,' I tell her.

Rubbish, but I love the cold.

Her eyes spring open in surprise. 'Really? Where did you live beforehand?' Eliza asks.

Geez, it's turning into an interrogation. Eliza has hardly spoken this whole meeting about my plans, and now she's interested in my life. Obviously just nosey, not curious. I want to tell her to mind her own business, but I don't have the balls. I spare her feelings and continue to answer her questions. A new trait I've adopted. I hate it.

'Britain.' I think that narrows it down, although my British accent probably already told her where I'm from.

She leans forward, her dark beady eyes fixed on me, and she asks, 'Your family must miss you both terribly?'

'I don't have any family, only Ava,' my voice now uncomfortably low.

'Husband?'

'No!' I reply more sharply than expected.

Nosey cow.

I let out an exhausted sigh, coughing lightly to clear my throat to let her know I don't want to continue with her line of nosey questioning, but her eyes fix on me, her lips slightly parted as though another question is about to release. I glance forward over my coffee cup to break eye contact. A face at the window catches my eye, drawing me to him, and I find myself unable to look away.

The face perched on a lifeless body, standing between the crowd of customers queuing outside. Rain drips rapidly from his jet-black hair. His dark marble eyes stare through me, as though he's looking through the window at an empty room.

I remember that face.

The collar of my dusty rose shirt grows tighter, squeezing my throat whilst I wait in anguish for him to move. My whole being is unsteady, throwing me off guard with my heart failing. A face that haunts me, making my nightmares become a reality, and I suffocate in his glare.

The background chatter in the restaurant dies, an eerie silence flare's and suddenly I'm alone. My heart thumping so hard and fast it's in rhythm with the buzzing in my ears. I sink further and further into my mind, my breathing frenzied beyond my control.

Breathe, for Christ's sake, breathe!

My vision blurs, I close my eyes tight, trying my hardest to focus on my breathing. Inhaling deep breaths through my nose, exhaling through my mouth, my hands trembling, trying to grip onto each side of the oak dining chair to ground myself. Squeezing tighter and tighter, until my fingers drain of colour and feeling.

Breathe!

I try desperately to revive myself, focusing on where I am, who's beside me. I'm not alone, I'm not alone! Focus. I'm at lunch, I can smell freshly brewed coffee, I can see a cup sitting in front of me, the cup I was drinking from. I ease my grip of the chair and loosen my top button with my aching fingers. My breathing calming slowly, I hear voices again, muffled in my ears.

'Stephanie, are you okay?' Eliza asks, panic clear in her voice.

My vision adjusts, and I can see her face clearer, a young blond-haired server standing behind her, looking startled.

'Will I get the manager?' the server asks, unsure of the procedure for dealing with anxiety attacks by crazy customers.

The mumbled conversations circulate the restaurant again. My breathing still troubled, along with my subconscious. My persistent mind still behind, trying to gather my thoughts. Wrapping my arms around myself, feeling vulnerable.

'I'm sorry, I think I just became overwhelmed with everything,' I say, my breathing exhausted, my heart regulating, leaving the start of a pounding headache forming behind my eyes.

'Are you sure? I thought I'd lost you for a minute?' Eliza asks, her face squinting to look at me, apprehensive of my useless excuse.

I'm not insane, I'm fully aware of the prying eyes watching me from the surrounding tables. Panic builds inside me again. I need to get out of here now.

Apologising profusely, I push my chair out and try to stand up with my trembling legs, leaving me unbalanced. The heavyweight man behind me offended with my surge of strength, firing him forward in his chair and nearly into his plate of lunch. I think he can afford to miss a meal.

Eliza stands with me, but I ignore her, gathering my bag and jacket, leaving as quickly as I can.

'I'll call you, Miss Shenton.'

Eliza's voice echoes behind me as I weave in and out from the cramped tables, my legs still trembling. The stares of strangers pushing me to walk faster. I rush out through the door, banging past the messy line of customers. I stand for a few minutes in the rain, trying to breathe in the cold air. Looking right and left, then again, over and over. Looking for his face, it's disappeared from sight as quickly as it appeared.

Was it really him?

The judgemental stares from strangers choke me, my unsteady legs feel like they're about to buckle under the pressure. I need to get away from here. Without looking, I run across the street. Blasts of horns loud in my ears, but I don't dare turn around, focusing on my car straight ahead. My hands tremble, desperately trying to start the engine, and finally, I pull away, semi-hysterical. Before I realise it, my car has come to a stop in a familiar place I have been so many times before, in the frantic panic I've driven to my safe haven.

Two

Stephanie

Sitting fretfully dreaming out of the side window of the car, I watch as the glistening frost forms after the rain has stopped. Stunning, perfectly imperfect shaped crystals cover the glass from the last days of winters frosty breath. The inside of the car so cold, when I exhale my breath turns to fog. But still, I sit here with the ignition turned off. Sharp chills of cold gushing through my skeleton, my wet ponytail dripping down my back, analysing my very public anxiety attack, not to mention my hallucination.

Hallucination or reality?

Shit, I don't know the difference anymore. The first time I thought I saw him wasn't like today, or any time after, but this time was horribly real, too real for me to process.

I would see his face blending between strangers in busy crowds, standing on street corners watching me as I drove past. Almost every night, my dreams would quickly snap into nightmares. His wicked face would come to me, standing firm wearing an erroneous smile that was shielding his evil mind.

'He should be in jail,' I mutter under my breath with apprehension, banging my head against the leather-bound steering wheel.

But what if he's not?

'He should be.'

And even if he isn't in jail, how could he possibly have found us?

I try to calm myself, taking deep breaths in and out, over and over. Telling myself no one knows where we are, no one should know where we are.

I enjoy being hidden here, invincible between the snowy Sitka Spruce trees. The trees so high that when you look up, you can't even see the lonely blue winter sky above the grey mist surrounding them.

My favourite time of the year, winter. The crisp fogginess of the dark mornings and early dark nights, sitting beside a hot burning log fire with the smell of searing wood circulating in the air. I love to sit and watch the snow falling outside. Winter all year round, or near enough. To me, it is simple perfection. How could I not settle here? Give me minus zero temperatures over a scorching sun any day. I was never one to lie on a beach with my pasty skin frying in the sun. Lobster red wasn't a colour that wore well on me.

My body's aching with the bitter cold, I turn the key and fire up the car engine. Rubbing my hands together vigorously, waiting for the heat to circulate the inside of the car. I should drive back to the cabin, but something is stopping me. What if it was him and he's waiting there for me? Maybe I should drive to Olivia's?

I feel sick.

The bile has been swirling in my stomach since I woke up this morning, I couldn't even look at my breakfast. Probably nerves. My overly embarrassing anxiety attack hasn't helped much.

My head tilts up and rests against the driver's seat, squeezing my eyes tightly shut. A memory of his touch flashes over me and a shudder of gut-churning regret follows. My eyes spring wide open. What the fuck was that?

Another memory follows. His weight on top of me, his heavy breath soaking into my neck. Fighting with myself not to cry, shadowing any sign of remorse. Bile swirls faster in my stomach, and it burns as it travels up my throat. Stinging wears over my skin as my mind floods with repressed memories I had locked deep down in the darkest hole of my mind. Sitting in the bathtub scrubbing my skin over and over and over until it bled. The blood diluting with the scalding water running from the showerhead, onto my disgraced body, then sucking away down the drain, along with his fingerprints and his scent. No matter how necessary it was to get that book from him, I will forever hold a fierce mortification in my heart for letting him touch me.

My arms console me in shame. Wrapping them around my shaking torso, begging my psyche to lock that memory back in the pit of my mind again where it belongs.

Rain begins again, fiercely smashing down around me. It had to be my mind playing tricks on me after Eliza quizzing me. It was my anxiety spiking under pressure. My heart races, I feel it thumping through my chest again as the scene from the restaurant sticks on replay and I'm unable to stop it.

A surge of bitter memories run instantaneously, forcing me to remember them. Ache clinging to them as they swirl unbidden in my throbbing head. My sanity fading as I'm abruptly thrown into a comatose of regret and sheer panic, wondering what has happened back home.

I need away from here. I can't be on my own. I'm driving down the highway towards Olivia's before I can catch my breath.

'Stephanie, breathe. What's wrong? What's happened? Is it Ava?' Olivia sounds worried.

I try to answer, but my words fail. My breathing laboured from the excruciating marathon being completed in my mind. Jumping over hurdles of past terrors, hidden away memories catching my feet, pulling me back as I battle forward to get away from them.

Olivia guides me to the kitchen, sits me at the table and rummages through a drawer beside the oven.

'Take this and breathe.' She hands me a paper bag. The old ways are the best, she always says.

I hold the bag tight around my mouth, taking long, hard breaths in and out, in and out, over and over. Following the drill. Ground myself, focus on my surroundings. I feel myself settling with Olivia beside me, her arm around my back, her other hand holding mines. My breathing now flowing softer into the paper bag.

'I'm going to call–'

'No,' I yell, shaking my head frantically before she can finish.

I remove the bag from my mouth. 'No please, don't. Ava is fine. I'm fine, I'm just being silly, please ignore me.' I force a smile, not very convincingly, and wipe my cheeks dry.

Olivia studies me, her eyes scanning my face and says, 'You wear that fake smile well, Stephanie. Fine is a bold word with a lot of meanings hiding behind it, and it's so easy to fake a fine smile. But one day the fake smiles and the *I'm fines* will become overpowering. They will consume you, and you will have no power left to do any of it anymore. Sometimes the best medicine is the truth.'

Olivia is right, there is only so long I can carry on pretending everything is fine. Fine is a bold word with so many meanings and a lot of responsibility clinging to it.

She waits for my next response. Her face is so calming, so friendly and warm that I can't control myself. A fresh wave of tears overtakes me, streaming from my eyes, dripping from my cheeks onto my shirt. The tears soak rapidly into the silk with every fresh drip.

'I thought I saw someone at the window when I was in Aunty Yum Yum's today.'

'Who sweetheart?' Olivia asks.

I shake my head, and tell her, 'Someone from my past.'

'Ava's father?'

I can't answer for fear of endangering her. I'm not supposed to tell anyone.

She pulls me tighter into her arms. 'Stephanie, please, I can't help you unless you tell me what's happened. You need to tell someone before the secrets swallow what's left of your sanity.'

I nod, defeated, Olivia is right. She waits patiently for me to compose myself as I fight back the tears. 'I don't know where to begin, Olivia.'

'The beginning is always the best place, keeps things simple and flowing.'

I let out a low-toned laugh, simple? 'Things haven't been simple for a very long time.'

'Then start with the good times.'

'The good times?'

'I know they're hiding somewhere in there. It couldn't have

all been bad,' Olivia answers.

They are in here somewhere, hiding from the darkness in the shadows of my heart, and I remember.

'There's only one place I can start,' I pause cautiously. 'With her.'

Olivia watches me tentatively, her expression never faltering, her warm smile pushing me to continue.

'With Freya.'

Three

Freya

Three months I'm gone, and I come back home to find Mum has taken in strays off the street, I feel my back teeth grinding together with irritation that I wasn't here to prevent it. Now I need to listen to her banging on about giving him, boy wonder, a chance. I take a deep breath in, allowing my jaw to relax before answering her.

'Sorry, Mum, not going to happen!'

'But Freya...'

'But nothing, he's not my type, simple. Besides, I thought you were more his type than mine?' I say, my tone sharp, serious, and I cut Mum off with my matter-of-fact question before she can say anymore.

Not amused, she squints her head at me in disapproval, narrowing her eyes to warn me from my mood. She's too easily wound up, and as entertaining as it is to see her flustered and annoyed, I know my limits. Time to back off.

'Please just come for me. See how it goes, then you can leave,' Mum pleads.

I know I'm losing this argument considering it's with the woman I take my stubbornness from. At five-feet, she towers over my five-feet-ten with her feistiness.

'Can't you just partner your new friend up with one of the cougar club since that's clearly his thing?'

'Freya! Enough!' Mum screeches and bangs her coffee mug

down on the kitchen worktop. She's not amused, her face stern.

Too far Freya, well done.

Shit.

My annoyance grows, and as hard as it is, I try to hide it. Mums always saw me as a bit of a flight risk since I've always taken off on last-minute trips alone. I say I'm more spontaneous, she would argue unpredictable. Now boy wonder is here I won't be doing that again in a hurry. Time for a slight role reversal; I can't trust Mum on her own. I must be the one to sort her mess out, whether she likes it or not.

The thought enters my mind as I sip another mouthful of coffee that boy wonder hasn't made an appearance today yet, not his usual behaviour. He's always hanging around somewhere, a foul smell that clings to me since I had the misfortune of being introduced to him. Why she offered him a room, I have no idea! She's too soft. Believing his story that his landlord sold the property he'd been renting. She was too quick to offer him the loft conversion. If I were home, he wouldn't have got one foot over the door. Yes, I'm a bit of a control freak, but my intentions are always good. One thing I'll say for my Father, he gave me the sense to see through bullshit.

Payday must have flashed before his eyes when he came across Mum's house, putting a leaflet through the letterbox offering his services as one of those cash in hand, handyman types. Preying on singletons of the older generation by my observations. Well, old-ish—Mum's only fifty-one.

I took it upon myself to ask a few of the neighbours if they had received any junk leaflets, to my displeasure they had. Maybe I'm wrong? I doubt he will hang around when he finds out Mum doesn't have any actual money—it's all tied up in the house. Passed down to her by her Mum, it's been in the family for ninety-eight years, or something like that. She's living in one hell of a nest egg, would never dream of selling.

I know she can't see it, though. I see the way she is around him, acting like the brightly glowing sun shines out from his perfect arse. And I've seen the way he is around her, handyman? Please! My skin crawls as I shudder at the thought.

Bastard!

My train of thought mutes by sky news, muttering in the kitchen's background. The story catches my attention.

'...suspected murder...'

I lift the remote control and turn the volume up a few notches.

'The remains of a man believed to be in his twenties was found early this morning by a neighbour. No reports yet on how or why the foxes were in the property. Our onsite reporter will have more to report shortly.'

What the hell? Why would anyone want to live with foxes?

Mum turns to face me. 'What a terrible world this is becoming.'

One of the many reasons I'm not having children, world's gone all the wrong shades of shit. I'll keep that to myself for now, though. I've had enough lectures for one day.

'Sounds fishy that,' Mum says, her phrase to most things she doesn't understand. 'Murder, I'm guessing.'

Hm, no shit Sherlock, the reporter did already say that.

'Yes, an extremely morbid one, so least we're safe up here in Stirling away from it,' I answer, trying not to sound sarcastic.

I stand from the barstool and drink what's left of my coffee. I want to leave before I bump into boy wonder.

'I hear its gang-related. The victim is only twenty-seven. Drugs, I'm guessing after listening to the interview with the neighbour,' a voice answers, echoing from the hall.

And right on cue, there he is, swaying into the kitchen like he owns the place.

'Not far off your age then, there's hope yet,' I smirk and wait for Mum's telling off, but to my surprise, she remains quiet. Embarrassed, probably guessing by the colour of her face.

'Morning Freya, looking as stone-faced as ever, I see.'

'Morning Nathan, sounding as dickish as ever, I see.'

Touché dickhead, can't even bring myself to follow through the pleasantries with him.

Mum's rolling her eyes, a warning, best play nice. I laugh into my coffee at the fact that was me playing nice. And gang-related? I didn't hear any mention of an interview with a neighbour.

Just as I part my smart lips with another sarcastic remark to ask where he heard this interview, he begins, 'TV was on while I was in the shower. Heard the full report.'

What the hell? It's like he's reading my mind, irritation is brewing. I tell Mum I'll call her later as I saunter from the kitchen to the hall to find my car keys. Walking past him sparks the temperature of my blood.

'Have a lovely day darling,' he shouts behind me.

All I can say through gritted teeth is, 'Oh piss off,' before closing the front door behind me as fast as possible before Mum chases me for a telling off. I've been at the receiving end of quite a few lately, feeling like I'm a teenager again.

Why the hell does he annoy me so much? No man ever gets under my skin as he does. There is no attraction to him, my defences are looking out for Mum. That must be it. I always make sure I'm in control with men, and I never entertain men... shit, boys, like him.

Mum's quick on her heels, I hear the door fly open and slam against the wall as I reach the side of my car parked on the driveway. Why can't she see him for what he really is, a gold digger? It's upsetting to think of anyone taking advantage of her, again.

'Freya, that was beyond rude,' Mum snaps, her shoulders relax, and her expression mellows. 'I'm not mad with you, sweetheart, I'm disappointed. What's happened to you since you got home?' Mum folds her arms and exhales loudly with a sorrowing sigh.

Shit. The guilt train crashes right into my heartstrings. It's disheartening, the upset this is causing between us. I know a lot of it is my attitude. For once I should put my stubbornness to sleep, for Mum's sake. As hard as that is, I will.

Really?

Hm, I'll try.

'I'm not interested in Nathan like that. Give him a chance. For me?' Mum asks.

I know Mum isn't interested in him romantically, nor sexually, but I also know he's not interested in me that way. He's interested in Mum. I wonder if I played even nicer, would it only be a matter of time before he made his move? Then Mum would see his true colours and kick him out of the house.

'Not every man out there is like Dad, Freya, you need to stop thinking they are and give someone a chance,' Mum reaches out with her soft voice and hugs me. 'You're twenty-seven. If you keep up that emotional wall then before you know it, you will be my age and very, very alone.'

And there it is, I sink into her arms and feel I'm five-years-old again. I let her know I will attend her party. I can't say no again. I walk away, turning back to smile at Mum before I step into my BMW X5 series. Black, like my soul.

As I start up the car, the Foo Fighters best of you sound through the speakers, I crank it up a couple more notches and instantly relax. Dave Grohl screams is someone getting the best, the best of you... No, my friend, Dave, they are not.

Four

Freya

Okay, time to wear a smile, exchange pleasantries, grab a gin and cranberry, then I'll go upstairs. Mum can't argue with that, at least I'm here.

My gut tightens at the thought Mum thinks I don't want to be here. Of course I want to be here. I so badly want Mum to do great and I know she will. Her talent for creating is rare, I'm completely in awe of her and her work. Nathan, I just can't stand to be around.

From a young age I've been unimpressed by a lot of shit, as I grow older it has only gotten worse. Nathan is the shit I can do without.

The large summer house Nathan's been working on looks spectacular. He's good with his hands, that's one positive thing I'll say for him. Not to his face though, I wouldn't give him the satisfaction of my gratification, nor degrade myself to give him a compliment.

Mum has created and hung an exquisite piece of copper tapestry, resting horizontally from the roof with thin weaved strings of copper lighting in between the rods to illuminate the room. The copper tree sculptures scattered around the room compliment the hanging piece. She really has outdone herself—never fails to amaze me.

'Freya, sweetheart, you're home,' Mum beams.

Her eyes roll over my clothes as she hands me a gin glass encased in copper lace. She knows me well.

'Sorry, work ran over.'

'That's okay, it will only take you ten minutes to run up to your room and get changed.'

Changed? What's wrong with my clothes? I'm not going to be here long enough for it to be worthwhile to change.

'My clothes are fine, Moira,' I say and give her a cheekily squint smirk.

She hates it when I call her Moira, she reciprocates with blue steel wearing on her face. You'd think my leather tunic was rags.

'Fine, petal, you're being sociable, I suppose that's something.'

Ignore it, Freya, breathe. 'So, how's it going tonight? Your works looking amazing, Mum. I'm so glad you showed some of it off. And the glasses are stunning.'

Another of Mum's original creations, making her own glasses. Mum has been creating art since I can remember, I think it's her release from the real world. I've been saying to her for years she should showcase her work again, but she forever declines. I don't think her confidence could take the hit of rejection. Until boy wonder showed up and mentioned it. Then she decided it was time. It's about the only praise I'll give him, seeing Mum this happy. Then again, he would suggest it, if it made Mum more money for him to get his hands on. I shake off the thought.

'Ah Freya, you decided to join us.'

Join us? Arsehole. Right on cue, he appears from nowhere, gloating with his smug expression. More deep breaths, Fee. Take big fucking deep breaths. In and out, in and out.

'No, I decided to join my mother,' I spit. I turn my back, smiling through gritted teeth, and walk away.

And with two large gulps, my gin and cranberry juice is gone. I'm going to need another one of these if I'm going to survive another hour of watching him floating around Mum's guests like he's her manager. Or even worse, her partner. Sick rises at the thought.

Double gin it is this time.

'Best go easy on the gin, didn't take you for much of a drinker.'

I jump as my lips are resting on my glass. Deep breaths, in and out. 'Christ, quite the magician you aren't you,' I say with haste.

'And why's that then?' He shuffles to the side of me and stands casually waiting for an answer, one hand resting in his suit trouser pocket, the other holding a glass of champagne.

He enjoys seeing me wound up. His eyes lit up in amusement.

'Because you seem to appear every time I think of trash, just like magic.'

His lips press together as he tries to sustain his smile, great now he's smirking at me. My irritation grows.

Game on, boy wonder.

'I think you and I got off on the wrong foot, Freya. I'm not sure why?' he asks, his expression plain, curious, waiting for an answer.

'You have no idea, do you?' I didn't take him for the stupid kind. That or he's an excellent actor.

I finish my gin and turn around to pour another as I search for the words to warn him off Mum and not sound like a psycho. 'I don't like people sniffing around my Mum, or around her money should I say. Especially people who are young enough to be her son and overstaying their welcome,' I say.

I think that was clear enough, quite proud of myself. Feeling quite giddy, actually. Must be the gin kicking in. The pressing smile falls away from his face, he looks pissed.

Good.

My stomach churns as I watch him straighten himself up and I wait for his retaliation speech, standing tall with my shoulders straight. I never was one to back down from an argument. Another trait I take from Mum.

'You have no idea how wrong you are, do you, Freya?'

What? How wrong I am? He has a cheek telling me I'm the one who's wrong. Deep breaths!

I laugh.

He takes a step closer to me, so close I can feel his breath on my face as he looks down to me and I feel a surge of irritation at how good he smells. He smells like expensive aftershave and sweet champagne. Probably some expensive aftershave his last conquest bought him. I have a flash of him cooing over some other woman who's double his age, splashing out on him like some extravagant pet.

'It's not Moira I'm interested in, or was should I say, well not romantically anyway. Moira treats me like a son, and I had no idea what that was like because I grew up getting shuffled from home to home. You're all she spoke about when I started working for her, and it intrigued me to meet her daughter with the heart of gold. I saw pictures of you about the house and felt like I had known you for a lifetime before we even met. I used to stand and look at your smile, how wide and sincere it looked. Then the day you come home from hiking all over God knows where, all I ever thought about you went right out the window. All you've done since you got home is throw your toys out of your pram like a spoiled little rich girl,' Nathan replies, stopping to take a drink of his champagne, looking drained.

I feel a pain like something sharp has just pressed through my skin into my stomach. Not a feeling I'm familiar with. Is it guilt? No, it's humiliation.

He continues, 'I had no idea how wrong I got you. The heart of gold is just a cold swinging brick in a dark space. I have never met someone as arrogant and judgemental as you, Freya.'

I'm speechless. My mouth drops open in surprise. When was the last time I was lost for words? I can't remember. Swinging brick for a heart? Is he insane? How dare he? He doesn't know me. Rage brews, but I can't find the words to defend myself. I know it's because he's right and the rage is quickly extinguished. I've never given myself a chance to get to know him because I was trying to protect Mum from him. I was too young to protect her from Dad, but I could protect her from him.

Mum used to be so full of life, and she put her love for life into painting and sculptures. She owned a small independent gallery in Stirling and did extremely well until her husband, my Dad, cleared her out and she was forced to sell up. I wasn't about to let someone else clear her out of what she has left.

With a large gulp, I try to swallow my pride, something I'm not familiar with and try my best to answer. How could I have gotten him so wrong and let him get me even more wrong in the process?

'Nathan, wait, please,' I call after him as he walks away, his head slouched down looking at the ground. 'Can we start again?' Not the best apology, but I'll work on it.

He stops and turns to face me, a half-smile wearing on his face. He shakes his head and continues to walk away. I stand on my own, embarrassed, brought down to size.

Emma is standing in the corner, watching, and looks just as embarrassed as I do, although she looks like she's cringing. She lifts her hand, gesturing for me to go after him.

'Idiot,' she mouths at me.

'Who cares if he's after money, fuck him then throw him out,' was her advice on our first catch up when I returned home.

Fuck, she's right. Not the fucking part, I am an idiot.

'Nathan,' I call again, and walk towards him, the heels of my shoes clicking as I go. 'Please, will you at least let me try again?'

He stops, facing me. I stiffen slightly as his eyes roll over me, waiting for the punchline I expect. 'Okay, I'd like that.'

The look on his face, the fact he's willing to forgive my behaviour or at the very least try to, tugs at my heart and it sinks to the bottom of my stomach.

He turns and walks back to the table behind us, lifting two flutes in one hand and a bottle of champagne in the other, gesturing to the patio doors with it and like a puppy I unconsciously follow.

Why do I feel so nervous? Light fluttering in my stomach. I sit on one of the iron chairs, overlooking the dark fields behind the house. The faint noises of the farm animals in the distance surround us, along with the glow of the fairy lights Mum has wrapped around the pergola and evergreen trees in the garden.

Again, I'm lost for words. Guilt of being such a moody bitch to someone I have never given a chance to play heavy on my mind.

Nathan hands me both flutes and pops open the champagne bottle, pouring it into both glasses, and I watch as the bubbles overflow from the flutes, running down my hands and onto the wooden decking beneath us.

He kneels beside me, sitting the bottle down by his side and cups his hands around my wrists. He lowers his head and sucks up the escaped sweet drink from my hands with his lips. My breathing hitches, hurting my chest, taking me by surprise. His lips are so soft, so gentle. A flash in my mind wonders what his lips would be like on mine.

Fuck, what is going on?

Less than twenty minutes ago I couldn't stand to be in his company, feeling nothing but hatred, and now I'm fantasising about him. About his soft lips in other places, anywhere on my body.

Get it together Freya, when was the last time a guy had this effect on you so quickly?

Never, definitely never. A new first.

'Thank you,' I mutter, releasing my wrists from Nathan's grasp and take a sip of champagne.

'What for?' he asks, taking a seat beside me.

'For getting Mum to do this, she has a glow about her I haven't seen in a long time.'

'Why did she stop?' he asks, turning to face me. His stunning, hazel eyes running over my face like he's trying to read my thoughts.

I try to compose myself. Coughing hard to clear my throat and nervously fix my eyes on my hands.

'Mum studied art before I was born, she fell pregnant with me and dropped out of uni. When I was three, she got back into it and eventually opened her own gallery. She was doing so well, the emotion she put into her work was beyond exceptional. I used to love watching her creating, I remember crying when she would complete a piece because she would cry. When I was four, she gave me my first camera so I could capture the moments that made me the happiest and her feel alive. That's when my passion for photography started,' I tell him and look up to see him still watching me contently.

'My Dad didn't work, he just lived off Mum. I think it was a relationship of convenience. My Gran and Papa were old school. She had made her bed, so it was her job to lie in it. I used to hear him when I was little smashing up her work. She found out he was having an affair with her accountant and kicked him out and he thanked her in return with two broken ribs and a bashed in face. Couple of days later she found out they had cleared her out and done a runner. Mum never pressed charges or chased them for the money, I think she was just glad to see the back of him,' I explain.

A lump has formed in my throat and I try my best to swallow it, not one for being an emotional wreck in public.

'And that's why you're so protective of Moira. I think that explains the ice queen act a bit clearer now,' he says, his voice is husky like he too is trying to swallow a lump in his throat.

I nod in recognition and we sit in silence, enjoying the serene night as though a great battle has just called a truce.

I wake with a start, a migraine is lingering behind my eyes, too much gin and champagne. This is exactly why I don't drink, the fear of absent memories, the fear of the unknown.

I need a coffee.

What if I bump into Nathan in the kitchen? I'm sure I dreamt of him last night, although the memory is hazy.

My phone vibrates from under my pillow.

Emma.

'Good morning sunshine, how are we feeling today?' Emma's voice is too high—it vibrates through my head, antagonising my hangover. 'I haven't seen you that drunk... Ever! What made you get in that state, anyway?'

'Fuck, I don't know? I can remember necking gins, then champagne. Must be mixing my drink.'

'Or the effect sexy Nathan has on you,' she teases.

I feel her smile through my iPhone.

'Ha, please. I've been a dick to him, he had every right to walk away from me.'

I shudder at my behaviour.

'Maybe that's what you've needed all these years, a man to kick you into shape,' she answers, and she's right.

Christ, I've never been treated like that before. I'm usually the one tossing them away.

'I'm going back to bed, text me later and let me know everything. Love ya.'

'Love you too, ace face,' I whisper.

I throw the phone down onto the duvet. God, I can't face him. I know it's inevitable since we live in the same house. How will I act around him? How will he be with me?

Get it together!

I throw myself back into bed, pull my pillow over my face and try to clear my thoughts of last night.

I'm pleasantly surprised at how tidy the house is when I head downstairs, you wouldn't even know there had been a party last night or that a house full of potential buyers for Mum's collection drank themselves through fifty bottles of champagne: very impressive. I would go as far as saying it was better than one of my tidy ups after the entire school had been at my house *studying* while Mum was away for an overnight break with Aunt Margaret and I was looking after my cousin Emma, four years my junior.

Rich people never say no to a freebie, probably why they have money.

I wonder if Mum's still sleeping. Not like her, she's usually up banging about somewhere in the house. She stayed up relatively late tidying up, though. And no Nathan? Maybe not a bad thing?

I fetch my travel mug, fill it with coffee, and head to my two o'clock photoshoot at Callendar House in Falkirk with a soon-to-be-married couple. Both very sweet, and not shy of public displays of affection. Wouldn't be me, not the public displays of affection, I mean. Well, that too actually, but the marriage part. Marriage, kids, no thank you. I like my freedom too much. Safety in numbers? More like safety with one. That's me.

There's unspoken beauty in photographing a part of the world that's not spoiled with concrete and human life. I love the serenity of outdoor life. Peaceful and pure, the way the world should be. But for now, capturing it in photo form is all I have, until my next trip at least.

Clasping my Nikon in my hand, my eyes closed, I draw the deepest breaths of air into my lungs. The best way to clear my thoughts—thoughts of Nathan confusing my feelings. My head is in turmoil and I have no idea why I'm tangled up in my own emotions. I don't like it. I open my eyes and shake it off. It's very frustrating.

In the distance I see the smallest of birds gliding in-front of a sheet of burning red sunset. I raise my camera eye level and snap a few shots. I can already see the developed pictures in my mind.

The colours bringing back my first emotions watching it with my Papa when I was young.

When my eyes are closed again, I relax. I can feel him close, almost as though he was standing next to me. Water fills my eyes and I'm quickly reminded he's gone. My memories are all I have of the gentleman in my life who never once let me down.

The grass crunches behind me, and I spin around. For a minute I think it's him. He knew how much I loved this place. I'm both disappointed and happy when I see who it is.

'Hey,' Nathan says cautiously knowing he's scared me. 'Sorry.'

'It's okay, I thought you were... never mind.' I turn back to the sunset and ask, 'How did you know I'd be here?'

'Moira. She said you came here every night before you went home.'

Thanks, Mum. Quite surprised she remembered. It's been a long time since we spoke of me coming here.

'That's quite a spectacular view. I see why you come.'

I nod but don't answer. My feet still trying to find familiar ground on how to act around boy wonder now the rage, to my surprise, has gone. Although I think my suspicion will always be on the back burner.

'Sorry again for last night,' Nathan says, speaking a little husky and I'm confused what the apology is for. My face must reflect this as he continues to explain himself. 'For you know, declining your offer,' he explains, flush showing on his cheeks, he's embarrassed.

My offer? My face again, speaking what I'm thinking.

'To come back to your room. I just, um, you know, think we shouldn't rush things, especially with me going away tomorrow. I'd like to get to know each other better first after the last few weeks.'

I'm lost for words, I'm on unfamiliar ground. My head is throbbing, trying to figure out what is annoying me more. That I came onto him and he refused my advances? That I can't even remember doing so? Or that he's going away tomorrow? Where the hell's he going? And I realise it's the third question, that he's going away. How long for? I need to play this calmly, keep my cool.

'Don't worry, it's only for three weeks. I'm going to help a friend do some building work on their house.'

I'm honestly believing he can read my mind. I used to pride myself on being a closed book, and it's looking like I've met the key to that book.

Say something Freya before he thinks you're simple.

'A friend? A secret wife perhaps?' I laugh, but inside I'm dead serious.

The words spill out before I can stop myself, and I suddenly pray to be swallowed up by a massive hole. I'm losing my grip around him.

He laughs and takes a step closer to me, his hands reach out and rest on my hips. He stands tall and looks down into my eyes. The red of the sunset reflects off the beautiful glassy hazel and I feel my heart flutter with excitement. His nose caved slightly at the bridge, the sign of a once broken nose. He doesn't look like he could hold himself in a fight, too much of a pretty boy, maybe why he ended up with a broken nose.

'No secret women in my life at all, I'm hoping the woman's attention I've been trying to get for some time fills that hole.'

My heart picks up pace as he holds my gaze. For the first time in my life, I long for a man to kiss me, for Nathan to kiss me. The urge to play my usual games and walk away, to leave him hanging slip away from me and I plead in my mind for him to read my proposition and kiss me. Just as I'm lost in my thoughts, I feel his right-hand slip down from my hip and into my hand.

'Come on, let's go home. It's getting cold,' Nathan says, turning to walk away.

He's read my thoughts alright, just not the right one. I yank his hand and summon him back. His eyes lock on mine, our smiles reflecting one another.

'But I can't wait another month for this,' he says, his voice breathy.

Nathan's hands are quickly on my cheeks, running into my hair and he leans in quick, wrestling his tongue through my lips, searching for mines. His hand wandering down my back, tickling gently as he goes until his hand cups my buttock and he pulls me closer to his waist.

My heart is racing, beating hard against my chest as my stomach explodes for him to never stop. In my head, I'm already counting down the days until he's back, back at home with me.

Five

Freya

Fast forward eleven months, I'm in a life I never thought I wanted. If I did, it was at the very bottom of my list.

That's a lie.

This life never made it onto my list. A few weeks after we got together, Nathan was offered a haulage job based in Edenbridge. I was so angry when I found out; I had no idea he had been looking for jobs so far away. We argued back and forth about moving away together and starting a life in England. He didn't want to stay in Stirling; he made that extremely clear, but I did because of Mum. I didn't want to move away from her.

I had already decided I wasn't moving to England but to pacify him we spent a weekend break in Amsterdam deciding what to do. If being together was a good idea? I can't say our relationship was plain sailing, even if it had only been for a short time. Nathan could make my temper explode sky high and then deflate all in the one breath, I knew it wasn't healthy, but the making up afterwards was worth it.

There were two options he told me over dinner on our last night in Amsterdam, move away with him and be together or stay in Stirling and call it quits on our relationship. I still knew I wasn't moving; I could be just as stubborn as him, but then little jellybean was discovered.

So, here we are, in a beautiful English cottage in the Kent countryside. Two floors high, the attic above, covered in medium-sized windows and colony red brick, a timeless classic, covered in wild ivy. Simply stunning, with wild greenery and vast fields of the greenest grass surrounding it.

I first saw it on the website of an estate agent, Nathan had been browsing on my laptop one day and left the website open. It was the name I fell in love with first, The Hollies. I think he secretly loved it and I think he knew I would too. It was a bonus Nathan had found it so close to his new job.

The only problem was the price; it was way over our price limit. When I spoke to Mum about it, she just smiled and nodded, not commenting on it at all. I thought she was upset at first because I was thinking of moving away, then the following week she sat me and Nathan down at the dining table in tears. I thought she was going to tell us she was sick, and I could feel the bile heating my stomach.

She handed me an envelope containing a cheque. A wedding present, she told me, after releasing equity on the house in Stirling. It was both amazing and stupid, but I'm still extremely thankful. If it weren't for her, we wouldn't have been able to buy this piece of heaven outright. I still give myself a shake every day, reminding me it's ours, and it softens the blow of not being near Mum a little.

'You're exhausted Fee. I don't think you should drive,' Nathan comments, shadowing me from the living room, up the hall and back into the kitchen, the heaviness of my wet turban wrapped around my hair weighing me down.

Even my feet are too tired to make an effort and function properly, leaving my slippers to shuffle along the hardwood floor.

'I'm not that bad. The showers woke me up, and I'm only going down the road to meet Layla.'

'Not that bad? So, you didn't put your phone in the microwave instead of Clara's milk?' Nathan frowns, one hand leaning against the worktop, supporting him.

'Maybe?' I turn my back away from him and scrunch up my nose.

Not that I can deny it since he was the one who pulled the phone from the microwave before it blew up, but I'm too stubborn to admit how much the lack of sleep is destroying me. That's like admitting I'm not coping, and I am. I think?

'I'll go pick up your prescription and grab you a strong coffee from Ali's. I'm sure Layla will understand. Please, go back to bed when Clara falls asleep after her ten o'clock bottle.'

A spark of frustration ignites in my stomach at his command, bossy shit. I hate it when he tells me what to do. My fist clenches and I take a deep breath in before I retaliate. I turn to face him, to tell him he's a bossy shit. He puts both hands on my arms and pulls me closer to him before I can open my mouth, planting a soft kiss onto my forehead.

'That's unless you try to heat your phone up again and feed it to her,' he says, teasing me.

'Ha-ha funny guy.' My eye's narrow at him as my fist eases, and I try my best to give him a somewhat cute penetrating stare.

'Please?' he whispers. 'I'll even bring a blueberry muffin back too.'

Anyone would think he was desperate to keep me home, away from Layla, but I really could do with the extra sleep.

Nathan and Layla never really hit it off. She is my soul mate from a different life. We both equally hate men. Well, some of them.

My eyes droop with the bright beam from the kitchen spotlights above us, bouncing off the white silk walls. Nathan is right. I could be a slight danger to myself, just a tiny one, I have never been one to function on very little sleep. I nod my head and agree to stay at home to pacify him.

'Good girl,' he whispers, moving closer to me.

I wrap my arms around his waist, squeezing him playfully tight. I ask, 'And what do I get for being a good girl and doing what I'm told, hm?'

His lips pout, he always pouts when he's thinking, the pout turning into a cheeky smile. Gliding his hands up my arms to cup my cheeks, he kisses me softly on my forehead again, then the tip of my nose and down to my lips, setting my long blonde hair free of the wet towel with a hard yank.

Rough.

His hands drag all the way down my back, clasping my buttocks into his huge palms he lifts me onto the kitchen island with one quick swoop, slowly sliding my legs apart and easing himself between them, the smooth polished quartz cool against my bare skin. My heart races as I unbutton his jeans and release his hardened arousal, his hands working fast as he unties my dressing gown revealing my stiff excitable breasts. His scratchy stubble rips over my skin with an aching pleasure with every kiss he plants on my neck. Excitement sparks all over my body, I feel my skin tingle. It's been so long since we made love, I could burst any minute just from his touch.

The wailing of a newborn baby screeches through the house, and Nathan's head drops on my shoulder with an irritated thud.

'Right on cue from our little distraction vacuum,' his breathing heavy through his words from excitement.

We both burst out laughing as the wails reach a higher pitch of tantrum.

'Stubborn like you. Wants what she wanted five minutes ago. I'll get her.' Nathan straightens up away from the embrace of my legs and walks from the kitchen, buttoning himself up.

'As soon as her eyes shut tonight, you're mine, Mr Lynn!' I shout after him, a laugh escaping him in acknowledgement.

'Ah!' Frustration is a killer, I jump down from the grey quartz, wrapping my dressing gown back around me.

Maybe I'm not exhausted, maybe its sheer sexual tension crying out for satisfaction. I hear a whip-cracking firmly in the back of my mind. Time to tighten the belt around here and show the little madam who's boss.

Adult interaction since Clara came firing into the world has been in short supply. We named her our little distraction vacuum. She was extremely fussy, always cried on cue, sucking up all our attention for herself. Not that I was complaining. As tired as I was, I embraced the exhaustion. Just not today!

I shuffle back up the hall into the living room after Nathan. The white porcelain walls nipping my eyes as I pass. They always seem to keep the house bright when the weather outside is misty and grey with winter unveiling its beautiful presence.

I badly need sleep. Insomnia kicks in with every blink, and I fight to keep my eyes open.

Nathan is sitting on the sofa, Clara wrapped in her marshmallow pink pom-pom shawl. The pom-pom's soft against her body as she sleeps in his arms, blissfully ignorant to the fact she's just disturbed the first spontaneously intimate adult time in weeks and isn't bothering her cute little butt.

'You're ruining her, you know, how is she ever going to learn to self soothe with you jumping at her every demand?' I ask.

He finds this funny, his laugh infectious, and I laugh back.

'Self soothe? If she takes after you, she will never learn how to do that.'

'Cheeky,' I say, curling up on the accent chair across from the corner sofa, watching her wrapping him around her little finger just by simply breathing.

'I can't believe we've had her for a full month. I can't remember life before her now,' he says, completely smitten with her as she sleeps, basking in the glory of being cuddled on demand. 'Happy one-month-old birthday, princess,' he whispers in his gentlest voice.

A smile widens on my face, watching Nathan with her, my perfect little world sitting before me. A perfect little world I wasn't aware I needed. Now I understand how his frustration for sexual attention has disappeared as mine evaporates into the air. If only the little madam would sleep at night, then it would be perfect.

'I want more.'

'More what?' I fear I already know the answer.

'Babies with you.'

'Well, the way things are going, our ickle dose of contraception here might not let that happen,' I say and transfer over to the sofa beside Nathan, he puts his arm around my shoulder.

Not that Clara was planned. I had been taking my contraceptive pill religiously since I was eighteen, so she was an extreme shock, and the shock is still lingering. Not that I would change her for anything. My Gran always said there's worse comes to your doorstep in a lifetime than a baby. I used to think that saying was ridiculous, I understand how right it is now.

'We could always take a trip up to Stirling and see your Mum? I'm sure she'd love to look after Clara while we caught up on some, um, sleep,' Nathan says, giving me a wink.

'Really?' A tearful smile forms on my face.

I miss Mum so much. Even more so now that Clara is here. She watched Clara being born and stayed with us until she was ten days old. That feels like a lifetime ago now.

'Yeah, of course, could even take a trip back to Derwentwater. Could pack the car up tonight and leave first thing in the morning?'

'Tomorrow!' I snap.

I sit frowning at Nathan, trying to figure out what he's up to? That's quick, even for him. At one point, I was sure he was trying to keep me from her until I realised I was hormonal to the point of insanity.

'Well, there is nothing stopping us, I'll need to pop into work early in the morning then we'll leave as soon as I get back. We'll stay with your Mum as long as you like.'

'You're going into work? But I thought you weren't planning on going back?' I ask, my face is quizzical as I watch Nathan's eyes run over me.

'I'm not, the boss is away this week on business, so gives me a chance to clear my stuff out with no hassle.'

'I still don't know why you're not telling him you're leaving. It's like you're running away.'

'Nah, my boss can be an arsehole, he doesn't like losing workers, easier this way,' Nathan explains, turning away from me, his eyes fixed back on Clara.

'Nathan, you haven't even worked for him for a year, it's not like you owe him anything.'

He sighs, his face serious. He takes his hand away from my shoulder and gently hands me Clara, still enjoying her cosy sleep.

'It's complicated, Fee, he's not a nice guy. If he knew I wasn't going back, he'd make my life hell. He's very private about his business, and from what the other guys are saying, he makes it difficult for people to leave. I thought while we're in Stirling we could look at new houses? Abroad maybe?'

'Are you serious? You love this place.'

'I do, we both do, but I love my family more. Listen, we'll talk when I'm home. I'll heat Clara's bottle up before I go, so at least I know the house will still stand when I get back,' Nathan says. His lips form a tight line as he stands to his feet. 'Will you please just get some sleep, and we'll pack when I get back and have an early night. Don't tell anyone we're going to Stirling. Not even Layla.'

'Why?'

Nathan was very seldom serious. He couldn't even be serious

when he found out I was pregnant, he just shrugged it off as *one of those things*, if I remember correctly. All I remember was a lot of crying, a hell of a lot of crying. Babies were never on my to-do-list.

'Um, because it will be a nice surprise for your Mum, that's all.'

The words spill out my mouth before I can stop myself. 'Are you in trouble, Nathan?' I ask, anger spiking.

He bends down in front of me, asking with a deep protectiveness in his voice, 'Do you trust me?'

I stare into his wide hazel eyes, trying to see what's going on behind them. 'Of course, I do, yes.'

'Then please do as I ask, we'll talk on the way to Stirling, I promise.' Leaning forward, he places a kiss on my lips then heads to the kitchen.

I can't help feeling he is holding something back from me, but I do trust him. And seeing Mum is the best thing I could wish for right now.

Clara is stirring again, right on time, 9:58. Little madam knows it's feeding time.

'Here you go,' Nathan says, returning with Clara's bottle, handing it to me with a fresh baby bib.

His face still looks straight, serious, a face I have seen little of. The last time I saw that face was the night we called a truce, and he gave me a reality check with my attitude. So, a face I know means business. Something is on his mind; it's unsettling me.

'I'll take your car Fee if that's okay? Can't find my damn car keys, sure I left them hanging at the door. I won't be long. Love my girls.'

The door opens and closes behind him before I can answer.

'Daddy's away, how does a yummy bottle of milk, nappy change and back to bed sound?' I ask in my new cooing baby tone. Completely out of character for me.

Clara is such a fussy little thing. I can tell by her whimpers going back to bed isn't an option for her. I suppose that's why I couldn't keep up with breastfeeding her, always unsettled, fighting the urge to sleep when she's tired and fights the urge to eat even when she's hungry. She's good at rebelling, like her Mother.

Karma has dealt her next hand.

Well played, bitch.

I change her into her lemon and white polka dot romper suit, everything Mum buys her is lemon, she suits it with her fluffy baby hair.

Cradling her in my arms as we stroll down our narrow hall, humming the tune to when I fall in love by Nat King Cole. It was always my favourite song my Papa used to sing to me when I was little.

Memories of a Sunday morning at his house fill my mind. Papa sitting peeling a huge pot of potatoes for the family coming for dinner, Gran preparing the Sunday roast, Nat King Cole playing softly in the background and my mood drops and lifts again all in the one breath. My heart still aches to think of him.

We stroll past our wall of memories, into the kitchen, around the kitchen island and back out to the hall, and she has finally given into a milk fuelled coma. I walk back to the lounge and lay my weary body down on the charcoal suede sofa, with Clara cuddled into my chest. I blink, and my heavy eyelids refuse to open again.

Six

Freya

The doorbell rings, short bursts repeatedly pinging, over and over. Clara stirs with the sound.

I open my eyes to a view of our vintage pendant light above me. It was here when we bought the house and Nathan loved it so much, I contrasted the living room interior to match it. A rustic solid sideboard rests against a plain white wall, making it pop when you walk into the room. It matches the wood surround for the log fire. I wouldn't say I liked it when we moved in, wanted the fire ripped away when we were redecorating, but Nathan couldn't bear to see it go. He suggested since it was a dated English country house, we should keep as many of the old fixtures as we could. Nathan loved the house, but if I had my way, I would've ripped it to the bare shell and modernised it. I like to be different. It drives him insane. I'm happy I listened to him, though. The house has come together so well.

The doorbell rings again, this time the short bursts extending. I sit up, cradling Clara in my arms, the stirring now light wailing. I feel refreshed; I wonder how long we've slept? I haven't woken up this fresh after a quick nap for a month.

It can't be Nathan; he has a key. It must be Layla. She probably didn't get my text to cancel our coffee date, she hardly ever takes her phone anywhere with her, it's frustrating. Or, she did get my text, and she's turned up to give me hell for cancelling on her.

The bell rings again. *Ping, ping, ping* as though someone's finger is bouncing on and off of the button.

'All right, Layla! I'm bloody coming!'

Like me, she has no patience. I think that's why we get on so well.

The clock catches my eye as I walk to the door, 14:54. God, we've slept for over four hours. Fuck, no wonder I'm refreshed.

Where is Nathan? There's no sign of him at home; my keys aren't on the console table perched beside the front door.

I open the door. Two men are standing on the porch, looking twitchy as their patience is draining, waiting for the door to open. One a police officer in full uniform, expressionless pale face. And the other a smart-looking middle-aged man in a black suit and baby blue tie.

He raises his hand, showing me his identification badge. 'Freya Lynn?' he asks politely.

I was expecting Layla. A wave of shock dissolves over my body.

Becoming quite concerned, I answer, guarded, 'Um yes, I'm Freya.'

'DCI Chalmers and this is Officer Banks,' he replies, returning his badge inside the pocket of his suit jacket. 'Could we possibly come in, Mrs Lynn?'

Why the hell do they want to come in? I don't want them to come in. My guard automatically pitches up a level. Is Nathan in trouble? Have they arrested him? I don't answer them, raising my hand instead towards the sitting room.

I follow behind them, watching Clara, who has fallen back asleep in her swinging crib in front of the unlit log fire, thank Christ. I couldn't listen to her wailing right now.

Both men have sat on the corner sofa. I cautiously take my place on the leather accent chair facing them. Nervously rubbing my hands together, their mannerisms making me think I'm in trouble.

'What can I help you with, Detective?' I ask with false confidence.

The uniformed man reaches into his breast pocket and retrieves a small black notebook, flicks through a few pages and hands it to the Detective.

'Mrs Lynn, I'm afraid I have some upsetting news about your husband, Nathan Lynn,' he says, stopping to glance at his colleague, Officer Banks, whose expression has now turned to one of dejection.

My stomach sinks into oblivion. The sensation you get at the top of a high rollercoaster that's just about to tip over the edge, just enough for you to see you're about to encounter a dangerously steep fall and there's no way of preventing it.

DCI Chalmers faces back in my direction and continues with a solemn sigh, 'I'm sorry to break this news, Mrs Lynn. Your husband was involved in a fatal road traffic accident at 10:07 this morning. I'm afraid he died instantly. There wasn't anything the emergency services could do.'

Every inch of my being has frozen. My mind on pause, not understanding the words I've just heard.

Am I still lying asleep on the couch, dreaming this horrible scenario? This can't be happening; it just can't! Nausea ignites in my stomach, my heartbeat undecided if it should beat faster or stop. Pressure builds in my head as my body trembles.

'No, I don't believe you. My husband has gone to get me a... He's out getting me a... He said he would be back with a muffin. He'll be back any minute,' I say, my words low to a whisper.

'I'm very sorry. This can be extremely hard to take in. Is there anyone you would like us to contact for you?'

I feel the pressure expanding behind my eyes, struggling to keep them open. I don't understand the words coming from the Detectives mouth, his lips move vaguely, but the sounds are strange, a foreign language I don't understand.

'Mrs Lynn, are you okay?' DCI Chalmers is now in front of me, one knee bent to the floor. I can't answer him.

The room is spinning around me faster and faster. Everything is mashing together into nothing but streaks of colour. I try to stand to my feet.

Everything goes dark.

My mind wakes before my body does, unfamiliar voices echo around me. Fragments of a terrifying nightmare linger in my thoughts.

There's a vague aching on my temple, I lift my hand, running my fingers over a piece of rough cloth. What the hell is that? I open my eyes sharply to rid myself of the terrible nightmare, my vision iffy, blinking to clear it.

I'm lying on my sofa, its dark in the living room, a glow from the small lamp perched on the iron side table at the end of the couch is struggling to light the room. At the side of Clara's crib sits a paramedic backpack, crushing the thick piled rug in front of the fire.

Clara! Where is Clara! What's happened to her?

Springing to my feet, I shout for Nathan. My head is now throbbing like I have struck it with a baseball bat.

I see a stranger standing in my hall. It's that Detective standing speaking with another officer, a woman holding Clara.

Reality hits hard. Our eyes lock on one another. My eyes silently asking him if this is all real, his eyes answering back a solemn yes. It freezes my body, empty of feeling. I don't know what to do. My mouth drops wide open with questions, but there are no words. My legs crumble to the floor. Tears flow uncontrollably, my heart dissolving from my body. The Detective heads hastily to me, trying to catch me.

This isn't real.

I'm behind a screen looking out to someone else's life, wishing with all my being this isn't my life I'm watching. Nathan can't be dead. He was just here. How could he do this to me! To Clara! He's just left us alone.

Anger consumes my body. I want to lash out. I want to punch, kick and throw the strangers from my house who have just torn my world apart. I collapse back onto the Detective, my face falls into my hands, sobbing with despair.

'My Mum, I need to call my Mum.'

Mum answers her phone with her usual chirpy *hello petal*. I open my mouth to speak to her, but my words are absent. She can hear me sobbing.

'Freya, you there?' Mum asks. 'Freya, you're worrying me, is it Clara? What's happened? Please answer me, darling.'

'Nathan,' I say, my voice shaky, unable to say anything but his name. I almost get the words out as a new flood of tears descend my cold cheeks, thinking of what I need to tell her next. 'An accident... He's gone.'

She goes silent for a split second, then screams exhale from the phone. I can't control myself any longer, sobbing uncontrollably.

DCI Chalmers cautiously takes the phone from my hand. 'Hello, ma'am. My name is DCI Chalmers. Your son-in-law was involved in a road traffic accident earlier today. Your daughter collapsed after we broke the news and got quite a nasty cut to her head that the paramedics have attended to. We don't think we should leave her alone. Would you be able to attend?'

He's done this many a time before; his professional stature beams years of experience from breaking horrifying news.

Mum composes herself just enough to speak to the Detective. 'I live in Stirling Detective. I'll pack and drive down as soon as possible,' she replies.

'I understand, ma'am. Does Mrs Lynn have any family or friends we could contact just now?'

'Layla, her friend, her telephone number is on the side of the refrigerator.'

'Thank you, Mrs?'

'Anderson, Moira Anderson.'

'Mrs Anderson, I will plan for Layla to be here until you arrive. And please drive carefully Mrs Anderson, you've had quite a nasty shock too.'

Mum is travelling down as soon as possible the Detective tells me. She loves Nathan more than I do if that's even possible? The son she never had she told him every time she saw him. It will crush her heart into a million pieces.

It's just after midnight, and mentally I'm exhausted. The house has been so peaceful since Layla arrived and everyone else left. The news hasn't fully sunk in yet. I've sat on the sofa watching the door, waiting for Nathan to walk in holding my coffee and blueberry muffin from Ali's, wearing a big wide smile on his face, ready to pack for our trip to see Mum. How can everything change so drastically in a few short hours?

I can still feel the tender skin on my neck from his stubble scratching over me. Tears trickle down my red, puffy cheeks again. I need a drink, my throat dry and scratchy.

My feet are unsteady as I walk to the kitchen, one hand leaning on the wall as I go. The wall opposite the staircase, leading to the kitchen, is host to our showcase of memories. Every inch of them covered in picture frames filled with our life's adventures for the past year.

Not one frame matched the other; I collected them from antique shops, charity shops, anywhere that didn't sell the same item in bulk. I liked one of a kind thrift items, some of them probably weren't though, their cousins hanging in a house across the country somewhere with their owner thinking the same as me.

I stop, Nathan's smile drawing me to the photos. Everywhere we went, we had taken as many pictures as we could, captured how we were in that exact moment in time. I could never walk through the hall without stopping to admire them. Always put a smile on my face, even in my bad days. He isn't dead; he can't be. Look at how alive he looks in all the pictures, fantastically full of life. He lit every picture up; I don't think I've ever seen a bad one of him.

The front door flies open, bashing abruptly from the wall, startling me from my wonderful daydream of Nathan's smile. Mum rushes in the doorway with Aunt Margaret in tow. They drove down as soon as the Detective hung up the phone. I don't have any words apart from tears. Her arms wrap tightly around me, and I squeeze her back. Everything said in a hug. She looks exhausted, she's aged years since I saw her a couple of weeks ago.

I used to believe her when she told me that life had a path for us, that everything happens for a reason. What path in life can you go down that possibly thinks that your husband, your best friend, can just die and you won't need them? It's just a load of crap.

Fuck everything happens for a reason!

'Where is Clara?' Mum asks, sobbing into a soaking wet tissue.

'In the sitting room with Layla.'

Mum dashes to the sitting room, I follow behind with Aunt Margaret's arm wrapped around my waist. Clara's sound asleep in another milk coma and oblivious to the fact her Daddy has gone, gone forever. I can't even bear to think about that right now, how I'm going to cope on my own?

'Mum, the Detective is calling back in the morning to take me to the hospital. I have to identify Nathan.' Saying those words doesn't seem to shake me one bit, I'm still expecting to wake up any minute from this hell.

Mum gives Layla a respectful look of gratitude, dismissing her from her duties now she is here. Layla has been unusually quiet. We've sat in silence most of the afternoon. Only when she offered me a cup of tea, I answered.

'I'll come with you, petal, don't worry. Aunt Mags can watch Clara.'

I nod in agreement as Aunt Mags arm squeezes tighter around me because I know by the time morning comes, I will wake up with Nathan beside me. He will hug me when I tell him my horrific nightmare and laugh it off as sleep deprivation and tell me to go back to sleep.

'Are you sure you're ready, Mrs Lynn? This will not be easy, so please take as much time as you need. You can leave when you need to,' DCI Chalmers explains.

We enter the morgue where Nathan's body is being held, his hand resting protectively on the lower of my back, guiding me through the heavy steel door into a room that looks like everything's sprayed with metallic silver paint.

The room is harshly cold, I feel the bitterness biting my skin, the first taste of death. The guilt of liking it makes me feel worse, twisting my emotions further into the pit of grief it has thrown me in. My mindset on autopilot, my body floating, watching from above as every part of me stills.

My wish to wake up from this nightmare beside Nathan didn't happen. Instead, nightmares of car crashes tortured me, along with blood and death. Deathly screeches of steel rebelling from being crushed on impact from its form linger in my ears.

Mum's trailing behind, her hand linked in mines for support, although I know she won't provide much. She spent all night crying, inconsolable. She knew Nathan before I did. She hasn't just lost a son-in-law; she's lost a friend. It makes me feel as though I should support her and not the other way around.

So many mixed feelings are taking up residence in my body that I struggle to control any of them, my head filling with a heavy pressure that I fear may erupt imminently.

They guide us to the side of a steel table, occupied by a white sheet resting on top of a shape resembling a body. My heart crumbles each second, and my breath empties from my lungs making me stumble. My reflexes kick in quickly, my shaky hands grab the table to steady myself. The table is smooth and icy, making my hands drop away to my hips.

I pray quietly into myself once again to let me wake up from this nightmare; I beg to let it be a dream, pleading with God he has tortured me long enough, but selfishly he ignores my silent screams.

Maybe it's a mistake; maybe it's someone else lying under that sheet and Nathan is lying in the hospital somewhere unable to tell me he's okay. Please let it be someone else, anyone else, just not Nathan.

Please, God, I beg, please!

The pressure in my head continues to expand.

'I must warn you, Mrs Lynn, your husband sustained some facial wounds that may distress you to see,' DCI Chalmers explains.

My head lifts to look at him. His words don't phase me. 'I don't think I have any feelings left in me that could shock me anymore,' I say, my voice defensive, trying to hold it together.

An eerie peacefulness blankets the room when the Detective places his hands on the sheet and glances in my direction. A deathly shiver runs down my spine. I don't like it.

He nods at me, waiting for the signal to raise the sheet. Taking deep breaths in and out, my heart skips a beat, then another. I try to steady my breathing, and I give the Detective an uncertain nod. I take a deep breath in, and it halts as I watch in horror as thick dark hair is revealed.

Mum lets out a painful screech, knocking her off balance and grabbing DCI Chalmers' right arm. Numbness overtakes my body, and I can't move to help her. I don't want to help her. I don't want to help anyone.

The shock snatches the colour from my face. My body trembles at the sight of the stranger lying in front of me. His skin looks so pale, a light shade of grey, deathly grey.

'Mrs Lynn, could you confirm if this man is your husband, Nathan Lynn?'

I release my breath. 'That's not my husband,' I mumble, not taking my eyes from the body.

Seven

Freya

The detective jerks his neck to look at his colleague and back to me.

'Mrs Lynn, are you saying this man is not your husband?' he asks, shocked.

He waits patiently for an answer, loosening his tie at the collar, slightly squirming. I've made him uncomfortable.

'It doesn't look like my husband, but yes, it's Nathan,' I say, tears drip from my face, and I can't take my eyes away from him.

I hear the light puff of air exhaling from the Detective's mouth with relief. I suspect relief that he's not made a mistake and mixed up some poor bastard's body, telling the wrong family their worlds now ripped from the roots and thrown away.

You hear people say they look like they're sleeping, the dead. Nathan doesn't look how he did when he slept. I watched him many a night, and that isn't how he looked. He looks empty; the spark has gone from him, his eyes aren't open and shining like I'm used to seeing.

I place my hand on his chest, scolding my fingers with the coldness of death, and immediately pull back. I try my best to see past the wounds, but it's impossible. A red slash of open flesh trails from his right temple, through his eyebrow and down his jawline, missing his eye by a millimetre. Is that what killed him? Was it that one blow to his face? What did his face hit to get such a deathly cut?

A surge of questions eats away at me. I need answers, and I need them now. I ache for them, the reasons I'm here in a morgue with my husband lying in front of me, dead.

'Did he die from those injuries to his head?' I snap.

'Freya not here, I think that's enough for now,' Mum says, reaching out, resting her hand on my arm, gesturing to the Detective to rest the sheet back down.

'No, this isn't right! Did he suffer? I need to understand why my husband's been taken from me!' I scream as I battle through the wretched lump forming in my throat.

Mum and DCI Chalmers exchange a look—neither of them knows how to deal with my outburst.

'I need you to confirm that the man in front of you is Nathan Lynn. Please, Mrs Lynn,' DCI Chalmers says, his voice is more authoritative now.

'Yes, that's my husband. I've already fucking told you, now answer me!' I snap.

My hand springs away from the table, grabbing the Detective's arm, stopping him from covering Nathan. He doesn't intervene. He folds the sheet back over Nathan's bare chest.

I take my hand from the Detective's arm as everyone watches me with blackened sympathy, feeling sorry for me no doubt. Watching and waiting for me to break as I run my shaking palms over his stubble, his stubble that was running over my neck only twenty-four hours ago, hurting my skin in pleasure, making me pine for him to wake up and hold me. I snap as it hits me hard in my heart that I will never feel his touch again.

I decide from this moment no more tears. No one will feel sorry for me. I have an uncontrollable urge to lash out again; I just want him back. I want that to be someone else lying on that cold table.

At this moment, my appetite for everything drains from me —my appetite for food, for sleep, for life. I'm hollow inside. Nathan's life has been taken away from him, but my cruel sentence will be to live on without him, only in body I will keep breathing, but my life will be over.

Please, God, please don't do this to me.

I feel Mum's arm slide around my waist, guiding my hands away from Nathan's body and gently urging me from the room. I don't fight it. I'm conscious of my behaviour. I'm trembling and cold. I just need home to Clara.

Mum nods to the Detective and signals it's time to go.

He turns his head away from me and rests the sheet gently back over Nathan. 'I think Mrs Anderson is right. I think that's enough for now. We will escort you home,' DCI Chalmers says, leading us from the room.

Clara is asleep in her crib, her usual daily nap after her 2 pm bottle. It's late afternoon, but my body's exhausted. I tiptoe over to watch her sleep. Her top lip perches out, covering her bottom lip, just as Nathan's rested when he was in a deep sleep. Is this the way it's going to be forever? Constantly reminded of him every time I look at Clara.

An unfamiliar ache fills my heart, crushing it from the inside. I can't look at her any longer.

'Hello, hunny. Are you okay?' Aunt Margaret approaches me with caution.

Mum must have told her about my outburst at the hospital, and now she'll start treating me like an insane person too.

'I'm fine,' I say, but I'm not fine, I'm exhausted.

My heart ripped apart along with my world, so what a bloody stupid question to ask me. I expect that's the first thing everyone will ask me; everyone's stupid then.

'Flowers have arrived for you. Layla and her family sent a beautiful bouquet. And some transport company sent two dozen red roses.'

I spin to look at her, shocked and ask, 'A company? Was it, Holmes Haulage?'

'Yes, that's it, who is it?'

'The company Nathan works for. *Worked* for,' I say, correcting myself quickly. 'I wonder how they found out so fast?'

'The accident was on the local news when you left this morning. A few reporters knocked at the door, but I've asked them to leave you alone.'

I nod at her. That would explain it. It's a small town; nothing stays private for long.

'The note was a bit strange though,' Aunt Mags says, shuffling about the lounge, tidying up and straightening out the sofa cushions. Her usual coping mechanism, keeping busy, trying to make herself useful.

'Strange how?'

'The words just didn't sound right when I was reading it. Maybe it's just me. It's beside the roses in the kitchen.'

I head to the kitchen and retrieve the flower card from the bunch of exquisite roses. They look and smell expensive. Aunt Margaret's right, the words don't sound right, but then what words do sound right for death?

So sorry to hear of your loss,
Take as much time as you need.
I'm here when you're ready.
Bryce Holmes
Holmes Haulage Ltd.

I'm here when you're ready? I don't even know you. Why does that bother me so much?

I toss the card back on top of the roses and raise my left hand to my forehead, rubbing vigorously. A headache is brewing. Now is not the time to be dealing with this crap.

Mum tells me to go upstairs, have a nap. I've barely slept since I got the news that Nathan... I shake away the thought. Sickness sparks in my stomach every time I think of him gone, and I swallow it back down.

I do as I'm told and make my way upstairs. I catch my reflection in the mirror ascending the stairs. I didn't know it was possible to age ten years overnight. Dark circles illuminate through the skin around my eyes. My skin is pale. I turn away from the mirror and head to our bedroom. *My bedroom*. The sickness wins, and I run for the bathroom on the top landing.

How can so much sick come from an empty stomach? I stand to my feet, my legs weak, and flush the toilet.

When I arrive back to my bedroom, Mum is there. She hands me two oblong-shaped pills and a glass of water.

'Dr Harper came by this morning when we were out with a little something to calm your nerves, help you get some sleep, sweetheart,' Mum says encouragingly.

Again, I do as I'm told. I swallow both pink pills at once and climb into bed. Mum tucks me in before leaving. I close my eyes and wish away the shitty day.

Flowers, flowers and more fucking flowers. Flowers are all I see as I descend the stairs. How long have I slept? Can't be that long, it's still light outside. Flowers seem to be the normal after death, like some ritual that will summon life to jumpstart. Rubbish.

An urge tugs at me, willing me to grab each bouquet, each posse and throw them away. Outside, over the Kent countryside, give them back to nature. Instead, the colours and beauty of them stop me in my tracks, when I realise I haven't even read the cards. Who are they all from? I haven't read any sympathy cards since reading the card attached to the red roses from Bryce Holmes.

I'm here when you're ready…

I make a mental note to ask the arsehole what he means, confront him about his choice of wording.

Mum has the flowers spread about the house, one bunch in particular, catches my attention. Not your normal neutral whites and creams, they're full of deep purples and reds, interesting choice.

I walk over to them. Taking the small cream envelope in my hands, I open it. My breath catches in my throat, a hard lump forms at my chest when I read it.

This house is full of tragedy, run away.

I turn the card over and over in my hand, as though this will make the words disappear and new, less frightening words to take their place. It doesn't work.

'Sweetheart, what's wrong?' Mum asks, appearing behind me with another bouquet in her grasp, looking for a spare worktop to settle them.

'Nothing, just overwhelmed with everyone's kind gestures.'

I slide the note inside my dressing gown pocket, careful that mum doesn't see. I don't want her worrying.

'They're all beautiful, aren't they? Some are apologies from

Scotland for not being able to attend the funeral, but I think he will still have a lovely send-off. Emma called early this morning on her way to work. She's getting away early and will get the train down.'

'This morning?' I don't understand.

Mum gives me a smile and explains, 'You've been sleeping since you went for a nap yesterday. Whatever Dr Harper gave you worked.'

Jesus Christ! I've slept for eighteen hours. There's so much to do. How could Mum let me sleep that long?

Calm down Freya, deep breaths.

I need to control my temper. I know none of this is Mum's fault. Relief settles me knowing Emma will be here soon. She's messaged me a few times, but I still haven't got round to replying to her, or anyone. They're all staying here for a few days, and for that I am thankful. It seems only right that the house is full of life.

I hear the creaks at night; the house settling down to sleep, but sometimes I think it's gentle cries of wanting to be full and live up to its full potential.

The card enters my mind again. *This house is full of tragedy.* I still don't understand. Who would write such a morbid phrase?

I notice how tired Mum looks. I ask, 'Did you get much sleep, Mum?'

'A little, Aunt Margaret and I took turns of looking after Clara so we could all get some rest. I've let her sleep on for now. Layla called earlier. She's coming round about noon to look after Clara. I think we should visit the funeral parlour, sweetheart.'

Mum's right, I have my husband's funeral to arrange.

I give Mum a nod and continue to read the other cards.

'He'd hate this,' I say, sighing long and hard at the silence.

'Hate what sweetheart?' Mum wipes her nose with her anorexic looking tissue that seems a bit overused.

'All this fuss,' I answer and gesture to the large posse of yellow roses at each side of the altar.

'It's not fuss, Freya, it's a beautiful send-off.'

'It's fuss. He used to joke that if something happened to him, just to bury him out in the back garden where he used to sit and have his coffee in the morning. He loved the view of the Kent countryside. I don't even know what his favourite was.' It doesn't matter what I say, it makes Mum cry.

'Favourite?' Mum whispers, confused.

'Flowers, the yellow roses are my favourite. He bought me them often, but I don't even know if he liked them. Or any sort of flowers.'

Mum's sniffing projects around the peaceful crematorium.

'This seems wrong, Mum, cremating him.'

'I'm sure he would love his ashes scattered in the countryside. We could do that if you like?' Mum blows her nose again. It's been a leaky tap since we sat down in the crematorium. It's irritating me and I breathe deep and loud, too loud for the crematorium.

Not the time or place Fee, relax.

Layla's sitting behind me, occasionally resting her hand on my shoulder. A welcome reminder that she is there, and also a warning to behave. She's been great through all of this. If I'm being honest, Layla was the reason I chose cremation for Nathan. She looked after Clara to allow Mum, Emma and I to go to the undertakers once they had released Nathan's body from the morgue. Confused about what to do about the arrangements, I was looking at every option. If I had him buried somewhere in Edenbridge, how would I keep up visiting him if I moved Clara and me back to Scotland? Layla suggested cremation, that way I could take him anywhere. She was right. I could scatter some of his ashes in the countryside surrounding the house, and some I could scatter in Stirling, over the edge of Stirling Castle? He loved the view.

The people who have come to pay their last respects, not that there are a lot of them, must think I'm the ice queen sitting here with not a tear in sight. I think I've dried myself out. They all look smart though, sitting in their Sunday best, black suits and ties. Some, I must admit, look rather official. Stoney faces that are not familiar. I did request everyone wore something a little less formal to match Nathan's personality. He hated wearing suits and ties. Said it made him feel like he was waiting for sentencing, whatever that meant.

Aunt Margaret has been standing at the crematorium doors greeting everyone since we arrived, a wedding receiving line at a funeral. She handles death tremendously, I must admit. She was like an undertaker at Papa's funeral, very professional and courteous, never even seen her shed one tear.

'Do you think he's here?' I ask Mum.

'Who sweetheart?'

'Nathan.'

'Um, yes Freya, he's there in front of the altar,' Mum whispers.

'No, Mum, do you think he's actually here? Like his spirit, attending his exhausted body's service.'

Mum blows her nose into the same tissue again that's now ripping apart from the fresh flood of tears and leaking nose. 'Oh Freya,' she answers, trying to battle through the lump in her throat and petted lip.

I know she thinks I'm losing my mind. She slides her hand over my knee and links her fingers with mines. 'I think he will be here in spirit, yes, sweetheart,' she says, giving my hand a squeeze.

I'm living in limbo. I'm sitting at my husband's funeral service, but it doesn't feel like I am. He's dead, but it doesn't feel genuine enough to be true. I'm so confused I want to stand up, straighten myself and sit back down. The restlessness is painful. Painful to sit through a service that shouldn't be happening, or I should be attending. I've not been sure of much since Dr Harper gave me something to settle my nerves and try to prevent another panic attack. I'm completely fine, though.

'We could pick up a Chinese for dinner.'

'Excuse me, sweetheart?' Mum replies.

'Chinese food, for dinner? I think by the time we get home it will be too late to cook.'

Mum doesn't answer, she just squeezes my hand tighter and wipes her nose with the final scrap of tissue. My irritation growing that much I'm about to offer her my sleeve.

Light footsteps enter the service room, heels tapping in rhythm with each other walking up the aisle. I turn to see Aunt Margaret sit beside Mum. With Emma on my other side, everyone stands as the hymn Here I am, Lord begins.

It was a small, intimate service. Rushed and short. It was our relationship down to the simplest of details. Thinking about it, it's quite ironic actually. We went full speed since the word go, from falling in love until an aching halt at death. Our life together had been on fast forward, giving us more in one year than most people experience in a lifetime.

It feels surreal standing shaking hands with guests who came to say goodbye to Nathan. Most of them I had never met until now. I'm thankful for their well wishes and support, though.

Layla stands at the bottom of the stairs with Mum, shaking hands with departing guests. I watch her, in awe of how calm she is, how well she's holding it together. I find myself slightly jealous, wishing I had some of her strength. I see a lot of myself in her; she doesn't take crap from men either. She's been at the house every morning, trying to help, but just her presence is enough. She knows me that well I swear we were friends in a previous life. I'm thankful we met.

Then there was Bryce Holmes, standing in front of me, finally introducing himself after the service. He isn't what I expected; he's calm, dignified, unfeigned.

'What a truly significant loss to you and your family, Mrs Lynn,' he comments whilst shaking my hand.

Have we met before? I feel like we have; he seems familiar. Too familiar, in fact. My spine tingles, and not in a pleasant way.

'If there's anything you need, you call me, anything at all. And when you're ready, there're some things I need to discuss with you, regarding finances.' He reaches inside the smart black suit pocket and retrieves a business card.

Finances? Maybe some employee life insurance or wages still due? It can wait.

Either he's a good, in fact, I would stretch that to a great actor, or he wasn't what Nathan made him out to be. I would go for the latter as Nathan wasn't a liar. I put it on my mental to-do list to find out.

Mum and Layla meet me at the top of the stairs, waking me from my thoughts as I watch Bryce Holmes walk with confidence in his expensive suit, down the crematorium steps.

'Who was that, sweetheart?' Mum asks.

'That, Mum was big businessman Bryce Holmes, Nathan's boss.' I fold my arms across my chest, I stiffen just saying his name.

'He seemed nice and genuinely upset,' says Mum.

'Yes, he seemed too, didn't he?' Layla's lips form a tight line as she stands by my side.

I feel her anger radiating towards Bryce. A small spark of anger ignites in me too, both of us projecting the blame onto Bryce Holmes for Nathan's death. Mum pats me on the back and I soften at her touch, my arms falling from my chest, quickly making me come to my senses. Bryce isn't at fault, I know this. My anger is looking for culpability.

'No one is to blame, Freya. It was an accident,' says Mum, who must be reading me. She used to be the only person who could until Nathan.

'Heaven isn't too far away sweetheart, every day you live on is a day closer to seeing Nathan again.'

'I hope so, Mum, I really hope so.'

The path leading up to the house looks long, ever-expanding with fear of reaching the door. I never thought returning home to a house I have walked into a thousand times over could suddenly flip to fear of going in. It looks different now, slightly unfamiliar. My legs come to a halt; they won't take me any further.

Mum's at the front door, still sobbing into a wet tissue as I stand at the bottom of three small steps under the light drizzling rain, watching her.

'Freya,' Mum says, her voice warm, welcoming but yet I'm frozen in my footsteps. 'Come on, sweetheart, nearly home.'

'Home?' I answer, saddened at the thought that it isn't our home anymore. It's just a house I'm going to live in, surrounded by all that space.

A sense of vulnerability grows inside me, an emotion that's unknown to me. I wrap my beige belted trench coat tightly around my body, shuddering, trying to shake it off. 'I can't go in there, Mum.'

'Why, sweetheart?'

'Because going in there means the start of me being on my own. Having to cope on my own. I'm not ready to live my life without him.'

Mum walks back to the top of stairs, stretching out her hand as guidance. 'You don't have to do anything on your own, I will be here as long as you need me. We'll do this together.'

I take her hand, making my way up the steps and through the front door. Returning home to start a new life without Nathan. My soul is empty.

Eight

Freya

Bryce's text message he sent to me the day after the funeral, has played on my mind all week. He needs to speak to me. I don't remember giving him my mobile number? I assume it was on Nathan's employee records as his next of kin.

Nathan's boss, the man he warned me to trust him about. I don't know what Nathan had on him, maybe I should ask. He seemed so normal at the funeral and genuinely concerned about both Clara and me.

I replied to his message yesterday, accepting his invitation to meet for coffee, but on my terms. I told him to come to the house this morning, leaving no opening to negotiate the arrangement. He replied to my message almost instantly, but I haven't taken the time to read it. He either accepts or he doesn't. What harm could it do to meet with him? I need answers why Nathan was dead set on leaving.

'Thank you for seeing me, Freya,' Bryce says as he glances around the house, his eyes skimming every inch in front of him. 'Sorry, you don't mind if I call you Freya, do you?'

Well, I suppose not since you've taken it upon yourself to call me it, anyway.

'Of course not, Bryce. You're okay with Bryce aren't you, since you've already decided we're on first-name terms?' I answer, relaxed, an unapologetic smile on my face.

He smirks and drops his head, trying to hide it. 'May I?' he asks, pointing one finger at Clara in the sitting room, already walking towards her before I can answer.

I follow him, my arms folded. 'Well, since you already are.'

He stops and turns to face me. 'Have I offended you, Freya? Mrs Lynn, if you would prefer?'

I don't know, have you offended me? Or my dead husband? Who isn't here to defend himself, so I intend to?

'Freya is fine,' I answer, sharply.

His body language is off, different from the funeral. Am I making him uneasy?

Yes, good.

'I won't hang about. Could we sit for a moment?' Bryce asks.

I nod towards the furthest away chair from Clara's bouncy chair, who is still sleeping. Good girl, keep it up for mummy.

Bryce rubs the palms of his hands together. He sits perched at the front of the chair for a moment before settling back, crossing his legs, then uncrossing them and sitting forward. I keep my gaze on him. A frightening sense of déjà vu stifles me, and I struggle to put together any words. I remain silent.

'Okay, first, I apologise for what I'm about to tell you as I know you've just lost your husband and believe me when I say I had become very fond of Nathan.'

Fond? Is this guy ninety?

I hold my gaze, my arms still folded.

He continues, 'Nathan was one of my best workers, kept his head down, made deliveries in great time, never any bother, until...' his voice trails off, his eyes fixed on the floor.

'Until?' I ask.

'Until he stole from me,' he answers, lifting his head, his eyes find mine.

'Ha, I'm sorry, but what? What exactly has my husband *supposed* to have stolen?'

'Money, quite a large sum actually.'

I hold myself, not showing that I want to punch him right in the face and throw him from my house. 'Do you have any proof of this *theft*, Mr Holmes?' I ask.

He doesn't, I can tell by his expression, taking a moment to answer my question.

'No, but I think you do.'

I don't answer, accusing a dead man of theft who can't defend himself against these accusations, disgust me. The way Bryce is so calm disgusts me.

'Nathan told you he got a bonus about the time you gave birth, yes? Bought you that glorious white Range Rover?'

I sag mentally when I realise he's right, Nathan told me the month before Clara was born that he had gotten a bonus for delivering a load of stock to Spain two days early. Clients of Bryce's kicking up hell if I remember correctly after one of the other guys messed up. I remain silent.

'That wasn't a bonus, Freya. That was money he had taken from my clients. A cash payment meant for me for getting the goods there, a compensation so to speak for express delivery. He told me they never gave the money to him, but I have witnesses that say otherwise. I will not pretend I make all my money in haulage Freya. I have sidelines the same as everyone else. I found out two days before he died, when I was in Germany on a business trip, tried to contact him, but he ignored my calls, my messages. Was he planning on doing a runner, Freya?'

I would never tell you if we were. 'No,' I answer, remaining stern. This guy almost has my temper at boiling point.

'Freya, I don't want to play games, but there're things I think you need to know.'

Bryce hands me a beige file. I hesitate, but then accept it without argument. 'I will look over it when I have time.'

His tone changes, he's irritated. I sense his real persona is struggling to stay hidden.

'I think you need to look over it now,' he tells me, pushing his shoulders back, and he straightens, trying to show his authority.

This is my house. He has no authority here, and I will make sure he knows that.

'I will look over the file when I choose to do so, Mr Holmes, not when someone tells me. Don't come into my house, make accusations about my dead husband, expect me to believe you, and then jump at your demands. You know where the door is,' I say, pissed.

I stand firm, my eyes zoom to the front door then back to meet his. Big boss man Bryce looks flustered, his mouth twists and he leaves without saying another word.

What an arsehole.

This day has just begun and already I wish it would fuck off. I feel the pressure of the tears forming, making me squeeze my eyes tight shut, forcing them to stay in.

The house is silent, everyone has returned home to Scotland. All apart from Mum, who I sent out for shopping this morning before Bryce arrived. Clara is unusually still asleep. I take advantage and head for the kitchen to make a coffee.

My stomach rumbles with a fierce roar, reminding me I haven't eaten since breakfast yesterday. If you can call one spoonful of porridge breakfast. I have no appetite. I'll add sugar to my coffee to substitute. I don't take sugar in my coffee, I never have. Milky unsweetened coffee tastes so much better.

I close my eyes, walking past the wall of memories; I hold it together better when I don't look at Nathan.

The door knocks, a gentle knock. Mum, she must have forgotten her keys. That or her hands are full of shopping bags and she's given the door a kick with her toe to summon help, gently, so she doesn't wake Clara from her 10 am nap. 11:10 and she's still in the land of nod.

I open the door, ready to laugh at Mum balancing on one leg, with the other airborne ready to kick the door again.

I freeze.

Two men in suits stand formally at the door. A rush takes me back to the day I was told Nathan had died, and automatically I think the worst. Mum!

I remain silent.

'Mrs Lynn, sorry to bother you. I'm Chief Superintendent Mathews. I believe you've been acquainted with my colleague, DCI Chalmers,' says the older man. He's not a stranger to this sort of greeting, I can tell.

All my functions have frozen, my heart is pounding.

'Could we speak to you about your husband, Nathan Lynn,

please?'

'My husband is dead Superintendent Mathews, what is there to talk about?'

My heart rate steadies, and I thank God it isn't anything to do with Mum.

Chief Superintendent Mathews doesn't answer but invites himself in. I lead them to the kitchen to avoid disturbing Clara. DCI Chalmers has brought himself back up this time. The big, big boss. I didn't think he was that scared of me.

My bitchiness level has cranked up a notch today and do I care? No, absolutely not.

I don't offer any drinks. I get straight to the point. My mood already scratching the surface of a meltdown and I don't fight it. 'What can I do for you, gentlemen?'

'Mrs Lynn, how long have you known Nathan?'

'Long enough,' I answer, short.

Where is this going? Is this when I find out he has a secret wife stashed somewhere looking for life insurance? If so, she can dream on. There was no life insurance.

Chief Superintendent Mathews continues, 'Not long enough to say you know someone that well?'

'I knew my husband better than anyone.'

Rude, my teeth begin to grind together.

'Is that so? So, you would have known about his criminal record then?'

I feel my jaw drop to the floor, catching my balance with it. Criminal record? This idiot has made a massive mistake. 'I think you have my husband mistaken. He had no criminal record.'

'We have been looking for a man named Nathaniel Emmert for quite some time. A notorious fraudster shall we say. Every time we had a lead, it would wind up being a dead end. It had been for years. Until your husband's DNA from his autopsy matched Emmert's. So, we ran some more tests. 100% match.'

DCI Chalmers hasn't said a word yet, but he looks smug at this.

My hearts thumping, I slide myself onto a breakfast stool. I can't hold my composure, not this time. I pride myself for breaking and bouncing back, hit after hit. Now, I have no strength for this. My gut always told me there was something mysterious about Nathan, but he was genuine with me, or I thought he was. I never doubted he had a past. Who doesn't? People deserve second chances. I was just never sure what I was giving a second chance to? Conning some old lady out of her dead husband's fortune?

'He owes some wicked men a lot of money, Mrs Lynn. If we've found out who he is, *was*, it could just be a matter of time before those wicked men find out too,' Chief Superintendent Mathews explains, taking a long breath. 'I can't guarantee your family's safety, Freya. We need to know if Nathan ever discussed moving?'

'Yes, yes, he did. The day he died. He seemed shaken, he wanted to leave as soon as possible. He made out it was his boss he needed away from.'

'His boss?'

'Yes, Bryce Holmes, he owns a company called Holmes Haulage. Does he have something to do with all this? He was here this morning accusing Nathan of stealing money from him.'

I can tell from Chief Superintendent Mathews widening eyes, that name is familiar to him.

'I can confirm Mr Holmes isn't part of our enquiries. If Nathan was planning on doing a runner, and in your words shaken, then it's a possibility these people could have already found him. If he has also stolen money from Mr Holmes, then he may have been planning to do a runner for some time, with or without you and your daughter.'

I sit up straight on the barstool, keeping calm, unnerved on the outside. 'What do you suggest I do?' I ask, not showing I'm desperate to ask so many more questions, but I don't want him to think I believe what he's told me, not yet.

'I will leave that for you and Mr Holmes to discuss.' He stands, handing me a business card retrieved from his pocket.

'Tell me something Chief Superintendent Mathews, does someone of your rank usually make house calls?'

Right on cue, Clara stirs, and I don't receive an answer to my question. Her cries penetrating the entire house in a split second. I make my way to the lounge and leave the men to make their own way out.

The nights are long, lonely. The house screams with silence and it tries to arouse my insanity. How did I get here? I feel like I'm still lying on the beach in Phuket, my body still wet from the afternoon of scuba diving in the Andaman Sea. My eyes closed as the sun is so bright, I strain them to see. When I've opened them again, I'm here, in this strange life that's gone so fast, I'm not sure it's even my life anymore.

Falling at a man's feet, becoming a wife at a flash of a wedding reception that lasted twelve minutes, becoming a Mum, becoming a widow.

Who am I?

My surge of thought annoys me. Bryce and his arrogance, that cocky Chief Superintendent, the morbid message on the flower card. *This house is full of tragedy.* My heads working overtime.

I get out of bed and creep downstairs, careful not to wake Mum or Clara. I close my eyes, walking past the wall of photos, careful not to open them until I'm safely in the kitchen.

I fill the kettle and switch it on to boil, grabbing my favourite mug, the one with the verse on the side that reads:

I'm Freya,
I'm not really a bitch,
Just kidding,
Go fuck yourself.

Nathan ordered it online after the advert popped up on the internet one day, said it was me on a mug. I pop a tea bag inside and pour the boiling water in. Even in the worst situations, a cup of tea isn't far away.

I head to the lounge and curl up on the sofa, pulling a knitted blanket over me that Aunt Mags made me when I was eight. The house is dark and cold—I welcome it.

The beige file Bryce left catches my eye, I forgot I had thrown it onto the sofa when he left. My mood is already at rock bottom, so I retrieve the file and open it. What have I got to lose?

The file is full of white sheets of paper, covered in grids and writing. The closer I look, the more I realise the sheets of paper are police reports, police reports covered with Nathan's name. I flick through them. There must be at least fifty reports, samples of fingerprints, mug shots of Nathan. I struggle to understand what I'm looking at?

I pull out a random sheet of paper, stapled to the far-right corner is a photograph: Nathan, only a lot younger.

The report reads, male, age twenty-one, address unknown. Date of conviction 07/05/2010. Narrative of the incident, GBH.

GBH?

Grievous bodily harm? Nathan? Nathan committed GBH on someone?

No, no! No, I don't believe it.

I throw the sheet of paper onto the floor and pull out another.

Male, age twenty-two, address unknown. Date of conviction 18/08/2011. Narrative of the incident, armed robbery, theft, GBH.

I throw it on the floor with the other, pulling more and more sheets, Nathan's name on them all.

Age, twenty-three. Narrative of the incident, GBH, fraud and theft again. The sentence, four years in prison.

Four years in prison at twenty-three. They released him in 2016. They released him the year I met him. It can't be right! It can't!

No, no, *no*!

I want to scream as my stability on reality frays. He was a criminal, Nathan, my husband. A convicted criminal. He played me.

Abhorrence overwhelms me, and for the first time since Nathan's death, it subsides my grief. Rage squeezes me with its tight grip, wrapping around my torso, wanting me to feel it. From day one, my gut told me what kind of person he was, and I was right. Was it my heart that led me astray? My head or my vagina? I don't even know anymore.

I lift my phone and try calling Emma. It rings with no answer until voicemail activates.

'Hey, it's me ace face, phone me back when you can, love you.'

I click the call off and look around. The house wraps its icy hand around my neck, suffocating me. I gather up all the reports from the file and rush to the hall, grab my car keys, jacket and escape the surroundings of Nathan.

Nine

Freya

Nathan's belongings still fill the rooms. Wardrobes filled with his clothes and shoes, cupboards filled with useless junk he refused to throw out. Even the junk that came with this house he refused to part with. He was a hoarder—it annoyed the life out of me. We had so many fights about it, and now I find myself able to part with it all. He has lost the right to a place here.

I sit on our bed, staring out of the window over the vast fields that stretch for miles. If I started walking outside, I would never stop, I would never turn back, but this is my house. The money Mum gave us, *gave me*, bought it. This is all mines. I need to remove every memory of him from it.

The wardrobe doors scream for me to open them. Without hesitation, I stand from the bed and pull suitcases from the bedroom cupboard. I open Nathan's wardrobe and begin ripping shirts, sweaters, hoodies and trousers from hangers and throw them roughly into the suitcases.

Once the wardrobe is empty, I move to his drawers, my hands working quickly, pulling underwear, socks, crap and disposing of them into the cases. I zip the cases closed, grab the handles and pull them from the bedroom. The cases slam down each step, thumping as they go. Inside me sparks with fireworks of restitution, my way of punishing him. I'm alive with rage.

'Freya, what's all the noise?' Mum appears from the kitchen,

Clara's milk bottle in her hand, her face a picture of horror when she realises what's happening. She follows me, asking, 'Freya what are you doing?'

I don't answer, my mind on autopilot, refusing to interact. I drag the suitcases through to the kitchen, then through the patio doors to the back garden. I throw as far as I can but unsuccessfully; the cases landing a meter away from me.

I jog back into the house and back upstairs, into one of the spare rooms that Nathan used as his personal storage space. I grab cardboard boxes and repeat the last journey of the suitcases, over and over, until there is a pile of miscellaneous junk that was Nathan's life in the back garden.

Mum's not intervening, and I'm thankful, I don't need a fall out with her added into this chaos.

I stop, take a deep breath, and look at the mess I've created. Not sure if I'm proud of myself or need committed.

I am proud, I'm ecstatic with myself.

All the anger of the last couple of days released and for the first time in weeks, I can breathe easily again. I'm me again, cleansed of the bastard that caused all this.

My thought process halts by the squeaking of the rope from the tree swing, hanging from the branches of the Sweet Chestnut tree that takes pride of place at the bottom of the back garden.

A woman sits on the swing, staring out to the field, oblivious to what's going on around her. I saunter towards her.

'Excuse me, can I help you?' I ask, cautiously thinking she might be lost, but still, she remains seated.

Her head rests against the thick rope harness of the swing. Her silver hair moves freely from the air as she gently sways back and forth. Her clothes are immaculate, expensive-looking white linen trousers, gold sandals and a matching gold silk scarf.

The closer I get to her, I realise she's not as old as her silver hair makes her look. She turns her face to me, her expression blank. She must be in her early sixties.

'Are you all right?' I ask again, kneeling beside her.

My defences evaporating as I look at her compact frame, she isn't a threat. Her lips part and she whispers, but I can't hear what she is saying. I move closer to her and see she's holding a small white stuffed rabbit with multicoloured spots. I spring to my feet, it's Clara's beanie bunny.

'How did you get that? Have you been in my house?' My heart picks up pace and I ask again, 'Have you been in my house?' My voice higher this time.

Silver-haired lady looks up at me, her lips forming a wayward smile. 'You are living my daughter's life,' she answers, and I hear her clearer this time, leaving me confused.

'I'm sorry, I don't understand.'

She stands to her feet and begins walking towards me. I stand firm and lean forward, snatching Clara's beanie bunny from her, and for a moment she does nothing, says nothing.

In a split second, she pounces at me, screaming slurs at me, and I feel her grab my hair.

'This life was my daughter's, my daughter's!' she screams.

Her strength is impeccable. She must be younger than sixty.

A man's voice shouts in the distance, tangling in with Mum's horrifying screams and silver-haired crazy lady is lifted from me. I sit up, pulling the hair and mud from my face and watch as she's lifted from the garden. I stand to my feet, my pyjamas wet, covered in mud, my eyes trying to focus and comprehend what has just happened.

The crazy lady disappears around the side of the house and then out of sight as Mum fusses around me.

Mum's finally calmed down. I sit on a barstool at the kitchen island with a cup of coffee, listening to her rambling on about today's events. I've showered the mud off me and put fresh pyjamas on. I still have no idea what happened, or why, or who the crazy lady was. Safe to say I hate her, but only because she destroyed my moment of finally feeling like me again, only to drag me through the mud and ruin it.

'I mean, if Bryce hadn't arrived when he did, God knows how I would've got that woman off you,' Mum mutters and perches herself across from me, a glass of white wine in hand.

'What was Bryce even doing here, anyway?'

'He said he came to apologise for upsetting you the other day.

Is that why you took off during the night? Because of something he said to you?' she asks.

I don't answer.

Mum takes a long drink of her wine with annoyance at the lack of information I give her. Maybe I should be truthful with her, get her off my back. Like that would even get her off my back.

'You know, Freya, it's things like today that make you realise you need to move back home. What if this happened when I wasn't here? What if it happens again?'

Christ, like a crazy silver-haired lady breaks into your house, steals one of your daughter's soft toys and then attacks you, happens every day. Typical Mum, worst-case scenario once again.

Calm down, Moira.

'Nathan was a thief,' I say. The words slip from my tongue before I realise I'm even contemplating saying them.

Mum's mouth drops open in horror.

'Bryce brought files round the other day. Remember, at the funeral when he said he had to speak to me about finances? Well, that was it. Nathan stole from him, and he had the paperwork to back up all his accusations.'

I take a drink of coffee and continue to tell Mum everything I read. 'So, my gut instinct about him at first was right,' I scoff.

'Jesus Christ, Freya! I mean, fuck!' Mum's voice is higher than I've ever heard it.

She never uses curse words. Her swearing is alien to me, and I fear the pressure is beginning to eat away at her. I'm sure she's dropped weight, but then so have I.

'My Granddaughter living with a criminal, Jesus, he could have done anything to you both.' Mum retrieves another bottle of white wine from the fridge and sits on the vacant barstool beside me.

I watch as her hands shake, trying to unscrew the cap. She pours the wine to the brim of the wineglass; the bottle clinking off the glass as she tries to steady her hand.

'I blame myself, you know, I pushed you into giving him a chance. I should have listened to you,' Mum says, rambling on, washing the words away with a large gulp from her glass.

'Mum, don't. He fooled us both.'

Bastard, what I would do to him if he were here. Mum takes a few minutes. I know her look. It's the I'm thinking, so don't disturb me look.

After what feels like an hour, but is only two minutes and a polished off glass of white wine, she asks, 'Ok, maybe he was after money at first, but before he died, did you have any doubts about him? About how much he loved you and Clara? I mean, were there instances when you thought he would hurt you? Were you ever scared of him?'

I tilt my head and narrow my eyes at mum, giving my best *he'd be dead sooner if he tried* look. It makes me think this over, though. There was no doubt in my mind that he didn't love us; I know he did.

'No, Mum, not one doubt.'

'Then, there's your answer. Everyone has a past, Freya. You can't hold it over him. Everyone deserves a second chance, and you and Clara were his. Even if he was a violent criminal.' Mum fills her wine glass up again at the thought. 'Bloody excellent actor too,' she says.

Mum's right, falling pregnant with Clara changed us both.

'Well, I'm not overly happy with my decision now. I asked Bryce to bring Nathans belongings back in. Wish I hadn't bothered now.'

I look at her, and she answers me before I can ask.

'He came back when you were in the shower. I asked if he could bring everything back in and he's put it all back up in the attic. I know that's the one place in here you won't go, and I wasn't sure if you wanted to be rid of everything, so at least this way, everything is out of your eyesight but still in the house. In hindsight, I wish I'd left it all outside now that I understand why you took a flaky,' says Mum, giving a half apologetic, half do what you're told if you know what's good for you smile.

I don't argue. She always knows what's best for me when I have no idea. She tells me Bryce will call by the house tomorrow night, and I'm surprised this doesn't make me angry at the thought of him coming back. Nathan screwed him over too. Everyone deserves a second chance as Mum said.

'Fee, sweetheart, I think we're going to need more wine. Today has been a lot to take in.'

I cuddle Mum and tell her I'll go to the supermarket.

Thank God for Mum.

Ten

Freya

I've spent most of the morning analysing my life, from the minute Nathan entered it, until now. Everything seems clearer to me after my blow out yesterday, I'm a stranger watching the relationship with an unbiased view. I needed to free myself, from myself to think straight for a little while. I've always found it easy to give my advice on relationships, to friends, on which there are very few, and family.

Take Emma for example, she is cautious, headstrong and won't let anyone near her unless they earn it, proving their worth to her, I'm not even half the woman she is.

Myself, I used men for what I needed, when I needed it and nothing more. Nathan played me, and I let him. Why? Because he treated me the way I treated men. Our relationship was blurry, now my vision is crystal clear.

I remember telling him I was pregnant; I was around five weeks gone when I found out. I sat on the toilet at home holding the test the day we came back from a three-day city break in Amsterdam. I knew myself I was pregnant before taking the test. Every time I put a drop of alcohol near my mouth, I would taste sick, travelling up from my stomach. I waited until we got home to do a home pregnancy test because I didn't want to ruin our trip. I stared at it for what felt like an eternity, waiting for the two blue lines to fade. They didn't to my annoyance. My first instinct was I wasn't keeping it, a baby didn't fit into my plan.

Nathan's reaction was simple. Worse things happen in life. He was like me, loved to travel, and staying with Mum in Stirling was just a stepping-stone for him.

A haulage company offered him a job which involved travelling for days at a time, and that was all he needed to know. The fact I was pregnant didn't change his mind, he agreed we should terminate the pregnancy.

The day of the appointment at the hospital I couldn't go through with it, Nathan told me it was my decision, but he had an upbringing with no Father, and it sucked. He told me he would support me if I moved to England with him and became his wife. He wanted to do it properly and let his child have the best life he could give it, with two present parents. Which now I realise meant he was only willing to have a life with me, with our baby, on his terms, the way he wanted it.

I told him under no circumstances would I move away from Mum, more so with me being pregnant. If he truly loved me, he wouldn't have followed with the ultimatum. Move to England with me and be a family or end our relationship and bring the child up alone. I think the shock of me not getting my own way together with Nathan willing to cast me to the side, made me decide and before I knew it, I was living in England with a newborn baby.

I would never change Clara for the world, but I wish I knew before I moved that I could cope on my own with a child. I never thought about the consequences of my actions, I didn't give myself time, I just acted and thought later. That later has now turned out to be almost a year later.

I never truly felt myself in England, the only time I used my camera was to take photographs of Clara, thought it was because I missed home so much, I know now it's because I never truly felt myself with Nathan.

I texted Bryce earlier, asking to meet and discuss what it is he wants from me. I feel a little sorry for him because it seems Nathan screwed him over too. Now I've given myself time to think, I'm mentally ready to deal with him.

He replied and told me to meet him in town tonight, for which I am happy. I don't like how uneasy I feel with him in my house, and it keeps him away.

Bryce is seated at the table when I arrive. He's trying to show off, booking us a table at Royal Silk, a swanky restaurant on the outskirts of London. I assume since he's trying to show off, he'll be paying the bill too. Fine with me.

I'm wearing my killer *don't mess with me* heels, chocolate brown leather pencil skirt and black turtle-neck sweater, my hair hanging loose and wavy. I've moped around in pyjamas and sportswear for weeks now, it feels good to be me again, even if it is only for one night. I can tackle anyone when I wear the right outfit, especially big businessmen like Bryce Holmes. I know what makes men like him tick, throwing their money around, bullying the smaller guys. He has the looks too, so I expect he has women falling at his feet.

A bunch of yellow roses sit on the table. Not your average bunch of Marks and Spencer's pre-packed roses, an expensive-looking bunch. Christ's sake, they better not be for me! I have no idea why this spikes my temper so much.

'I knew you liked them,' he says.

I narrow my eyes at him, not wanting to acknowledge the roses.

'I heard you at the funeral say they were your favourite.'

How could he hear me? I'm sure he was sitting at the back of the room, a few rows away from me?

I smile, that's all he's getting. This isn't a fucking date, I want to say, but a smile will do.

'How are you after yesterday? Not to shaken I hope?' Bryce asks, his eye skimming me for any sign of injury after the crazy lady attack.

'I'm fine, it seems you appeared at just the right time. Who was that woman?' I ask.

'I'm not sure, she seemed quite wandered. I walked her to the end of your drive and down the road a few feet and she didn't seem to remember what happened, even asked me why she was covered in mud. I drove her to the nearest police station, explained what happened, and they took over.'

Poor woman, I hope the police got her home safely. 'So, Bryce, shall we get straight to it?' I ask after I order my meal.

Lobster Thermidor, I've never tried it but sounds expensive. Bryce doesn't even bat an eyelid at it, seems he is more reserved than I have given him credit for.

'Yes, of course, you'll want to get home to the little one.'

The server arrives with our bottle of wine, some fancy name Bryce ordered, and pours us each a glass.

'Well, as I was saying to you on our last conversation, Nathan stole a sum of money from me. £500,000 to be exact,' he explains, then stops to look at me.

My mouth falls open, and I quickly close it. When Bryce said a large sum, I had no idea just how large. Why the hell would someone be carrying money like that around in cash.

'£500,000? That's a lot of money, and you say Nathan stole this, how?' I rest my elbows on the table and stare at Bryce.

Looking around this restaurant, it seems they frown at elbows on the table. Who cares, I'm never going to be here again with these people.

'My client handed it over inside a case, a case that was never returned to me. I didn't just lose that money, I also lost an excellent client and a business contract that has set me back quadruple that amount. I'm a businessman Freya, here to do business and claim back what Nathan stole from me.'

'Are you implying I know where that money is Mr Holmes because you are seriously mistaken,' I snap.

I had no idea about his bloody money or money Nathan stole, so I sure as hell don't know where it is. I continue, 'That is money I do not have to pay Nathan's debt back to you.'

Another server arrives with our meals, disturbing us. The last bit of conversation hanging in the air between us. The longer I wait to continue, the more my irritation grows. I sip a taste of wine, and to my annoyance it's delicious. I sip another and I feel the liquid slide down my throat, firing up the heat in my stomach. After another sip and the server has left the table, I've relaxed.

Bryce's eyes darken for a split second before a friendly smile appears back on his face. Did I imagine it? The wine couldn't be effecting me that quickly, could it?

'That's where you're wrong, Freya. Nathan has hidden that

money somewhere. Whether it be in a bank account or hidden in your house? I know you knew nothing about it, or I would speak to the police and not be having dinner here with you.'

'I think that's where you're wrong. You admitted to me you don't make all your money in haulage and if that money was legitimate then it wouldn't have been paid in cash, in a briefcase would it? So, let's not kid that you would have gone to the police.' I lift my glass and take another sip of wine.

When I sit my glass back on the table, it's met by Bryce refilling it with more of the delicious wine. I must remember the name. He doesn't look pissed at my comment, but more impressed, his mouth curved up at one side.

'Smart girl. I have a proposition for you that may work out to both our benefits.'

I lean back in my chair, my eyes widen.

Bryce continues, 'One option is you sell me your house, discounted with what Nathan stole from me, and I give you the rest. I think that should leave you with a tidy sum to move back to Scotland?'

Bastard, no way in hell is he getting his hands on my house. Even if I decide to sell, I'd make sure it wasn't him buying.

My face remains serious, unfaltering. 'And the other option?'

'Work for me,' he answers.

I almost laugh out loud, but the seriousness of his stare scares it back inside me.

'Shit, you're serious?' I ask.

I lift my glass and a large gulp of wine slides like silk down my throat. 'I don't want involved in any of your illegal work.'

'I never once said my work was illegal. I just said it wasn't all in haulage.'

He's right, I just assumed it is. I still think it is.

'You're a trained photographer, yes?' he asks, politely.

Everything about him is polite, I don't buy it, but I nod, my hand running up my wineglass.

'I flip a lot of houses, all over Europe. It costs me a lot of money to send photographers abroad to photograph all the work for advertising, for making portfolios. I always use the same company in London, but I want you to work for me.'

Fuck, how long would it take to pay back the money he's looking for? I would be under his beck and call. Would I need to travel with him?

'I need to think about this.'

Bryce nods and tells me to take all the time I need before tucking into his meal. My appetite has completely disappeared.

'Are you sure I can't get my driver to take you home?' Bryce asks.

His driver, ha, says it all. 'No, it's fine, I'll just grab a taxi.'

I turn around, walking away from Bryce, my hand digging around in my handbag for my phone. I hear him say something as I walk away, but I ignore it.

When I finally locate my phone and pull it from my bag, the screen lights up. Three missed calls and four text messages. One message is from Mum, telling me she won't go to bed until I'm home, classic Moira, still thinks I'm a teenager. The rest from Layla, asking me if I'm alright, then another saying she's worried. My fault, I told her earlier when I spoke to her, I would only be out for half an hour tops. I was only giving Bryce a chance to say what he had to say, but the truth is I enjoyed being out, being me, even if it was with company I wouldn't have chosen. But it was a break away from the chaos that is my life at the moment.

I swipe to my call list and hit Layla's name while I wait for the next taxi to arrive.

'Hey you,' I say, trying to sound chirpy.

'Hey you? Jesus fuck, I've been pacing the floor worried sick. I even thought about jumping in the car to come find you,' Layla snaps down the phone.

'Calm yourself, snappy cow, I'm fine. There was a lot more to talk about than I expected.'

That was me being polite, but as much as I love Layla, she isn't the boss of me, and she isn't my Mother. I understand she was just worried about me, so I'll let her cheek slide.

'I'm sorry Fee, just you said you wouldn't be long, and something in me doesn't trust this guy one bit.'

'And until tonight I agreed with you, but it seems Nathan has been playing everyone and he's screwed Bryce out of a lot of money. He's wanting it back. He's given me two choices. Sell him my house and he'll give me whatever is left after he takes his money back or work for him for free making portfolios of his renovation work.'

'Fuck,' Layla answers, sounding deflated. 'Fee as much as it pains me to say this as it's the last thing I want 'cause I'll miss you and Clara a tonne, but maybe you should just sell him the house, move back to Stirling and start fresh? Do you want to be in debt to this guy and having to work for him?'

'No matter how much I don't want to be in debt to him I am, thanks to fucking Nathan, but I'm not giving him the house. That was my inheritance money from Mum. If I sell the house, I'll lose a chunk. Working for him is the painless option.'

The mention of Nathan these days, even just the thought of him makes my temperature spike.

'Just make sure you know what you're getting yourself into, Fee.'

I tell Layla my taxi has arrived and I'll send her a message when I get home; I don't want to listen to any more lectures.

I step inside the black taxi and slide into the leather seat. I remember the day Nathan brought my Range Rover home, how happy he was with himself, how angry I was with him.

'I've got a little something for you,' Nathan says playfully.

Well, you can keep it, arsehole.

I'm standing at the sink, washing last night's dinner dishes, a wasted meal since he never came home from his work run to Spain like planned, three hours of cooking scraped into the bin. I sat watching my phone until midnight, with no phone call or message to say where he was or he was running late. My temper exploded to a new high, my stubbornness not allowing me to phone him. Must be the hormones. I promised myself if he came home safe, I'd make sure I would hurt him for making me worry, but since he walked through the door at eleven o'clock this morning, I can't even bring myself to speak to him.

I left the table set up, candles, wine glasses with non-alcoholic wine in them: if I can't drink alcohol neither can he. Purely theatrical, so I could scrape the wasted food into the bin in front of him and make him feel awful.

His hands slip onto my hips and I feel him pressing hard against me, his nose nuzzling through my hair to kiss my neck. I flinch, surprising myself at how much I want to kill him. I grab his hands, throwing them off my hips as I slip away from him, grabbing a dish towel to dry my hands as I go. 'Do you think you can just come home, try to seduce me, and I'll forget last night? I mean, what the fuck Nathan!'

I storm from the kitchen, the heat from my face burning with anger. 'Were you buried that deep inside some other girl that you couldn't fucking phone me?' I scream.

I feel him grab my wrist before my feet even reach the hall, pulling me back to him.

'Is that what you think I was doing? Cheating on you? Jesus fuck Freya, these hormones are really messing you up, making you paranoid,' he says, laughing.

Is he serious? He's turning this on me, making me look like I'm overreacting?

'Why didn't you bloody phone me?' I stare at him, waiting for his pathetic excuse.

'I thought you'd be sleeping. You're always sleeping early these days.'

'So, a text message would have been the sensible option then?' I ask, fuelled with rage.

'I was driving so I couldn't,' he answers, and leans in for a kiss.

I let his lips brush mines before I answer, 'Never stopped you before has it?' I shake his hand from my wrist, turn and walk away from him.

'Fee just look outside. You know that dream car you've always wanted?'

I stop, no way, there is no way we could afford a Range Rover.

'Got you curious now, haven't I? Open the door Fee, look,' he tells me.

My anger slides away by interest, and a little excitement. I've wanted a white Range Rover since I can remember. I saunter to the front door, still not turning to look at him. If he's bought me a white Range Rover, I will be the happiest woman alive.

I slowly open the door, there's no car in the drive, but a small parcel the size of a shoe box on the doorstep. I turn to face him, not understanding, and he gestures for me to lift the box.

I kneel beside it and lift the lid off. A mix of emotions rattle me, I don't know whether to laugh, cry or throw the contents at his head and chuck him out on the street.

Inside the box sits a model Ranger Rover, white and matching white interior. I jump hard to my feet, and spit the words, 'Is this a fucking joke?'

Nathan's laughing, just a little at first and then uncontrollably, hunched over like his sides hurt. 'You should see the look on your face. God, I wish I had my phone to take a picture.'

Something inside me snaps. I bend over with difficultly, a growing baby bump restricting me, lifting the model car from the box and throw it at him. He ducks, the car smashes on the wall behind him.

'Holy fuck Freya! You could've hit me!' he shouts.

Now he looks mad, his laughter exchanged for heavy breathing and narrowed eyes. He walks for me and for a split second I think he's going to slap me, but he doesn't. He walks past me and lifts the box from the doorstep, pulling out a card from the bottom. 'Read this,' he tells me.

I take the card from him.

Open the driver's door to reveal your dream.

Nathan brings back the wreckage of the model car and hands it to me. I pop the driver's door open and retrieve a key. A life size car key.

I look at Nathan, now sitting on the stairs, still glowering at me, I don't understand.

'If you had of just looked in the box and read the card before going off on one, you would've got it. You've just ruined it now with your temper. Your gift is round the side of the house.'

My shoulders sink and I feel that horrible brew of guilt in the pit of my stomach. Fuck Freya, well done.

'Nathan, I'm so sorry. I thought you were messing with me, and I thought, I...'

He interrupts me, before I can say anything else, and says, 'You just thought the worst as usual. I'm going for a shower then bed. I'll speak to you later.'

He stands, his body slowly stretching with exhaustion, and I watch him walk upstairs. I need to control my temper when I'm around him, Nathan has been the only person who gets me in this state. It has to be the hormones, hopefully when the baby is here our relationship won't be so heated.

I head outside to see what's parked at the side of the house.

The taxi stops outside The Hollies, bringing my thoughts back to the present.

Nathan knew how to play me. The more it becomes clear of that with every scenario replayed in my head. I still don't know where he was that night he was due home, or why he didn't phone or message me. That situation was quickly turned around onto me, to make me look like the bad guy. I'm so disappointed at myself for not seeing it all clearly quicker, before it all got out of hand. Now I'm indebted to a man I don't even think I can trust, that I don't want to trust.

I pay the driver and step outside the car, staring at the house. I can't sell it. If I sell it, I'll have almost nothing. I can't do that to Mum. I'll work for Bryce, for as long as it takes. I've made my mind up and now I need to live with it, there is no other option.

Eleven

Cassandra

The room is peaceful when I wake—my eyes open easier than before. I feel as though I have slept for a week. My body is tender but recharged. My baby, he must be fast asleep too.

I roll onto my side to watch him in his hospital cot. He's not there. I roll to my left, nothing.

I feel a pulling sensation. My hand wanders between my legs, and I feel a tube, a rubber tube, a catheter?

How long have I been sleeping? A few hours? It was late afternoon when I came to the hospital; I must have slept overnight? I wonder if he is with the midwife or his Daddy? I'm ever so glad he has come around and seen sense. I knew he would be by my side for the birth. He will be an amazing Dad.

I'm wearing a hospital gown, wet at my chest from my leaking breasts. I need a shower, but I need to see my son first. I reach for the nurse call button behind me and activate it. I wait a few minutes, but no one comes. I press it again, this time the logo lights up and I realise I didn't press it right the first time.

A fresh-faced nurse knocks and enters my room. 'Good morning, glad to have you back with us,' says the Nurse.

'Thank you. How long have I been out?'

The Nurse walks to the window and releases the blinds. 'Almost two days.'

The shock on my face prompts the Nurse to continue, 'You

had quite an ordeal. We thought we'd lost you, but you pulled through. If it weren't for Dr Hutton, I dread to think...'

The overly fidgety Nurse trails off, fixing my bedsheets, fixing them into perfect hospital corners.

Who is Dr Hutton? Why was my doctor, Dr Cox, not present for the birth?

'The Auxiliary Nurses have been taking good care of you, but we couldn't find your hospital bag, so you must excuse the fashionable hospital attire,' she says, giving herself a small inward laugh, as though she has said that exact line more than once and giddy with the memories.

She wasn't the Nurse at my bedside when I gave birth; she's shorter and dark-haired, older. My memory hazy but I remember that much.

'My son, Nurse, where is he? I would really like to see him as soon as possible. To meet him properly.'

The Nurse takes a few minutes to answer, studying the sheets first. 'Now, now, plenty of time for that, let's just make sure you're back to full health first. We don't want you overdoing it.'

That doesn't answer my question. 'Where is my son, please?' I ask, my voice more authoritative.

'Your son is with your husband.'

'He is not my...' I stop myself.

Has he told the hospital he's my husband? The thought warms me. Everything I wanted, a perfect family of three.

When I was in my late teens, I became very ill, bleeding badly, and had to go through a lot of tests. They diagnosed me with a condition known as PCOS. I had no idea at the time what that diagnosis meant. Safe to say I was heartbroken when I did some research.

Polycystic ovaries, harmless follicles that grow inside the ovaries. *Harmless*, the doctor told me that too. Harmless if it weren't for the fact it made me infertile.

'Don't worry, all that means is you will most probably need some fertility treatment if you go down the path of wanting to have children,' the doctor commented.

At nineteen, that wasn't a question that was on my mind, but from then on, I stopped using my contraceptive pill. And the doctor was right; I was infertile for eleven years.

I shudder at his reaction when I first told him, *my husband*, I was pregnant. That look on his face—disappointment? No, more like disgust, pure undignified disgust at me. Disgust at me for thinking I lied to him about not being able to have children.

The doctor said it happens; people fall pregnant naturally, they're blessed. I didn't feel blessed after telling him.

'Are you trying to ruin me? Ruin what we have? How can I ever trust you after this?' he scowled at me.

The memory makes me feel sick.

'Would you tell him I'm awake, please Nurse?'

Nurse Fidgety nods and leaves. I rest back onto my freshly plumped pillows, feeling relaxed and excited that I get to see my boy. He's two days old, but I have waited a lifetime to meet him. My stomach roars with hunger. It has been at least three days since I've eaten. I glance at the clock on the wall, 11:40. Gosh, I've missed breakfast. I expect lunch should be soon. I've never been a fan of hospital food, not my usual fine dining experience, but I plan on eating whatever is on the lunch menu, need to keep my energy up for my baby boy.

I cannot wait to meet him.

Twelve

Freya

In my head, time has stood still. Every night before I sleep, I say a small prayer to my Papa, wishing the last year away. I would wish away the parts of my life that included the moment Nathan chapped on Mum's door if it wasn't for Clara being the best thing to come out of an unpleasant situation.

Ideally, I would wish away the split-second decision to book a next-day flight to Thailand on a silly whim, leaving Mum on her own for three months. If I hadn't of done that, I would have been there to send Nathan packing when he first arrived.

It hasn't stood still, though, and I can't wish away any of the poor decisions of my life. Clara is the reason I can deal with the bad.

Clara's first birthday has been and gone. Her Daddy has missed it, and her first step, her first word, every major milestone to date. But I don't care anymore, that is his punishment even though he's probably burning in hell for every bad thing he has done in his life. I hope he is burning in hell. Clara doesn't need a thief for a Father in her life, a manipulator. I've read about girls with Daddy issues, ending up falling in love with someone exactly like their deadbeat Dads.

Ironic really, isn't it? I fell in love with him because he was different, different from my normal type of weak men who fell at my feet. He made me chase him in bewitchment. He was a fraud, just like Dad, minus the violence, or would it eventually have gotten like that? It won't happen again.

I keep myself awake, frequently tossing from side to side. My mind decided it wasn't ready to shut down and sleep almost four hours ago. Instead, it went ahead being selfish and hosting a party of random thoughts and memories that I completely forgot were sneaking about in there, along with thoughts on where Sammy ever disappeared too?

Sammy was my childhood pet dog. Well, when I say my childhood pet, he was my Papa's dog, so naturally, I stole him and classed him as my own.

My Papa used to walk for miles every day. He would wake up, make Gran's breakfast, and then take him for a walk for hours. Sammy used to disappear and turn up hours later, scratching the back door to summon someone to open it for him. One day, he never came back home. I know it upset my Papa as the days went on, said he probably fell down a hole in the hills they walked and could never get himself out. Of course, Papa walked the same route every day after, but there was still no sight of poor Sammy.

Strange, isn't it? The thoughts that haunt you only at night-time.

I hear a creak on the stairs, and I sit up, eyes focused out to the dark hall. Third stair from the top. We learned to bypass that step when Clara started sleeping in her own room; the slightest noise would wake her up.

I listen contently, no more noise. I relax back into bed. I feel myself drifting into sleep, thanking the creek of the stair for evaporating my head party.

Another creek sounds, a distinctive creek this time making my eyes spring open, it's the floorboard outside Clara's bedroom, across from my room.

I climb from the bed and head out into the hall to investigate. I look to my left towards the stairs, nothing. I turn to my right; the top of the hall is dark under the attic hatch, nothing. I sigh low with relief and turn back around into the bedroom.

I'm stopped in my tracks, spinning back around as movement from the top of the hall startles me. I screw my eyes up, trying to adjust them to the dark. Again, a dark shadow moves, a silhouette of a body.

'Nathan?' I whisper.

I take a step forward, my heart racing, but I'm not scared. 'Nathan, is that you?'

I spin around and head down the hall to the top of the stairs for the light switch. I flick it on and turn as quickly as my feet allow me. The hall glows from the light, and to my displeasure, it's empty. The attic door sits closed, silent. I'm alone.

Jesus Christ, I'm losing my mind.

I run my fingers through my hair; my breathing is harsh with adrenaline. I need sleep. Thank God Mum will be here in two days, maybe then I will get some proper sleep.

I hope that creepy old man isn't at the pool today. There's something about him that makes me feel uneasy.

When he first started hanging around, I thought I was paranoid, that maybe he was sitting in the spectator's box as he was waiting on someone in the pool. A Grandchild, possibly? Or his wife, who was maybe in my swim class? I tried to shrug it off until I noticed him looking down at me every time I looked up to the window. He would sit with his open newspaper, always peering around from behind it. It was putting me off teaching my clients; I would lose focus when I felt his eyes fixed on me. I tried covering myself up in my swimsuit, thinking he could be some sort of pervert.

The first few times I caught him, he would quickly look away. Now he stares right back at me, determined to get my attention. Part of me wonders if it's the wicked men that Nathan had dealings with deciding to make their move now the police have backed off. There was never any sight of him when I'd finished work. I don't like it. If he's about today watching me, I'm telling Bryce.

The showers are directly underneath the spectator's box; I stand under the cold shower before entering the pool. I can't see if he is above me, looking for me. He is always there, waiting for me to leave the changing room. I don't know if he drives here or what he drives so I can't even check for his car or confront him.

Right Freya, shoulders back, chin up and walk to the pool like you've never noticed him. I take a deep breath in and make my way to the adult's pool, to the left side of the showers. I keep walking, smiling at Dan, the on-duty lifeguard sitting on his tall chair overlooking the full pool area. He's here every Tuesday morning. He gives a friendly wave back. I only need to scream, and he'll come running to my rescue.

I don't think I've ever had a tall, blond, tanned Australian come to my rescue before? I remember a time when I wouldn't have said no.

I get to the top of the pool closed off for my 9 am, over fifties swim class. Slowly turning around just enough to have a quick glance up at the spectator's box. I can't believe my eyes, it's empty. Not one person in the concrete grey box.

It has two levels of seating, with twenty-four red plastic chairs. The box is on the upper main wall of the arena, centred and full glass front so you can see the entire pool area. There was nowhere in there for him to hide.

Feeling a little stupid, I've been so paranoid the man was something sinister. An immense sense of relief that I can put my full concentration into my class today eases me. A part of me still wondering where he's gone, though.

10:50 and the class was finished. My two elderly regulars didn't stay for their usual chat after class, not that I was complaining. Plenty of time for steam therapy.

The steam attacks my body as soon as I open the door to the sauna. I sit down on the wooden slatted bench, throw my legs up and lay down. Closing my eyes, allowing the soothing heat to melt into my skin.

'Just what the doctor ordered, isn't it,' a strange voice begins.

I don't open my eyes yet. Annoyed, thinking I was alone, I let out a loud sigh. The man probably isn't talking to me. If I didn't see him in here then there could be more, I don't reply.

'I was hoping to catch you. I know you sometimes don't have time if your class runs over,' he says, this time it's definitely me he is directing the conversation at.

I don't know this man's voice, but I'm feeling uneasy. I open my eyes, sit up and put my feet on the floor. With my hands holding onto the bench at each side of me, I lean forward, focusing my vision as the steam settles to see who the unknown voice belongs to.

A figure sits in the far corner, I look around but can't see anyone else.

'I'm sorry, are you speaking to me?' I ask, slightly disconcerted.

'I apologise, please excuse my manners. My name is Collins, Albert Collins.'

I don't answer him. My vision is still trying to focus on his face through the mist. It can't be him, can it? Is this why the spectator's box was empty? I haven't seen him up close, only from afar, but my gut is telling me it's the creepy old man from the spectator's box. He doesn't have the khaki green, worn-out looking trench coat on, and his normally scruffy hair is flat with the steam making him look younger, but it's him I'm sure of it.

I'm in a sauna with a man who's been practically stalking me for almost five weeks, and I really should get to my feet and leave, but I pause.

'Sorry, Detective Albert Collins, I should say.'

Detective? I'm slightly less afraid and more intrigued, so I get straight to the point. 'Why have you been watching me, Detective?' I try to make myself sound fearless but note my voice is shaky. 'Have I done something wrong?'

'No, I'm sorry, I had to make sure you were who I'm looking for, Freya? Freya Lynn?' he asks. His voice is strong English and polite, very gentlemanly.

'Yes?' I answer, my intrigue growing.

Trying not to seem interested, I relax back against the wooden bench. Inside, I'm far from relaxed.

'I'm sorry about Nathan's accident.'

Firing forward to the edge of the bench, I snap before I can stop myself, and ask, 'How do you know my husband?'

'Your husband was helping me with my enquiries, Mrs Lynn. He passed away before I concluded my investigation. I was hoping you could help me?'

The steam fades, I can see his face more clearly. It looks bloated and red, and I realise he's been sitting in the sauna for much longer than is healthy, waiting for me here rather than the spectator's box. I'm hesitant he's telling the truth, my faith in the police in short supply.

'I'm sorry, Detective, but Nathan has been dead for almost a year. I don't see what I can help you with.' I stand to my feet and walk to the door as I feel my eyes swelling.

Detective Collins stands to his feet like a gentleman gracing a lady when she leaves a room. He's a lot taller than I thought he was. Maybe around six feet, well-built and not intimidating at all. I pictured him with a well-fed belly hanging over his trousers, short and scruffy, but he's none of those things, he's just a normal man.

'I didn't mean to upset you, Mrs Lynn, I understand I have made you uneasy. I have left my card in an envelope at reception for you, put it somewhere safe and out of sight. Call me. I think we have a lot to talk about.'

I give him a nod and turn away, with no plan to call him. I'm confused, though. What does he want to talk about?

Deep in my mind, I don't want to know. I need to get away from him; I don't want to speak about Nathan anymore. I put my hand on the misty door and push it open when I hear him again.

'Oh, and Mrs Lynn, I think it's best all-round if you don't tell Bryce anything about meeting me today, or anyone else.'

I quickly turn my head, narrowing my eyes to look at him. My mind going into overdrive now, what the hell has gone on? I turn my back on him and leave the sauna.

I change and leave as quickly as my legs will take me and sit in my car.

The car engine is running, waiting for me to go home but I can't bring myself to drive away, something stopping me from going, my curiosity maybe?

I don't want to contact that Detective. Nathan is dead, leaving me to deal with the aftermath of his secret life, his illegal shit. Whatever dealings he was having with the police I don't want to know, but why did he mention Bryce? Why did the Detective not want anyone to know he had approached me, that he had been stalking me? Now I'm torn, torn between trusting the Detective or telling Bryce about my encounter with him.

I need to know everything before I decide.

I turn the engine off, leave the car and run back inside the building. Heading towards the reception, I ask for the envelope the Detective left for me.

Thirteen

Cassandra

My patience is growing thin. Three hours have passed since the Nurse left. There has been no sign of my boy yet. I don't need this much bloody rest. I need my son.

I press the Nurse call button again.

Without my hospital bag, I have nothing. I packed my mobile phone into it when we left for the hospital.

I press the Nurse's alarm again, nothing. Again, I press, but I don't remove my finger.

Ping, ping, ping rings around the room, and I hear hurried footsteps arrive at my door.

'Miss Chesterfield, is everything okay?'

A different nurse, slightly out of breath, walks by me and resets the Nurse alert.

'The Nurse that was here before, she went to get my son. I haven't met him yet, why hasn't anyone brought him to me?'

The Nurse stops me before I continue, her voice calming, 'Shh, it's okay. You've been asleep for a long time. I don't think seeing your son is best right now. You've just woken up.'

My temper snaps, but my voice doesn't raise. 'Enough of this rubbish. I have been awake for hours. Your colleague already checked on me and said she was going to arrange for my son to come to me.'

The chirpy young Nurse looks startled. I can almost see the wheels in her head-turning, trying to find something to say to me.

'There must be some mistake, Miss Chesterfield, the only Nurse that has been checking on you is me since I started my shift at seven o'clock this morning, you have been asleep every time I have been in.'

'Are you accusing me of lying?' I snap, trying to prop myself up in the bed, surprising myself with my outburst.

'Hey, hey you, calm down. It's okay, Nurse. I'll take it from here.'

The Nurse looks just as relieved as me, and she hurries her tiny frame out of the room.

'Ben!' I yell.

He's finally here.

The tears burst free and run down my cheeks as he sits down on my bed beside me. I wince in pain, trying to hug him, my catheter stings below. He pulls back from me; his hands reach for my shoulders, and he gently eases me against the pillow. I'm thankful he has given me some relief.

'Our son, no one will bring him to me. I'm so worried he is sick, or something terrible has happened. Where is our son? The first Nurse said you were with him?'

I watch him, his face intense. A face I have never seen him wearing in the six years we have been together. Fear shocks down my body when I realise its sorrow, he's sad, but why?

'Ben, what's going on? You're scaring me.'

He shuffles his body closer to me, as close as he can get. I ignore the stinging of the pain this time.

'Cass, he's gone,' he tells me, his voice choked with emotion.

He can't look at me once the words have fallen from his tongue.

'Gone where? Have they taken him to another hospital? Is he sick?'

His head doesn't lift; my patience now alerting an empty tank.

'Answer me, Goddamnit!' I scream.

I freeze when I realise I've raised my voice at him—at Ben. I have raised my voice once at him in the past. I have never done so again. He made sure of that.

He ignores my outburst for the time being.

'Our son was stillborn, Cassandra. The Doctor said the umbilical cord got wrapped around his neck,' he explains as his head lifts to look at me, his eyes glazed, watching for my reaction as the words hang in the frosty air between us.

I search his face for the truth; I know what he is saying cannot possibly be the truth. It just can't.

I sit in limbo.

Am I still sleeping? Stuck in a nightmare?

'But I heard him crying. I remember his soft whimpers breaking into cries. I heard him crying out for me.' I can't fathom any of this. There must be some mix-up. I straighten up, push him back and say, 'You were there, you heard him too. I remember you there.'

'I was by your side the whole time, Cass. He didn't make any noise. His eyes were closed; it looked like he was just sleeping. I know how hard this is, I've been with him every minute, so he wasn't alone.'

I refuse to answer him. None of this is true. I heard him crying. I heard his whimpers. I knew he was my own as soon as I heard him.

'I want to see him,' I say, the tears swiftly stopping.

I won't believe any of this until I see him.

'Cass, I don't think...'

'I don't care what you think. You either bring my son to me, or I will go to him.'

Ben stands up by the bedside, his shoulders straight, the way he stands when an argument is imminent. I push myself back into my pillows, looking for them to wrap around me and shield me from his reaction. To my surprise, he nods and leaves.

I breathe hard, deep breaths, and I wait for my heart to give out. None of what he has told me is real. I will know this when I see my baby.

Fourteen

Freya

A few days go by before I find the courage to call Detective Collins. It was so close to Nathan's anniversary that I couldn't bring myself to call him before that.

Sitting on the edge of my bed, I stare at the card in my hand, contemplating what to do, telling myself phoning him would just open up old wounds.

It wasn't a printed business card with all of Detective Collins' credentials on it; it was a small piece of ivory coloured card with a mobile number written messily in pencil, nothing else. How strange for someone in a profession such as a Detective?

I've sat here since I settled Clara in bed at 20:30. Quarrelling with myself about what to do. Would I regret calling him? Or would I regret not calling him? I knew what the answer was. I needed to know. As much as I didn't want to admit it to myself, it was eating away at me inside.

I glance at the bedside clock perched on a chest of drawers beside my bed. 23:10. Was it too late to call? I know if I don't do it now, then I'll never have the confidence to.

My hand trembles picking up my phone, I try to steady my fingers to dial the number on the card. A man answers almost instantly. Was he watching his phone, waiting for it to ring?

'Detective Collins?'

'Mrs Lynn?' he replies.

He has the same polite manner on the phone, a well-polished

professional tone to his voice. It almost doesn't go with his scruffy, laid back look.

'Yes, I'm sorry for calling you this late. I hope I haven't disturbed you or your wife?' I ask.

'That's all right, Mrs Lynn, you haven't disturbed me.' He pauses for a moment, then continues, 'I didn't think you were going to call me. It has been almost two weeks, and you haven't been at work. I was worrying.'

He sounds genuinely concerned.

'I took some time off, Detective. This isn't a good time for me.'

It would have been better if he hadn't approached me and made things worse, I could've sailed through the past two weeks better.

'I see. Understandable, Mrs Lynn, but I'm glad you're safe. Have you had time to think over my request to meet? I have a few things I wish to discuss with you. It would be best for us both to do it face to face, sooner rather than later.'

'Is this about Nathan's past, Detective?'

'How so Mrs Lynn?'

'His criminal record? The charges for theft and assault?'

'What makes you think Nathan had a criminal past?' Detective Collins asks, sounding shocked, almost as though this information is new to him, which answers my question if he needed to speak to me about Nathan's past.

'I think we need to meet Mrs Lynn.'

'I think that would be a good idea.'

I need to know why my husband was helping the police. Detective Collins sounds pleased and slightly relieved that I have agreed to meet with him.

'I will meet you tomorrow after your morning swim class. You usually leave around eleven o'clock, so I'll meet you in the cafeteria around then if that suits you?'

He knows so much about me, it's unsettling. The quicker I find out what's happened, the better.

'Yes, that suits me fine, Detective, I'll see you tomorrow.'

Just as I'm about to hang up the phone, he quickly adds, 'Oh, one last thing Mrs Lynn, you may wish to delete my number off your calls list, goodnight.'

The phone goes silent.

My mind won't shut down. My train of thought is going full speed ahead, and I can't reach the breaks to stop it. I don't think I've slept a wink all night. My mind filled with every scenario possible about Nathan. Who was he? Who was the man I shared a bed with? Shared a life, and a daughter with?

My bed shakes, Clara is trying to climb onto my bed beside me. My eyes open but I feel worn out, I'm not ready to deal with her energy just yet.

'Cuddle into Mummy baby and close your eyes. Mummy just needs your big squishy hugs.'

She giggles and does the opposite. Going back to sleep is clearly not an option.

'Go, werms,' Clara says, pointing at the window.

Mum must still be sleeping. She usually stirs when she hears Clara. I'm thankful she still makes the long trips to visit us, staying for two weeks every time she visits. This time she plans on staying three weeks, and I couldn't be happier to have her longer.

It was 03:13 the last time I checked the clock on my phone. What time is it now? I lift my phone from the bedside unit, 05:46.

There's a text message from Bryce asking if I'm okay. I didn't call him last night; I didn't feel up to it. I hit reply and text him back, telling him I fell asleep early.

A reply vibrates on my phone as soon as I send the text message, a curt reply saying he'll call tonight. Does he know the police have been in contact with me? Is that why his reply was short? How could he know?

I need coffee; I get out of bed, lifting Clara with me, trying to shake off my train of paranoid thoughts. I need to get through this morning's meeting with the Detective before I worry about Bryce.

'Okay, Clara, let's go dig for worms.'

Fifteen

Cassandra

I met my son today—my beautiful, long-awaited baby boy. A child I made peace with never being able to have.

Today I met my dead baby boy. He was small, helpless, cold.

They brought him to me, wrapped in a blanket. A stranger's blanket, but it didn't contain the cold. It sunk through the fibres into my skin, leaving a burn of death on my naked arms. I held him for a long time—I didn't want to let him go. I silently prayed for him to open his eyes, to let everyone know he was just holding them shut until his Mummy woke up, so I was the first thing he saw.

I prayed to God to let him live, for always being a good person, a kind person. A person who done no wrong in life, who only wanted to make his Daddy happy. Was our son being born asleep what Ben wanted? Did he secretly pray for this? I shake off the sickening thought.

I cradled him; his frame was so tiny. I don't even know what weight he is, *was*? I don't know if I should talk about him in past or present tense.

I ran my fingers ever so softly over his face, taking it all in so I wouldn't forget how perfect he was. He didn't look like me; he didn't look like Ben. They say that though, do they not? Babies don't look like anyone when they're born. Although, according to my Mother, I was so identical to my Father when I was born; it was as though he was the one who carried me for nine months, then spat me out—a clone of himself. An unlikeable way to describe it, but my Father's taste in sentences was relatively more relaxed than Mothers. Mother used to get annoyed. All that hard work for nine months, morning sickness and stretch marks and I come out looking like him. To this day, she doesn't find it amusing; the stretch marks she wears are a constant reminder. Daddy finds it funny. I do a little too.

Something swiftly changed in me today. He didn't look like his Daddy or me. He couldn't be ours. That baby was not my son.

I opened the blanket at his neck. A blue-ish purple line visible on his bird thin neck. My heart ached for the poor baby, but he wasn't my baby to mourn. I think back to Ben, his disgust at me.

'Take him away, please,' I say to Ben. 'He is not my son. Take him back to his actual Mother.'

Ben looks in horror at me. No, I'm mistaken, he's embarrassed.

He opens the door and asks the Nurse to come back in, his face twisting as irritation at me brews. I hand the fragile baby back to the nurse gently, as though I'm scared to wake him, thanking her for taking him away. Careful not to make eye contact with Ben. Eye contact that will tell me what's in store for me. Just one glance from him will diminish my small fragment of credence.

My tears have dried from my eyes, but the residue remains on my cheeks and T-shirt. 'Cassandra, this isn't healthy, I thought you seeing him... I thought seeing Jasper would help.'

'That is not his name, that is not our son. Our son is alive somewhere in this hospital, and there has been a terrible mix-up,' I say, my posture remaining gallant.

Bens patience is wearing thin, I'm taking up too much of his time. Funny, we are back to our old ways. His stance is tall, authoritative, and I know he wishes he was elsewhere. He has no time for my crap, sorry not a word I use often, but Ben seems to use it around me a lot. I have heard this line from him so many times in past years, I've lost count.

'I'm sorry, Ben. Am I eating into your time? I can take this from here if you need to leave.'

'I don't need to leave, but I think it's for the best if you have some time on your own to reflect on your behaviour.'

I laugh sarcastically. I can't give a dignified response to that statement—my behaviour. I'm allowed to act however I like considering not even three days ago I went into labour and woke up in a different hospital room, with people trying to tell me I imagined hearing my son. That I was hallucinating because of medication they gave me, which I didn't consent to be given. I must remember and ask my Doctor, who gave consent for me to have pain relief. My Doctor! With everything that's been happening, I've not even thought about my Doctor.

'Could you tell Dr Hutton on your way out I would like to see him, please? Thank you.'

I don't give him the opportunity to answer; I wasn't asking, more commanding. It's about time I met him.

'I think I should be here to speak to the Doctor with you as you said, he was our son.'

Ben's stance has not faltered, staring from six feet tall. It used to be intimidating. Now I realise he is just a small man regardless of how tall he is.

'Well, have we not changed our tune? Tell my Doctor I would like to see him on your way out. I won't tell you again,' I say.

Ben's face changes, his lips tighten. He takes a step forward towards the side of my bed, and I tense. He notices. He laughs, takes his hands from his pockets, and crosses them over his chest. 'That's what I thought, don't push me, Cassandra. We both know what happens when you get too ballsy, don't we?'

Yes, I know all too well. Does he have the guts to lay a hand on me in the hospital? Do I have the guts to find out? I sink back into my pillows. No, I don't. I need him more than ever.

'I can speak to the Doctor when you come back. I'm so sorry, Ben. I didn't mean to make you angry; I'm so sorry. These past few days have been the worst of my life. Please, forgive me,' I say, fighting with myself not to cry.

He doesn't like me crying.

'Oh baby, I'm not angry, not this time. I'm sad, very sad at what's happened. Who's here to look after you? Me, no one else looks after you like I do, do they?' He sits on the edge of my bed, cups my cheek in his hand, and I melt.

I whisper I'm sorry into his hand before he kisses me on my forehead and leaves. Promising me, he will bring my hospital bag and mobile phone when he comes back. Mother doesn't know.

She'll be out of her mind with worry.

Sixteen

Freya

Detective Collins sits in the far right-hand corner of the cafeteria, a lonely table in an area that you can't see from the entrance nor any windows. He's clearly trying to be discreet and keep out of sight—his face hiding behind his newspaper. It's the khaki green trench coat I first notice, and the wild silver hair like he has just gotten out of bed and ran his fingers through it. Fingers or a branch, I can't quite tell.

He sees me and waves me over, looking relaxed with his legs crossed. Glad one of us is. He's dressed in black suit trousers and a pair of black Adidas trainers. What an odd dress sense he has. Anyone would think he's homeless. Maybe he is?

'Good morning, Mrs Lynn, would you like to take a seat?'

It seems my tongue is still asleep. He slides a chunky white mug in front of me and asks, 'White and one sugar if I remember correctly?'

What? How the hell does he know what I take in my coffee? Completely knocking me off guard with one sentence, the first sentence. It provokes my temper, making me worry about how the rest of the meeting is going to go.

Give the man time to explain Fee, relax.

'I'm sorry, please forgive my ignorance, traits of the job, an excellent memory. I met Nathan a few weeks before his accident, and he ordered a coffee to take home to you. He explained you were exhausted with the baby and you were living from day to day on coffee,' he explains as his eyes meet mine.

I came here today intending to be confident, optimistic, friendly and give this man a chance to say his peace. But after one mention of his name, Nathan, I crumble in annoyance.

I thump down, sliding deep into the red plastic bucket chair across from him. I try my hardest to stay focused without projecting my disgust. 'Can we just get straight to it, Detective?' I ask firmly, but still friendly.

'Of course, please bear with me.'

His hand reaches inside the trench coat and retrieves a black paper folder. He hesitates before placing it on the table. The Detective continues, 'Three years ago, I began working on a case, a case that seemed completely impossible at first. A young woman approached me at the station one summer afternoon in 2015. She must have been around twenty-four. She told me how she had given birth to twin baby girls, but one of them was sadly stillborn.' He stops, his face growing serious.

My stomach already in knots, unconsciously tapping my left hand on the table, wondering what this has to do with Nathan. I ask, 'I'm sorry, Detective, but I don't see what relevance this has to my husband or me?'

'If you let me continue Mrs Lynn, you'll understand shortly. I just want to make sure I don't leave any crucial information out.' He pauses and looks at me, waiting for me to allow him to continue.

I nod my head at him.

'As I was saying, the young lady explained to me she had given birth to two healthy baby girls. They had given her Diamorphine, so she was extremely drowsy and fell asleep almost instantly after the girls arrived. She woke up three hours later to find her husband holding only one daughter, breaking the news to her that the youngest twin had been stillborn. Understandably, the young woman was completely grief-stricken and asked to see her daughter, but the Doctor refused. After arguing with Doctors for some time, they allowed her access to her dead daughter to say goodbye, but after seeing the child, it convinced the woman she wasn't her daughter. She had come to the police station with the hope I would investigate her concerns. She explained that during labour, the heartbeat monitor showed two healthy heartbeats, but the Doctor said the baby died in the womb at around thirty-five weeks and that the second heartbeat was her own. I applied for a warrant to have the dead child's DNA checked, but they had cremated the baby with the Father's consent. We couldn't take the case any further, so it was closed. Then the most peculiar thing happened. I did a bit of digging, and a woman had made another complaint of the same nature after giving birth to a baby boy a few years before, in 2011. The death certificate stated stillborn, but the Mother was adamant she heard her baby crying after labour. Again, there were no further leads as they had cremated the baby. It played on my mind for a long time afterwards, so I did some private investigating on the side, seeing if there was any connection to the dead babies. I found that both Fathers worked for the same company, Harris Haulage.'

Detective Collins opens the folder and places two birth certificates in front of me, both stating where the Fathers worked. I don't understand what this has to do with Nathan; I want to stand up and leave. I'm exhausted with the last year, I'm exhausted hearing his name. It seems trouble follows it, even in death. My head tells me to stay, to listen.

He continues, 'After a lot of digging around, I found another two similar deaths reported at different hospitals spread over the Kent area. Three years apart but one with the same Father as the complaint made in 2011, who was the owner of Harris Haulage and the other Father an unfamiliar name. I hit a dead-end when I discovered the company had been closed and there was no sign of Mr Harris or his two employees. It was as though they had vanished. In August 2017, I received a phone call from a private number asking me to meet as he had information about some missing babies. You can understand my surprise at the phone call that I had to meet with this stranger. I met with him, and he told me he had suspicions that the man he worked for was running an illegal trading company covered up by a home makeover and delivery company. He told me this man was trading babies, and that he had evidence to back up his allegations.'

I sit frozen in my chair, eyes wide and fixed on the Detective.

'Mrs Lynn, the man I met with, was your husband.'

My mind goes blank. Anger sparks in my stomach and a cold, deathly shiver travels up my spine. Nathan worked as a truck driver for Bryce's company, transporting goods abroad to the homes Bryce's team was renovating.

I gulp hard as reality hits. 'Detective, are you telling me that there is a possibility that Nathan travelled abroad with one of those tiny babies hidden inside his truck? Did Nathan know he was doing it?'

I feel a lump forming in my throat, I'm not sure I'm ready for the answer.

'No, Mrs Lynn, Nathan had no idea. Another employee brought it to your husband's attention, and when the owner found out, he tried to bribe Nathan to keep quiet. Nathan contacted my station, and an officer gave my number to him. He was very helpful in our enquiries.'

The lump in my throat drops back down to the depths of my stomach, and I let out a relieved sigh. 'Why didn't Nathan tell me any of this?'

'He didn't want to put you in danger,' says Detective Collins.

'I'm his wife, Detective. He should've trusted me with everything.'

And then I remember the conversation the day he died. He was desperate to leave Edenbridge. I remember how he spoke about his boss being a bad guy. 'Nathan and I were planning on leaving Edenbridge. He wouldn't tell me why, but he said he was done with working. Something about his boss being a bad man? He was going to explain to me when he got home that day.'

'Before Nathan started working for Bryce, another young man who worked for him approached me. The lad explained he could get me evidence, but he went missing and turned up a month later, dead in his flat. Wolves had eaten the poor lad. Strange case, I knew it was murder but couldn't prove it to my annoyance, as though there was someone on the inside covering up leads.'

The news, in Mum's kitchen in Stirling, the boy discovered by his neighbour. Eaten by wolves in his own home.

My body cripples with anger, at Bryce, at Nathan, at myself for allowing these people into my life.

'Yes, well, if Bryce had done anything to Nathan, he had it coming. They both sound as bad as each other!' The comment hisses, and I shock myself at the level my anger has just hit.

Jenny and Dan appear at my side.

'You good, Fee?' Dan asks while looking Detective Collins up and down, and I nod while he hovers, suspicious of the Detective.

I don't introduce him to Dan or Jenny. I suspect they think he's some down and out harassing me. Jenny gives me a look of uncertainty, she doesn't believe me, but turns to head back to the office. 'You know where we are if you need us,' she tells me.

Detective Collins leans forward, his elbows resting on the table, not phased in the slightest with his brief encounter with Dan, who is at least three times the Detective's build and could probably squash him with one punch.

'Freya, what have you been told about Nathan?'

I explain to Detective Collins about my encounter with his colleagues, the files Bryce had shown me, all of Nathan's criminal background. Not once does his facial expression change, his poker face is perfection, and I can't tell if the names of the police officers are familiar to him.

'Bryce had police records regarding Nathan's life before he met you? I never once doubted Bryce didn't have police officers on his payroll, or he wouldn't have gotten away with what he has. Let me ask you this, though. If my colleagues thought Nathan was Nathaniel Emmert, shouldn't all the police records have been in this notorious criminal's name, and not your husbands?' asks Detective Collins.

My heart fastens at this because he's right. He is completely right. My heart thumps in a frenzy in my chest.

'Detective, are you telling me Bryce falsified who Nathan was? Why would he do that?'

'Honestly, I can't say why at the minute because there are a few unanswered questions I'm trying to figure out. That's where you come in Freya. Bryce is a devious man, perilous. You cannot trust him. He has a lot to answer for, but he's intelligent, so he knows how to cover his tracks. I surmise that he knew the police were onto him, so he had his inside men plant the seed that Nathan was a criminal. He's kept his head down this last year.'

'Why now, Detective? Why after all this time have you come to me? Why not come to me when Nathan died? What do you want from me?' I rant on, my nerves steering my line of questions.

Detective Collins takes a deep breath in and explains, 'Because I know one of his employees has gotten a girl pregnant after a one-night stand and my gut tells me it is all wrong.'

My face freezes. Bryce is doing all of this. My skin crawls thinking I have let this man, this evil man into my house, called him a friend. I have spent the last year hating my dead husband, not grieving him like I should have been. I want to be sick.

'I think that's enough for one day, Mrs Lynn, I'll give you some time to get your head around all of this, it's a lot to swallow in one go. When you're ready to talk further, call me.'

Detective Collins assures me he'll be around whenever I'm working, and I can call him anytime.

He stands from his chair, sliding the folder back into the trench coat, and a thought passes through my mind, wondering what else he has in there.

Before he leaves, he turns to face me and says, 'Oh, one last thing, Mrs Lynn. Bryce has had someone following you for weeks now. We need to be very careful where we meet. If anyone asks you who I am, my name is Jack Tully, and I'm the husband of one of your swim clients. He's the only person who's build I can pass as. You must not act any differently towards Bryce for the time being. He already suspects the police are following him again. That's why he has had someone following you, in case we contact you.'

I nod as he walks away. Why does he always leave with, *'oh one last thing?'*

There are many unanswered questions from Detective Collins' statement, but it's left me scared. Scared of my temper and the damage it can cause. My head and heart feel broken and bruised. Do I have anything left in me to confront Bryce? No, I can't confront him! I need to keep him away. How can I carry on as normal? He has let me believe Nathan was a criminal. He has let me tarnish my life with him with pure hatred. It's going to be punishing on my sanity.

Seventeen

Cassandra

Yesterday, they introduced me to a sleeping baby, a dead baby. Not my baby.

Today, young Nurse Chirpy tells me I'm free to go home once they have carried a few tests out, my blood pressure, I suspect. I don't know. I'll ask her when she comes back to take my untouched breakfast away. No point in keeping my strength up, is there? I've spent the last two hours rearranging a small bowl of cereal around the hospital table. I tried the so-called freshly squeezed orange juice. It confirmed what I thought when I first saw it, fresh out the carton, with no juicy bits.

My tolerance for lies today is low, no matter how insignificant. I still have not seen my Doctor, or any Doctor, and Ben didn't come back into visit me last night. My punishment for challenging him. Time to think about my behaviour, he said, after I thought we'd turned a corner. I wonder if things had been straightforward and our son had not died, sorry, been mixed up with a dead baby, would we have been better? Possibly perfect?

I miss my possessions. My new Chanel pyjamas I purchased for the hospital, still folded neatly in my hospital bag somewhere, cuddled beside baby blue Stella McCartney sleepsuits, covered in beautifully animated giraffes. My mobile phone so I can call Mother.

However, I'm glad Ben didn't come back last night, it's given me a lot of time to think about my behaviour. I haven't put my foot down and demanded to speak to my Doctor before now. It's been four days, and he's not graced me with his presence. Hiding something from me, perhaps? Does he know he's messed up? Mixed up babies?

Also, I need to find out who was with me in the delivery room; I paid for a private delivery room, which I suspect I gave birth in, so why was I moved to this shoebox closet of a room? By my observations, I'm hidden somewhere out of the way as I hear nothing or anyone. No footsteps, no Nurses, no Doctors speaking. When I activate the Nurse's alert, it takes what feels like an hour for someone to come. So far all I have seen is the first Nurse who apparently doesn't exist, Ben, and now young, full of life Nurse chirpy.

I have never been in this situation before, so I have no idea what the correct procedures are, but I'm clever enough to know something is not right. Mother will know, I cannot wait to speak to her.

The light tip-tap of feet echo outside the door. It's Nurse Chirpy. I have become custom to know whose feet are entering my room next.

'Hello, Cassandra. Aww, are you still not eating? Doctor Hutton said he would rather you were eating before discharge,' she tells me, fiddling with my breakfast dishes.

'Well, Nurse? Sorry I don't even think you told me your name?' I fix my eyes on her with a cheerful smile. A forced, cheerful smile.

'I told you it, don't you remember? You have just been so exhausted.'

'Yes, I have, haven't I? It seems everyone insists on reminding me.'

I hold my gaze at her. She looks away first, walks to the window and fiddles with the blinds.

'Nurse?'

I'm always astounded at how peremptory I am when Ben is not with me.

'Oh sorry, it's Angelos, Nurse Angelos,' she answers, her voice still chirpy.

She walks back over to my bedside and lifts the tray.

'How nice, you are of Greek origin?' I say, my voice still trying to match my forced, cheerful smile.

Nurse Angelos looks spangled, like a deer stuck in headlights. She is speechless, searching for words. I swiftly realise she has no idea her surname is Greek. No identification badge is visible either. When did trained Nurse's job roles involve serving meals and clearing up dishes? She smiles and leaves as quickly as her feet take her.

Stop it, Cassandra, it is not the young girl's fault. She's probably here on work placement.

Yes, yes, that is what it is. She can't be over twenty.

I ease back against the pillows again, running my hand through my hair. I feel how greasy it is, unwashed, neglected. I need a shower. Maybe that will make me feel slightly better, clean body, clean hair, clean clothes, clean mind. Yes, that is the first thing I need right now.

Where is Ben with my hospital bag?

I wake with a start, a knock at my room door disturbs me. Ben walks in before I answer, followed by a short man with fair, thinning hair and Nurse Chirpy-doesn't-even-know-where-her-surname-belongs trailing behind.

I reposition myself up the bed, pulling at the shoulders of my bland hospital gown to make myself more presentable. It doesn't help one bit.

'Afternoon beautiful,' Ben comments in an upbeat tone, as though he has arrived to pick me up from the airport and not a hospital.

As though he's forgotten the last few days, maybe even the last nine months.

He plants a kiss on my lips, leaving me dumbfounded by his public display of affection, not his usual style. Perhaps he has some good news? Perhaps he's found out I'm not mad and agrees something's not right about this total mess.

'Cassandra, this is Doctor Hutton.'

Ah-ha, the famous Doctor Hutton finally shows himself. The Nurse promised he would check on me.

Ben stands aside, allowing the Doctor space to squeeze in beside us and shake my hand. I greet him vacantly, and I'm aware of Ben side-eyeing me to behave. I now realise his public display of affection was to play lord of the manor, to show everyone he is running this circus, showing he runs me.

'How are you feeling, Miss Chesterfield?' Dr Hutton's voice sounds strained, rusty.

I suspect from the raspiness in his throat he is a heavy smoker. He wraps a blood pressure monitor around my left arm, and I watch as it inflates, tightening, then gradually deflating again.

'Blood pressure is perfect, so I'll just check your stitches, and if all is fine, you can go home.'

He pulls two blue latex gloves from his pocket, blows air into them from his mouth and begins sliding his fingers into them.

Stitches? That's right; I have stitches. I felt them when I first felt the catheter. I must have torn when I gave birth? With everything that's happened, it has completely escaped my mind. That explains the endless stinging down below.

'He must have been a chunky little thing,' Nurse Chirpy comments from the doorway and I'm sure I catch the end of Ben rolling his eyes.

Doctor Hutton has already made himself at home on the bed. I close my eyes and try to shake off my private parts being prodded at. He emerges a few moments later, retracting the catheter with him. The yucky feeling makes me wince.

He asks a few more questions about how I'm feeling. I tell him I feel fine, that I'm a bill of health. He gives Ben a nod and tells me he's happy for me to go home. Just like that, I'm supposed to go home and carry on with my vacant life.

I retrieve my bag, my wonderful bag with my clothes, my wash bag and head to the ensuite shower room. When I'm finished, a new lease of life has taken hold of me. I'm ready to face the world and get some actual answers, proper answers from somewhere far away from this twilight zone hospital, mourning no longer for someone else's dead son.

Eighteen

Freya

I've been trying to process every bit of information over the weekend. I'm not sure how long I've been sitting on the stairs, staring at the wall of photographs. I went to bed with my head bursting, the pressure of secrets making it ache, and now I'm here.

Sitting, watching, thinking.

Thinking about how long I can keep up the made of tough stuff act. How many bounces back have I left inside? I fear there aren't many.

Bryce has called me repeatedly, and although Detective Collins said to act normal for now, I can't. I've ignored every phone call, every text. Just his name resting on my tongue makes me want to vomit. Every inch of me wants to confront Bryce—but I can't.

A thunderstorm is brewing inside me, and I fear just how far my temper may go. That bastard has let me hate Nathan, let my grief switch with enmity. I've cursed him, thanked God he is dead, and now I hang my head in shame that I've allowed myself to believe it. Mum believes it, and I can't tell her the truth. I can't tell anyone the truth. It kills me I can't make amends, but not as much as it should.

I thought I would begin grieving again, pick up where I left off. The truth is, a part of me still hates Nathan for not being honest with me, for leaving me with all his crap. There's nothing I know to help with this investigation, and although I don't want to deal with it, I must.

The only thing there is to do now is to help the Detective. It's time to arrange another meeting with him.

I retrieve his card and dial his number, again he answers almost instantly. He sounds relieved when I ask to meet again. Same place, same time tomorrow morning.

Detective Collins is sitting in the same seat, same position, newspaper propped in front of his face and that ugly green trench coat. Surely, he can't have a wife because she would be mental to let him out in public looking so jumbled.

Two chunky white mugs are steaming away on the table, a coffee I could do with right now, the lack of sleep is killing me.

'Thank you for calling again, Mrs Lynn.'

'Please, it's Freya, just Freya.'

'Just Freya,' he smiles, and for a moment, I see past his scruffy demeanour. He's properly out of place in those clothes.

He notices my eye's running over his coat as I sit across for him, making him drop his head a little, and I sense a smile forming on his face.

'You must think I'm potty with my attire,' Detective Collins says, crossing his legs and resting his clasped hands on his knee.

It refines his polite persona, and I wonder who the real Detective is because so far, I'm getting mixed vibes from him. He projects class and dignity but looks unhinged.

'I, um, no, of course not, I...' His laugh stops me, he finds my stuttering amusing, and for a moment, I forget why I'm here.

'My coat was a gift from my wife when I became a Detective. She said every good Detective needed a disguise like Columbo,' he explains as his features soften, and I know he's reminiscing.

'So, what you're wearing is not your normal clothes?' I want to laugh back, but a smile will have to do. It makes me relax, and the tension lifts from me.

'Goodness no. If I had to meet you in my suit and polished derby shoes, then I would stick out like a sore thumb. No one can know we've met Freya.'

I quickly realise he has been in disguise the whole time he has been coming to my work, and I finally see the real Albert Collins. The fear I have for him, the uncertainty, it all subsides. He really is a Detective.

'What is it you want from me, Detective?' I ask, much calmer than our first meeting.

'Please, call me Albert. I want your help.'

He digs inside his Columbo-style trench coat again and pulls out a small, tattered looking grey notebook. 'Please let me explain?' he asks, sitting the grey notebook down in front of him and starts flicking through the yellow sheets of writing paper inside.

'When Nathan last called me, he told me he had evidence that would put Bryce behind bars, evidence that would connect him to the newborn babies. Babies that might still be alive. The last phone call was the morning he died, Freya. He called me when he pulled away from your house.'

Last week the very mention of Nathan made me rage, now it makes my heart hurt, really hurt.

Detective Collins slides the tattered notebook over the table for me to read, clearly worried in case anyone is listening. It reads Nathan had found out that Bryce kept two ledgers of all clients he had done business with in the past ten years, including client contact details and everyone else associated in business dealings with Bryce. It says the ledgers are kept in a safe inside his apartment, along with a laptop detailing all of his bank account transactions. It also reads Nathan had stolen the safe passcode from Bryce's personal phone.

'Does the lake of creation mean anything to you, Freya?' Detective Collins asks.

The Lake of Creation. I haven't heard that for a very long time.

Nathan and I had gone away for a romantic holiday after Christmas 2017 and stayed into the New Year. We travelled to Derwentwater, part of the Lake District in the North-West of England and stayed in a secluded cabin right beside the lake. The scenery was stunningly breath-taking, all around it covered in a blanket of fresh white powdery snow. Quite surreal when you start a new year naked in a hot tub drinking fine wine, making love as the clock struck midnight, looking at the untouched snow and a frozen lake. It was one of the most romantic times of my life, just the two of us, enjoying one another. It almost felt like we were the only two people left in the world, a world of our own with no one to bother us.

I snap back from my moment of nostalgia. 'It does, Albert, it means a great deal to me.'

'Nathan made a copy of that safe code. He told me he put it away in a place which he referred to as the lake of creation and said no one would know where to look other than his wife if anything happened to him, that's you, Freya. What does it mean?'

I can tell by his resigned expression I'm his last hope, the last lead in the investigation. I think how I would feel if I was one of those poor Mothers. If someone had any evidence or knowledge that my child was still alive, I would pray that they would come forward and help me find them. I can't turn my back on the Detective; I must do everything physically possible to help now.

'I don't understand, the lake of creation is miles away. There is no way Nathan could have driven there and back home in a few hours without me knowing.'

Then it occurs to me that's why he was desperate to leave for Stirling before he died so that he could stop at the Lake District on the way there? He died before he could tell me, so I need to figure it out. 'I have no idea what any of this means, Detective, but I'll try to make sense of it. I promise you, I will.'

Driving home, my thought process works overtime, and I feel my anger towards Nathan tenfold. How could he be doing this behind my back and not share this with me, something so serious and fucking dangerous? I'm his wife, for fuck's sake, he could trust me. I want to hit the son of a bitch.

'Freya, are you all right, sweetheart?' Mum asks.

I'm so glad Mum is here. I love having her around. She is a great help to both of us. If it wasn't for her, I think I would have had a nervous breakdown by now.

'Yeah, I'm okay, Mum. I just need this month to be over.'

She hugs me. 'I know sweetheart, but you're doing so well, better than you know.'

'I couldn't have done it without you Mum, you've been the

glue that's held me together.'

'Don't you maybe think it's time to let go, start afresh and come home, back to Stirling?' Mum asks.

Mum and I had spoken a few times at the start about Clara and I moving back home with her. It would have seemed like the most logical thing to do, but I couldn't commit to the move. Did I want to? My head said yes, my heart was a strong yes. If truth be told, I couldn't leave even if I wanted to. I was in debt to Bryce, a false debt.

'Just you and Clara rattling around in this big house isn't healthy though.'

Mum's right, I know she is, but how do I make her understand I can't, without telling her what's going on?

I still hear his voice echo through the house sometimes. His shadow dissolves into the gloom. He haunts me, and I scream inside for him to leave.

'I'll think about it, Mum. Maybe you're right. Maybe it's time to move on.'

Mum gives a comforting nod, but I suspect fireworks are going off inside her. There's been a lot to think about this past week.

'Whatever is changing your mind is good for you and Clara,' Mum says, kissing my forehead.

It's not good for me Mum, it could destroy me.

I smile.

Mum leaves the kitchen, chasing Clara as she zooms up the hall, shouting for Mum to chase her, her infectious giggles reflecting off me. Suddenly, I'm on my feet joining them. The past few day's events forgotten for the time being, and I bask in joy with my little family, or what's left of it.

I can't sleep. Sleep is becoming a thing of the past. Today's meeting with Detective Collins bothers my anxiety. I don't know if this man is lying; I don't know if what he's told me is another lie, like Bryce. Although my gut tells me he's sincere, I have to be sure, but how to find out is going to be hard.

I swipe my phone open and search for the number for Edenbridge police. Making sure my number is withheld, I hit call.

'Edenbridge police station, how may I direct your enquiry please?' answers a female voice.

'Could I possibly speak with Detective Albert Collins, please?'

'Hold please,' the young woman replies. The line beeps, placing me on hold. 'Sorry, but Detective Collins isn't at his desk, but I can direct you to another member of his team?'

'No, thank you, I'll call back later.'

I hit cancel before the young woman can further the conversation. Well, at least I know he's a real Detective.

I go back to the safari app on my phone and search news stories on newborn babies.

Too many search results load up, new mums boasting about their babies being born. I try again but search dead newborn's in London area. I scroll past some articles, nothing reflecting the information Detective Collins has given me.

Just as I give up, ready to click my phone back to lock screen I see it. A local newspaper for Edenbridge reported a new Mum's conspiracy theory into wrongdoings at her local hospital.

The story reads how the local woman gave birth to a son, but unfortunately, the baby boy was stillborn. The woman had called for an enquiry into her son's death, accusing the hospital of covering up wrongdoings as she claimed she heard her baby son crying after birth.

I lock the screen, my head bursting with information. I know now what Detective Collins has told me is true.

Nineteen

Cassandra

It has been four weeks since I left the hospital. I have been to the police; I have taken my complaint to the head of the health board; I have been to a lawyer to see if there is any legal action I can take, but no one will help me.

Ben thinks I should seek some medical help, his patience with me is non-existent, and I know I'm on thin ice with him, very transparent thin ice.

Do I need psychiatric help?

No, not at all, I think?

Well, possibly. I don't know anymore. I don't know who I have become.

Sometimes, I wake in the night with the sound of a baby crying. My baby. The same cries I heard when I brought him into this world. I feel his little heart beating through me. I feel him—not a dead presence, a strong, healthy one. He is not dead; he just isn't.

I need help.

I need someone to tell me how to sort this mess out. Ben was angry with me earlier when I got home and told him I had been to the police. He disappeared from the house for hours. How could I not go to the police? I gave birth to a baby that tore me so severely I had to get seventeen stitches and catheterised. But the baby I met was so frail; he could not have weighed more than five pounds.

The Detective I spoke to said he would check it out but held little hope after I told him Ben had given his permission for the hospital to cremate the baby. I was so angry, words fail how angry I was, but when I challenged Ben about deciding without me, he accused me of shutting him out, of not allowing him the chance to look after me. I thought he was just taking the lead like he usually does, but I see now he saved me more heartache.

When Ben came back, he was calm. He even brought me back a gift: a necklace, delicate platinum chain with a platinum feather. For our lost son, he said. For a moment I thought it meant he agreed that they lost our son, but I understand now he meant lost to death. Such a thoughtful gesture, though.

Christmas Eve is tomorrow. He said that it is going to be our best Christmas yet, just the both of us. Of course, it would be perfect if our boy was here. I don't say those things to him anymore; they make him angry. I still get scared when he's angry. I try so hard to make him happy.

Tonight, the house is peaceful. The sound of wood cracking on the fire echoes through the house and the smell of hot chocolate floats through the air.

'There you go, gorgeous, just how you like it. Milky and covered in whipped cream,' he says, handing me the cup. 'Things will get better. I'm going to make sure of it. You didn't deserve any of this, and I'm so sorry it happened.'

I take a sip. The warmness of the milky chocolate runs down my throat and into my stomach, the heat radiates through me, settling me.

He can be so protective, so affectionate when I'm not making him annoyed with me. I promise myself I will try my best from now on, to do what I'm told and be a good partner for him. I drink more of the hot chocolate, relaxing with every mouthful.

'How are you feeling?' Ben asks, kneeling on the floor beside me, stroking my face.

'I feel so... I feel a little sleepy.'

My eyes are closing, but I don't fight it. I have been so tired, using all my energy to find out what happened to my son. Tonight, I agree is for rest with Ben.

'I need to close my eyes Ben, thank you... for looking after me,' my voice drifts off with my mind.

I feel Ben take the cup from my hands. One last time my eyes open and I see him in front of me, his dark eyes wide, smiling, stroking my cheek.

My nemesis, my protector, my love.

I smile back before I succumb to sleep.

Twenty

Freya

The attic? Nathan knew I hated going up there, so I don't know why he would hide anything for me, but Mum stored all of his belongings up there. Why didn't I think before?

It wasn't the fear of what creepy beasties had taken up residence in my attic, or fear of some old ghost haunting it. It was Ataxophobia that stopped me. Boxes containing God knows what, covered in God knows what, old bric-à-brac thrown everywhere, age-old clutter, no thank you! I shiver at the thought. But Mum had Bryce move all of his belongings up there when I chucked them outside. Maybe the code was in amongst something that reminded him of Derwentwater? But what?

'What do we think Clara, some Foo Fighters and we'll tear this place apart?'

Clara claps her hands in excitement.

'Yip, I agree, let's do it,' I say in the goofiest voice I can.

I ask Alexa to play a mix of the Foo Fighters, and my determination jump starts at The Sky is a Neighbourhood.

Yes!

Mum rolls her eyes, not her taste, but she goes with the flow. She thinks I'm having another one of my episodes, so I suspect she's treading carefully.

The attic smells of oldness. It enters my nose as soon as I open the attic hatch. Boxes of various shapes and sizes scattered across the wooden floor. Miscellaneous items of house furnishings, photo frames, ornaments. It's as though the last owners didn't move out, they just moved up, up into the attic. There must be a full house worth here.

Above, cobwebbed beams meet a series of arches, illuminated by the small window cut into the roof. I'm amazed at how tidy it is. Anyone would think a housekeeper had been doing weekly visits. I feel out of place, trespassing almost in someone else's house. I don't let it stop me. I push myself forward towards the organised clutter.

Do I even know what I'm looking for? No, but I pray I will when I come across it, if I come across it, that is. Where do I even start, there must be at least thirty cardboard boxes and the rest?

I wander slowly, past a collection of portraits, leaning one against the other. They must be at least one hundred years old.

A small photograph in an antique brass frame rests in front of them all. A stone-faced woman in her thirties, possibly early forties with a baby around one-year-old resting on her knee.

Clarissa and Benedict, 1973.

I haven't been afraid of much in my life, people, scary houses, but I relax at the thought I will never cross paths with that woman. A shiver runs down my spine.

I walk towards the gable end of the attic; I can still feel her eyes burning into my back, a warning not to go through her things. Well, if she is still alive now, I doubt there is much she could do to stop me. I stop when I see a mahogany ottoman, its high varnish coating catches the light. It's stunning, I think to myself, and shouldn't hide up in this stuffy old attic. Another thing added to my mental to-do list, move it downstairs.

The ottoman lid opens with ease. Not one bit of rust on the iron hinges, well-oiled it seems. It's filled with old newspapers, and I can only assume they meant something to an old owner at some point, old rubbish to me though. I flick through the rest of the content and find myself surprised when I come across official-looking papers, dated and stamped. One is a birth certificate.

Jasper Louis Hewitt, born November 21, 2011, stillborn, Mother Cassandra Chesterfield, Father Benedict Hewitt.

Behind it, a certificate of death for the Mother, Cassandra Chesterfield. Date of death, December 24, 2011. Suicide.

My stomach churns, the sick getting ready to travel up my throat as I realise I know that name, Cassandra. I've read it before. Where? Where have I seen that name?

I type Cassandra Chesterfield, Edenbridge into my phone and instantly another report from the same newspaper as before appears. Dated a week after the initial report.

Her partner, Benedict Hewitt, had found 30-year-old Cassandra Chesterfield, dead following a breakdown after the birth of the couple's stillborn son. Chesterfield had sent a text message to her Mother, Dee Beaton, stating how she found life hard to cope with after losing her baby boy. Beaton raised the alarm with Chesterfield's partner, and he found her hanging from a tree outside the couple's home. The enquiry into Edenbridge and District War Memorial Hospital has been closed.

A painful lump forms in my throat. I struggle to swallow it down with my saliva. This woman killed herself at my house on Christmas Eve after her baby boy died. I wonder if her partner sold the house after she died?

My knees weaken, and I thump down onto the floor. My head feels woozy, and I decide that's enough attic for one day.

'Did you find whatever you were looking for, love?' Mum asks, sitting on the sofa with Clara.

I hesitate to tell her about my discovery. Does she need to know? She's already gathering enough ammo to get me to move back home. 'Nothing much, Mum, just a load of old junk. It could do with a good gutting up there.'

Like my life.

'I bet there are a few things worth a bit of money. An old house like this must have years of secrets up there.'

You have no idea, Mum, but nothing you need to worry about. 'Probably,' I answer.

I'm lying in bed with Mum beside me, watching TV. Clara's sound asleep between us. All I've thought about is finding the passcode for Detective Collins. He said time was of the essence. The pressure of it all is building up inside me. Everything is depending on me finding that code.

My anger towards Nathan is hitting boiling point. I had no idea it was possible to detest someone that much you would kill them with your own hands if they were still alive.

I need to get out of here; The house is suffocating me.

I leave the bedroom and go downstairs, past our hall of memories towards the kitchen. I stop dead in my tracks when I see Nathan's smile. I glance at another, then another. He is smiling in every picture. No matter how I move, his eyes follow me, mocking me. I wish he would stop. I wish he were here to fix all of this. He had no right to leave. How dare he! Did he know that poor girl killed herself here? Did he know anything about the previous owners? In my head, the answer is yes. He knew everything, and everything was his fault.

I grab a frame from the wall and throw it down the hall. A rush of satisfaction sparks in me. Throwing that frame was like a mini release of anger.

I grab another frame and throw it, then another and another. I can't stop myself. The rage drives me.

Mum appears beside me, silently shouting at me to stop. Her mouth moving, I can't hear her words. Trying to hold me, to console me.

For a moment, I forget all that has happened. Peace blankets me, and a veil of darkness drops. I look around the hall, smashed glass and broken frames carpet the floor.

Clara is sitting at the top of the stairs, looking through the wood of her baby gate, her sleepy eyes watching me. She looks scared, upset. Mum's arms wrap around me.

What have I done?

The noise of glass crushing fills the house, waking me from my restless sleep. For a moment I think I'm stirring from one of my dreams, nightmares of Nathan's crash, but I don't think I dreamt at all. Not after Mum spoon-fed me sleeping pills to shut me up.

Mum's in the hall downstairs cleaning up the glass when I emerge from my bedroom. She must have gotten up early and taken Clara to playgroup. I have woken up like I had a heavy night of drinking, thumping sore head and blank patches in my mind of what happened the night before. The fear of facing Mum overcomes me. She has put up with a lot over the past years. She doesn't deserve any of this.

I creep down the stairs, stopping in the middle to sit down, peering through the wooden slats. She sees me and gives a sympathetic smile but looks away. I know then she isn't angry at me.

I stand and begin my descent in mind and body. She meets me at the bottom of the stairs and wraps her arms around me. That one hug is all I need right now from her.

I examine the mess, the mess I created, all the damage I've done.

Mum has gone to make me a cup of coffee when the doorbell rings, but I slouch on to the bottom step. I don't care who's there; they can fuck off. I turn away, my head looking for support from the wall, but the door slowly creeps open in front of me.

'Morning, anyone home?' a male voice asks.

It's Bryce. Great, as though the morning can't get any worse. I feel a snap inside me, subdued thunder inside my entire body. He enters the house and looks right at me. I must look like a deer caught in headlights.

There's an unmistakable air of blind panic in the room. I've not seen or spoke to Bryce since my meeting with Detective Collins five days ago. He knows something isn't right.

His eyes glance over the mess, then back to me. His shoulders straighten, towering above me, and I'm not sure if he's thinking crazy bitch or I feel sorry for the crazy bitch.

'Everything okay, Fee?'

He walks over and sits beside me on the stairs, then slides his arm around my shoulder and pulls me closer to him, I freeze with disgust but try my best to hide it. Sickness spikes at his touch and I swallow it hard. I don't want his hands anywhere near me. His touch, his smell, everything about him makes me want to vomit. Disgusting human being, he puts on a friendly act. World-class actor. I can't make it obvious what I know.

Don't cry, don't cry, for Christ's sake!

Tears fight to flow with the frustration of not being able to push him away from me and scream what I know.

Mum leaves the kitchen, holding two cups of coffee. I jump

to my feet to take a cup from her. Her eyes connect with Bryce's, I can see they're communicating through facial expressions. *She's finally cracked then?* I imagine he is asking Mum. Her reply: *God no, she cracked years ago.*

The words hang on my tongue, of everything I know about him. I want to tell Mum. It kills me, everything I have kept inside me, every dirty little secret of Bryce's. I want to warn him to stay away from Mum; I want Mum to know what sort of animal he is. His time will come, and when it does, I will love every minute of his downfall.

'She got a bit overwhelmed last night, Bryce. This time of the year is very hard for her, you know,' Mum tells him, sympathy now sounding in her voice, sympathy for her insane daughter.

'I thought I would pop in before work. I haven't heard from her. I know she hasn't been right. I feel terrible I haven't popped in before now to check on her,' he tells Mum.

He sounds that concerned that if I wasn't aware of what he's done, I would think he was sincere.

'I go away next week to meet with a potential new client and was hoping we could have dinner one night next week. I need to talk to Fee about something important,' he says, talking to Mum like they're the only people in the room.

His voice is painful in my ears.

'Jesus Christ, I'm right fucking here! Don't talk like I'm God-damn invisible!'

I take a few moments to realise the words have spat from my mouth and not just passed through my head. Mum watches me, not shocked, not embarrassed, just blank and blinking. I expect she's used to my crazy bitch ways by now.

What could he possibly want? I don't think he knows I've been meeting with the Detective, does he? 'I'll call you later, Bryce. I need to get things sorted here,' I say, bluntly.

I can't help but be blunt with him. He knows I'm under a lot of pressure; he just doesn't know why.

He gives me a disgruntled nod, raises his hand to Mum, which I take as *a good luck with her today* kind of wave, and heads for the door.

His foot catches one of the wooden frames on the floor, the

frame snaps. He bends down and picks it up, holding it, examining the picture. 'We still miss him around the office, you know. It's not quite the same without him,' he says, sounding sad.

He hands me the picture and leaves, looking sorry for himself. Excellent actor in-fucking-deed.

It's the picture Nathan had taken of us both in the hot tub outside our cabin in Derwentwater. The camera in his right hand, his left hand around my waist. I remember that moment well, that was the minute before he removed my bikini. It was the only picture we had taken the entire time we were away.

Carefully removing the shattered glass and broken wood, I notice a piece of folded up paper fall to the floor. Strange, I don't remember that being there when I put the picture in the frame.

I unfold the piece of paper. I don't believe it. It's been in front of me the entire time. Hidden in the frame from our breakaway at the lake of creation. It's the passcode for Bryce's private safe.

I need to call Detective Collins!

Twenty-One

Freya

Monday, November 5, 2018

Detective Collins was ready and waiting with a plan when I called him, as though he never doubted I would find the passcode, but more a case of *when* I found it.

He has given me instructions to follow and I will call him every night with an update. Phase one begins today, Monday.

The pit in my stomach has been swimming with nerves since I read the instructions, I've done everything Detective Collins told me to do.

I ordered two wigs, not cheap ones as they have to look as real as they can. One to be completely different from my lengthy blonde hair and the other as close to my real hair as can be. I bought an untraceable pay as you go mobile phone and planned to cancel my daily swim classes. Packed the new jacket and clothes he told me to buy into my gym hold-all, making sure they were different from my normal style of dresses and skirts. I don't think I've worn a pair of jeans since my early twenties.

'You need to look as unlike yourself as you can,' Detective Collins told me. And he is the master of disguise.

My style has always been classy, today I am aiming for unpretentious. So why am I sitting in my car, my hands wrapped around the steering wheel, holding on for dear life instead of going into the sports centre? My mind is nudging me to go in, but my body has frozen.

I'm scared. I thought I was strong enough to do this, but I'm not. Every inch of me oozes weakness. I need to act normal. I know Bryce will have that car following me again, and I can't have it suspecting anything.

Taking a deep breath in, I step out from the car, lifting my hold-all from the passenger seat. The same as I do any other regular day. I struggle to keep my balance walking through the car park. The strongest urge comes over me to turn around, to check no one is following, but I need to fight it, so I focus on the road straight ahead. The car park stretches with every step I take, forcing the building in front of me further away. I fight with my inner being not to run. I'm panicking, my feet picking up pace. I'm finally in the building, my breathing erratic as I head to the changing rooms.

Before I know it, I'm locked in a cubicle crying uncontrollably with fear. I can't do this. What the fucking hell was I thinking? I'm too weak to do this. Clara is my weakness. If I fuck any of this up, it puts not just me at risk, but her too.

Panic sets all over my body. It aches, trembling from my head to my feet. My hands go numb and I shake them vigorously to get the feeling back in them. I check the time on my iPhone, 09:24. I have to meet Detective Collins at 10:30 on the other side of town.

Still sobbing, my psyche gives me a mental slap, telling me to pull myself together. I am not feeble, I can do this, I can fucking do this.

Kicking my trainers from my feet, I remove my black and fluorescent pink sports leggings and vest; I gather all my hair and wrap it tightly in a flat bun to the back of my head. Next, I pull the new clothes from my hold-all, putting the dark denim, ripped knee skinny jeans on, Chelsea boots and black jumper. I carefully place the short shoulder length brunette wig on and pack everything else back into the hold-all. Everything goes into a guest locker, including my iPhone switched to flight mode and I take the new mobile with me.

Detective Collins also encouraged me to get coloured contact lenses to disguise my piercing blue eyes. They're my one standout feature. Nathan always told me that was the first thing about me that caught his eye. They needed to go. I spent last night learning how to put the contact lenses in, bloody fidgety slimy suckers, but I think I got it.

Wasn't easy to get everything organised with Mum staying with me, she can smell something off ten miles away. I don't even know this woman staring at me from the mirror. Dark eyes and dark hair make my complexion look whiter than usual. This was my chance to play a woman full of confidence, to play a woman I used to be before my life flipped upside down.

A splash of water over my face and I think I'm ready to go. I hope I'm ready for this. There is no room for error now.

I can't believe it, I left the sports centre and walked to the taxi station a ten-minute walk away. No one batted an eyelid, but I noticed the black Audi parked at the very back of the small car park as I left. It hasn't followed me.

That was easier than I thought it was going to be, but still a long way to go. My psyche, I'm sure, has been doing star jumps in celebration for making it this far without fucking up.

The taxi takes me to the nearest supermarket. He doesn't wait; I didn't ask him too. Running in quickly to use the photo booth, I get passport pictures taken of this stranger who I'm getting acquainted with. I walk from the photo-booth, passport pictures in hand, staring at them. I look—real.

As I glance up from the photos, I see a face I know, walking towards me and alarms pitch my breath.

Layla is walking towards me.

Keep your head down. Shit, I can't do that, I'll look suspicious. Just say hello and tell her you're in a rush.

I prepare myself to speak but she drifts past me. In my panic, I forgot she wouldn't recognise me.

Hurriedly, I get into the next taxi waiting outside at the taxi stand and drive to the address Detective Collins wrote on a small piece of paper.

Sickness has been trying to escape from my stomach since I passed Layla. One of my closest friends, I was sure she would recognise me. Not sure why she was shopping so far away from her house, though? Strange, I can't even ask her later because I would need to explain why I was there.

The taxi slows down outside a mid-terrace three-story townhouse with slate grey exterior. I'm pleasantly surprised, it has put me at ease. I imagined a slum full of drug users who would do anything for money to pay for their next hit or robbed before I could get to the door.

'Please could you drive forward another few yards,' I ask the driver.

Detective Collins told me under no circumstances to get out right outside the front door or get the same taxi back to the sports centre, making sure I covered all my steps.

I step out from the taxi, walk back down towards the house and walk up the three small concrete stairs to the door. I knock, looking around me. My guard is well and truly in force today. No sign of the black Audi either.

A small gold plaque on the door reads, *Samuel James Leighton, Master of Fine Arts*.

An elderly man opens the door. He's a fine-looking man in his seventies with slimline glasses and a grey defined beard that covers most of his face. He's dressed in corduroy green trousers and a cream Arran sweater vest that hides a navy blue checked shirt. It makes me wonder if he has a wife, and if he does, does she allow him to dress like that?

'Ah good morning, you must be Freya. Come in, child,' the man says, extremely polite and welcoming, holding his hand out to show me into his home.

I stand in his hall waiting for him to close the door, already in awe of his home. It's beautifully kept, vintage pieces of furniture and priceless paintings taking up residence in the hall. He was a man of fine taste, a collector of ancient artefacts. I decide then he must have a wife to keep the home looking this stunning. He gestures to take my jacket and I accept.

'I'm Samuel to my colleagues. Albert has told me everything you need. Did you bring passport photographs of yourself?' he asks.

'Yes, sir, I have everything here, and every penny in cash as you requested.'

'Thank you, dear, come, have a seat and I'll get us some tea.'

He walks towards a door to the left of the hall and I follow. Relaxation has consumed my body. I'm at ease. The presence of this stranger settles my nerves in a way I can't understand. For the moment, it's like meeting an old friend for tea.

Mr Leighton returns from the kitchen with a tray balancing a teapot, two teacups and a small jug of milk. Above his grand fire surround showcasing an open coal fire with brass grill, hangs the most eye-catching portrait of a young woman, it's mesmerising. Bold, vibrant colours surrounding her. I can feel her happiness beaming from the colour.

'A painting of a very young Mrs Leighton, wasn't she exquisite? The choice of colours represents her true nature perfectly. Never went through life without a genuine smile,' Mr Leighton explains.

'She is exquisite, Mr Leighton. You must be extremely proud.'

'To have her as my wife made me extremely proud. I never asked for a single thing from life after she said yes to marrying me. She made me the richest man to walk the earth. True love is the only fortune that gives you true happiness, Mrs Lynn. That's from any relationship, whether it be friendship, marriage, family. I married my best friend.'

His eyes light up when he looks over at the painting. Mr Leighton is quite the old-fashioned gentleman and somewhat the romantic. Something that's scarce in present times. It makes me think, did I have true love, true friendship with Nathan? I'm not sure anymore. If I doubt it, then I know that's my answer.

'Please forgive my rudeness, Mr Leighton, but Detective Collins gave me the impression he'd be joining us?' I ask.

It had only gone 10:21, but from what I knew of Detective Collins, he was always earlier than he needed to be.

'It will just be you and I, Mrs Lynn. It will be better that way. We have a few things to discuss.'

He holds a piece of paper in his left hand with a detailed list of itineraries. Starting with the first detail on the list, he asks me for the passport photos and £15,000. I give him both. The amount in mixed notes as he requested through Detective Collins.

I had a fair idea of Mr Leighton's role, but I ask, 'Mr Leighton, may I ask what it is you do?'

He places the piece of paper onto his lap and removes his reading glasses to face me. 'Officially, I'm an antique dealer and auctioneer. Unofficially, I help certain people begin new lives. I have a very distinctive circle of clientele and have never done business with the same person more than once. I have a very strict process of interviewing people before we talk business. I have an instinct for reading people, and my instincts tell me I can undoubtedly trust you. On Wednesday morning, you'll come back here and collect your new lives.'

Wednesday morning? I had no idea it would be so fast. I know Detective Collins said a few days, but it's all so fast. My head is spinning at 100mph and my nerves are struggling to keep up.

'When you leave, you'll be carrying a package, I'm an antique dealer so we must make it look like you've made a purchase. You'll fill out an order form for the item just now and sign it with the name I have written. This will leave evidence of a purchase in your new identity so they can't associate us together.'

I can't help but think how strange this all is. My subconscious telling me this is not legal, which I already know. This man can't be working for the police. You wouldn't pay the police for witness protection, now would you?

I have to ask; the whole situation has me troubled. 'Please excuse my curiosity, but you don't work for the police, do you? The witness protection unit Detective Collins told me would help me and my daughter.'

'Albert only asks for my help with special cases, which I admit doesn't happen very often. He is one of the best Detectives I have had the pleasure of knowing. If Albert smells a rat, then something's definitely off. All I can tell you, Mrs Lynn, is that you can trust Albert with your life. He has told me you and your daughter's safety is imperative, so we must work fast and with caution.'

I ask no more questions after that. I hold every faith in Detective Collins, and whoever he trusts, I trust too. When I first spoke with him, he told me he thought Bryce had a lot of officials working for him, so if Detective Collins is doing this unofficially, I know he suspects the police.

I give my full cooperation to Mr Leighton and head back to the sports centre. Sticking to my normal daily routine is paramount.

When Nathan and I first bought the house, a building developer was desperate for our land. As I recall, it got heated between him and Nathan as the man wouldn't take no for an answer. He offered a considerable amount of money that anyone in their right mind would be insane to turn down—but we did. We were living a blissful life and no amount of money could have encouraged us to move.

I know his business card is around here somewhere. I need to find it, harshly pulling drawers out, rummaging through every inch of the house.

'Freya, what's going on? Are you all right?' Mum sounds worried, she probably thinks I'm having another one of my episodes.

Not surprising, I usually have one daily.

'I'm looking for a business card, my colleague from work is looking to have some work done and I know I have a number for a builder somewhere around here.'

I shuffle down the hall, my slipper boots dragging along the floor towards the drawers of the sideboard at the far side of the dining room. Mum right behind me, ready to intervene in case I break more valuables. Love her confidence in me. *Not*.

Pulling everything out onto the dining table, then moving on. Mum shadowing over me, carefully putting everything back in place as we go.

'Sweetheart, could you please not be so rough, you'll wake Clara up, and the rest of the street,' Mum whispers.

She's right, I need to calm down. Even if I found the card, I can't call him until tomorrow when I get the untracked mobile phone from the locker at work. I left it there alongside the two wigs; I didn't want to risk bringing it all back home and Mum discovering it. She was quite the detective herself. Never in my younger days did I get away with anything without her figuring it out. If it wasn't for my shaky nerves and moments of insanity, I'm sure she would be onto me by now.

'Is it Jai Chandra Stone Masonry by any chance, Freya?' Mum shouts from the kitchen, tidying up my mess.

'Yes! That's it!' I yelp with a sigh of relief. 'Where did you find it?'

Don't know what I'm going to do without Mum. A wave of emotions come over me and I can't control it. I shuffle back into the kitchen, hanging my head. 'I'm sorry, I'm exhausted. You have no idea how much I love you.'

I wrap my arms around her and squeeze. I know it's our last week together, but she has no idea. My tongue on the verge of revealing what is happening, but I stop myself and head upstairs to call Albert with an update of my day. We'll be lost without one another.

Twenty-Two

Freya

Tuesday, November 6, 2018

A woman answers on the third ring. 'Mr Chandra's office, Ella speaking,' her voice bordering on ignorant.

I called the mobile number on the card, expecting him to answer himself. I had the entire conversation rehearsed in my head, so this throws me off. Panicking, I hang up the phone.

I'm irritated with myself for hanging up, irritated at the silly receptionist for answering the phone and making me hang up.

Cow.

Christ, Fee, get a grip of yourself. Shake it off.

There's no time to lose, the only option is to call back. I dial the number again, this time it answers on the second ring.

'Chandra speaking.'

It's him, Nathan would hate me speaking to him of all people, but I know it will be a quick and easy sale. Nathan doesn't get a say anyway, does he? He made sure of that when he died, running around keeping secrets from me.

'Mr Chandra, I don't know if you will remember me? My name is Freya Lynn. I live in The Hollies, the country house in Edenbridge.'

'Ah, Mrs Lynn, how could I forget. Your husband was quite the hothead, as I recall. How is he?' he asks, still sounding as cocky as he did when we first met.

It almost makes me want to hang up again.

'As I remember, so were you.' I pause for a second to hear the annoyance of my comment. A deep breath washes down the line. This makes me happy. 'My husband passed away two years ago, Mr Chandra,' I tell him.

Saying this doesn't have the same sting as it used to. He's gone quiet; I can imagine him in his office waiting for the ground to open up and swallow him, no annoyed breathing this time.

'I was wondering if we could meet, I have some business to discuss with you, if you're interested of course, but only if you agree to discuss this with no one,' I explain.

'I'm intrigued, Mrs Lynn. I have meetings all day today, but I could meet tomorrow afternoon. When and where would you like to meet?'

'Today, in the next hour, I can assure you it's an opportunity you won't want to miss.'

I try to sound confident that this is not up for negotiation, leaving the ball in his court to accept or decline. He's that far up his own arse, I know he won't turn me down when it involves The Hollies.

'Could you give me a moment?' he asks, his voice muffled at the other end.

He must have his hand over the phone, speaking to his assistant about cancelling his appointments for the morning. Even his muffled voice screams dickhead.

'I can do that. Where?'

'Edenbridge sports centre. I'll be waiting in the cafe for you. And please don't discuss this with anyone, Mr Chandra. If I discover you have, the offer is off the table.' I hang the phone up before he replies.

The cafe is emptier than usual for a Tuesday morning, not that it's a bad thing. Fewer people to witness the meeting. Chandra's office is based in Marlpit Hill, if I recall correctly, so it should take him ten minutes to get here. I order a coffee and get myself comfortable at the same table Detective Collins and I use, up at the far end of the cafe, a bit more private, but not by much. It seems to be my personal office these days.

Time seems to fly by and before I know it, he's at the entrance to the cafe. Dressed in a white shirt, the collar undone and black suit trousers. No jacket, of course. He probably thinks he's too cool to wear one, even though it's pouring with rain outside, and yet his shirt looks dry. This irritates me.

He notices me and walks towards the table, none of us making any gestures to the other. He's here on business, and so am I, so we skip the pleasantries.

'May I?' he asks, pulling the chair out from under the table.

I give him a semi-friendly nod. 'Would you like a coffee, Mr Chandra?'

'No, thank you.'

I smile and there's an awkward silence while I think of how to start the conversation. He's going to think I'm insane or in financial trouble and looking for the simple way out.

'Freya, I'm very sorry to hear about Nathan, truly. I know we had our differences, but it was just business. I made an offer on the house and he blew mine out of the water. Can't say I was best pleased about it. I had been trying to buy the house for years. It lost me a potentially massive investment.'

The awkward silence tsunamis away, spiking my curiosity.

'I don't understand, you had been trying to get the house for years? It had been empty for almost six years.'

'Strange, isn't it? I made an offer the first week the house went on the market in 2012, but it got declined. I thought someone must have made a higher offer, so I made another, that got declined too. A year later the house was still vacant, and the for-sale sign was still there. I contacted the agent in charge of selling to see what the owner was actually looking to make on the house, but the agent said every time he emailed the owner with an offer, everything came back declined. About six months later, the for-sale sign disappeared but no one ever moved in.'

'That makes little sense?' I say, curious.

'Like I said, strange. I had to listen to my wife nipping my ear off every time we got declined like it was my fault. I figured the owner changed their mind about selling. I initially asked the agent for the seller's email address, but he couldn't give it to me, data protection.'

I nod, a bit of a pain in the arse data protection. And wife? So, Mr Chandra isn't the boss at home, it seems. Could explain why he's an arse to everyone else.

'Then January 2017, I was driving past, and the for-sale sign had returned so I made another offer, a lot higher than my other offers and yet again, it came back declined, really pissed me off. Next thing I know, you and your husband had moved in. Like I said, everything with Nathan was just business.'

I watch his face twist, thinking.

Just business, he says. As I recall, he wanted to *break Nathan into pieces*. My back teeth grind, and I shake off the thought and get back to business. No point in bringing it all up now though, all water under the bridge.

'Well, Jai, I'm here to make you an offer to rectify your loss. If you're interested.'

He sits forward in his chair. I have his full attention; he's already rubbing his palms together.

'I'm looking for a quick sale on the house,' I say.

His eyes widen, and he answers instantly, 'How quick are you thinking?'

'Wednesday afternoon tops.'

His face goes into shock, his mouth dropping wide open, staring at me. He thinks this is a joke, watching me, waiting for me to laugh and break my serious face.

I don't.

'Holy shit, are you serious?' he asks, running his hand down his stubbly cheeks and onto his chin.

He looks uneasy at the offer. Maybe he doesn't have as much money as he likes people to think he has? I must play it like he's not the only one interested.

'I have another buyer, but they can't complete the deal until Friday afternoon, and that's too late for me, but if I need to take it, I will. Perhaps you need some time to discuss it with your wife?'

Chandra snorts at my last comment. 'Now I didn't say I wasn't interested. I know how much that house is worth, so it won't be easy getting the money together by Wednesday afternoon. How much has this other *investor* offered you?' He emphasises investor like he knows I'm lying.

Shit, I didn't think of a number. I'm not entirely sure what Nathan actually paid for it.

I remain stern, my face reading I have taken offence to his question. 'Just what we paid for it. Like I said, I'm looking for a quick sale, so I'm not interested in any sort of profit. But part of the condition is you don't come near the house until Friday afternoon. My Mum is staying until Friday and I don't want her getting upset.'

I keep my confident composure as Jai rubs his hand off his cheeks, down to his chin again. He's thinking, hard. I can tell by his eyes.

Sitting back in his chair, he crosses his hands on his knee. 'If I recall, my offer was for £850,000 and it got declined because of a higher offer. Your husband's higher offer,' he says.

He looks at me, head slanted, waiting for me to answer him. In my head, my jaw has just dropped wide open, smashing to the floor. How much did Nathan pay for our house? My mind draws a blank.

He's a businessman, used to playing hardball, I can't let on I have no idea how much we paid. I give him a nod to say that's right, holding my cards close to my chest. Poker face on point. 'I will accept £900,000. I'll sign everything over to you when I receive the money in cash. The house will be all yours Friday afternoon. Do we have a deal, Mr Chandra? I would prefer an answer now.'

For a couple of minutes, he looks blank, then asks me if I'm in any sort of trouble. I don't answer the question.

Keeping my face serious, I ask again if we have a deal and with no hesitation this time, he rocks forward in his chair and holds out his hand. 'We have a deal, Mrs Lynn.'

We agree to meet back at the sports centre tomorrow at 6 pm when I return for Clara's swim lesson. Mum will be with me, so I must be discreet.

'Oh, and when you come back tomorrow afternoon, wear something less conservative and bring the money in a gym holdall,' I say.

He nods and leaves. I sit back down in my chair and let out a massive sigh of relief. Phase two completed.

The window of the cafe overlooks the car park. I glance out as I walk past to leave the room. The door to the black Audi is sitting open, I jump to the side of the window, peering out, intrigued. For the weeks the car has followed, not once have I seen the door open. A man appears, tall, extremely well built, bald and dressed all in black. Shit, he's walking to the centre. Did he see Chandra entering and leaving? Do they know one another?

I'm panicking, my heart thumping in my chest. My thoughts disappear into a grey cloud of nothing.

Run and get into the pool, Freya. Now!

My subconscious is right, I need to make it look like I've been in the pool the whole time. As quick as my feet can take me, I run to the changing room, throwing off my clothes and into my swimsuit. I leave my clothes in the cubicle, no time to sort them into a locker.

Jumping into the pool, my breathing heavy, I quickly burst back up through the surface of the water, trying to catch a breath. Holding onto the side of the pool, until I calm down.

Dan walks towards me, he looks worried. I don't blame him; he must think I'm completely mad.

'You doing okay, Freya?' he asks, kneeling at the side of the pool.

My breathing slows down, and I answer, 'Hey Dan. I'm fine. Just having a quick dip before I go.'

'I thought you had cancelled your swim classes this week?'

'I did, I just didn't feel up to it. It's not been a good few weeks.'

Not for the reasons you would think.

He smiles sympathetically and stands up. 'Listen, if you ever fancy grabbing a drink, let me know. I'm a good listener,' he says in his gorgeous accent.

His smile is so warm, it would be awful to turn him down but bitterly terrible to say yes knowing I'm leaving. If I was staying, I might even consider having a drink with him. He's so kind and extremely fuckable. He would have made a great friend with benefits if we knew one another under different circumstances.

'That would be great. We can get something arranged next week.'

God, I'm an awful person. I'm probably going to hell anyway, so why stop now. Lying to people is not something I usually do, it's not me. I take pleasure in telling the truth, giving it to people straight. I'm losing a grip on myself. He looks pleased though; I think he's been trying to ask me for months.

Suddenly, I have an urge to look up at the spectator's window. The same urge I used to get with Detective Collins. My heart can't take much more of this, I'll be dead before Friday.

Casually, I push my feet off the wall of the pool and swim backwards, giving Dan a wink as I go. He's there. The bald man all in black is in the spectator's box looking down at the pool. I can't let him know I see him, so I try my best to concentrate on my swimming.

By the time I get to the other end of the pool and swim back again, he's gone. That was too close. The danger level is firing up with every new action of the plan I execute.

I need a drink.

Mum looks so peaceful on the corner sofa reading her book. Her short blonde pixie cut tucked neatly behind her ears. Her tanned skin making her look younger than she is, she's a hot momma.

Dad used to say I took my looks from her side of the family, the Anderson side, but my pasty skin came from his side, the Longcrofts. Luckily for me, I didn't take his shitty attitude and love for violence. Well, maybe a little shitty attitude, but only when needed.

Mum took a lot from Dad. The first time when he pleaded was just a drunken mistake of battering her black and blue, throwing her down the stairs, which she covered for him, saying she slipped on one of my toys and fell by accident. Everyone knew it was rubbish, but no one would dare speak up.

The second I remember, another alcohol-fuelled attack on her for not having his dinner waiting on him returning from the pub late at night. I must have been about three, listening from my bed as he tortured her and threw her across the room like a used beer can. I can still hear whispers of her quiet screams, trying to hold them back to protect me from hearing.

Black and grey memories of him fill my childhood, a man I wanted to steer clear of for the rest of my life. It would explain why I ended up so fussy with boyfriends.

Tears cloud my vision, not now! Not in front of Mum.

'Sweetheart, you okay? What's wrong?' Mum asks.

I wipe the tears from my eyes, trying to gulp away the lump that's formed in my throat. 'I just can't believe it's almost the end of our three weeks. Feels like you've just arrived.'

She signals me to sit beside her on the couch. 'You know you could always come home. I know I keep asking you, but I really would love to have my girls where I could look after you both, full time.' She places her arm around me and gently pulls me closer.

Home sounds the most amazing place now, how I long to be there. I have every regret for not going home when Nathan died, for not giving the house to Bryce out of stubbornness. I wish I could turn the clock back on so many things now.

'It's time to think about it, Freya,' she says in her soft voice.

We cuddle silently, enjoying the closeness. Our relationship has been the same since I can remember. Mum was never shy with her emotions.

That's it, the idea has just entered my head. All the things I want to keep, I could get Mum to pack them into the car and take them home. Clara's baby keepsakes and some photos. Just enough for her to think, I'm thinking about moving home.

'Mum, maybe tomorrow night, when Clara's in bed, we could look out some stuff you could take home to Stirling with you on Friday. I could move gradually.'

Her smile grows, a genuine smile of imminent happiness, and she kisses me goodnight on my forehead before heading to bed. She looks like she could cry. My stomach sinks, I'm going to burn in hell for hurting Mum.

I make sure Mum and Clara are sleeping before I call Detective Collins with my daily update. I settle myself at the back door, wrapped in a blanket, and dial his number from the burner phone. He answers instantly.

'How did today go?' Detective Collins asks.

He always sounds so sincere. I can speak to him about anything. I need to, there is no one else I can speak to now. 'It went ok. Mr Chandra has accepted my proposition about buying the house. It's just... something he said just didn't make sense though,' I tell him, hesitating to go on, I don't know why.

'Really? How so?'

I need to tell him, to get his thoughts and give me satisfaction that I'm not going off my head.

'Well, when we were discussing numbers, I let him take the lead and be the first to say an amount. I can't remember how much the house was exactly, but I know roughly. He said Nathans offer blew his offer out the water, I said I would accept what he offered to pay for it and then...' I stop, sighing.

'It's an expensive house, I'm sure however much his offer was will be plenty to start over afresh, to keep you and Clara going for a while?'

'Well, that's just it, Albert, it will. It will be more than enough. More than I could have dreamed. And that's what I don't understand. He said he offered £850,000 but his offer got declined.'

'Good heavens, that's a substantial amount Freya,' Detective Collins says, but he doesn't sound shocked.

'Yes, yes, it is. Considering Nathan told me we paid around £450,000.'

Detective Collins remains silent, as though thinking this over.

'Mum released equity on her house and gave us it as a wedding gift. She told me it would all be mine someday and to make the most of it just now. She gave us £500,000 to buy the house, Albert. The money left we used to furnish it, and some went into my savings account solely in my name. It just doesn't make any sense.'

'No, it doesn't, but I'm sure there is a reasonable explanation for it.' Detective Collins sounds off, not surprised in the slightest. 'Don't think too much about it, Freya, however much Nathan paid for it you're doubling your money. Maybe it's Mr Chandra who is mistaken?'

I doubt it. The man seems like he wouldn't pay a penny over the price if he didn't have to.

'Yes, possibly, but I guess we will never know now, will we?'

We leave the conversation at that. Detective Collins tells me he will check in with me tomorrow.

His reaction bothers me. He didn't sound surprised. It's never occurred to me he could have something to do with all of this, could he?

Freya, get a grip.

I'm tired, it's almost 22:30 and I haven't eaten today yet. My nerves won't allow it.

Twenty-Three

Freya

Wednesday, November 7, 2018

I slept well last night. I've woken up refreshed. The sleeping pills work a treat. My mouth feels like I've been sucking cotton wool all night, even though I brushed my teeth twice after my shower.

Mum got up early with Clara and took her to playgroup. Today I feel like I could conquer the world, but for now, I need to settle for visiting Mr Leighton again and picking up our new lives. Starting with a trip to the sports centre to change my identity for a few hours.

Mr Leighton welcomes me with the same gentlemanly gestures and offers me tea. He doesn't fail with his attire today, and I can't help but smile at him. Red chino style trousers, a plain royal blue shirt, buttoned right to his neck. I wonder how he's able to breathe? The same cream Arran sweater vest finishes the look.

I like Mr Leighton. I wonder how his wife died? If they had children? Or if he devotes his life to helping others because he's alone. I think he would've made an illustrious father. You can just tell sometimes, can't you?

'There you are, my dear, please take a seat,' Mr Leighton tells me, his manners impeccable, and I imagine him pulling out the chair for his wife at dinner, letting her sit first before he did.

'Thank you. You have a wonderful home, Mr Leighton. I was looking forward to seeing it again.'

It truly is wonderful. Mum would have a field day in here. I wish I could have brought her here under different circumstances. The whole place screams Antiques Roadshow. Yeah, I'm not ashamed, I watched it. I was a geek.

I sip my tea and notice the plastic folder on the coffee table in front of us. If I wasn't feeling nervous before, I am now. That plastic folder holds our new lives. Amazing, isn't it? How it only takes two days to get someone a new identity and how cheap it is.

'The tea is very nice, thank you, Mr Leighton.' It really is, it's not Tetley, that's for sure. Some fancy morning tea, I expect.

'I know you're on a tight schedule dear, so I'll get right to it if that is okay with you?' Mr Leighton asks, smiling, a warm, friendly smile, and I know he is sincere. He continues, 'In the folder, there are two new passports, for yourself and your daughter. A driver's licence, British of course. I can't have you as an American citizen, your accent is too strong.'

American?

Am I going to America? It's never occurred to me; I have no idea where I'm going. Albert said he would reveal all nearer the end of the week. One step at a time.

I nod in agreement. Born and bred in Scotland, but I always say my accent is more British than Scottish.

'There are also birth certificates, national insurance details, and your photography qualifications changed into your new identity.'

Wow, how did he get those? How did he know I was a photographer?

'Mr Leighton, how... I mean, where did you get my qualification certificates? That isn't possible. All my certificates are at home.'

'Freya, I was given everything I needed over a year ago,' he explains, sitting down his teacup.

I can tell by his face there is more information that I haven't been told.

'Albert introduced your husband, Nathan, and me just shortly before he died. The reason it's only taken two days to get you everything you need is because I already had it. Albert thought it was best to use new pictures of yourself and your daughter for the passports, though, to be extra cautious. In the folder, there are also bank account details Nathan had set up for you both along with your destination details and flight tickets. Nathan was on his way here the morning he died.'

I can't breathe, the information is choking me, expanding in my throat. I can't take all of this in. Nathan had arranged everything. He was doing all this behind my back. The more I hear about him, the more I dislike him. It's been an emotional train wreck since the beginning with him. Hating him, loving him, finding out he was a criminal, hating him again, discovering he wasn't a criminal, guilt of hating him, then all the secrets.

I loathe the man.

Just expecting me to up and leave Mum, go into hiding with him and Clara when he told me nothing. My teeth grind, and I hear it loud inside my head.

'Freya, I'm sorry dear, I really am. Your husband was just trying to protect you and your daughter.'

I take a deep breath before answering, 'Sorry Mr Leighton, please forgive me, but if he was trying to protect us, he should have been honest and not put us in this position. I appreciate your help, though, I do. I must get going now. I can't be over my time.'

I'm trying not to be a bitch, but I'm failing miserably. It's not Mr Leighton's fault. I'm pissed off with Nathan.

Mr Leighton nods and hands me a package. 'Your purchase, dear. I hope you like it. Nathan mentioned your Mother was an art lover and artist. He chose something he thought she might like, as a gift before you went away. I wish you and your daughter all the luck in the world.'

You and me both, we're going to fucking need it. I wonder what my wonderful husband chose? A gun perhaps? To finish Mum off before he took her daughter and grandchild away for good?

We shake hands, and I leave with my expensive folder and

package that could contain a paper-maché frog for all I know.

This day can fuck off.

My patience has been in short supply today since I met with Mr Leighton. My irritation has been plentiful.

'Freya, what has gotten into you?' Mum asks, angry, after I snap at Clara for being too loud, instantly making me feel terrible.

The rain battering every inch of the house is louder, but my temper doesn't snap at that.

I lift Clara, hugging her. 'Mummy's sorry my little cookie. I'm just tired. Are we ready for toddler swim class?'

She yelps with excitement, her eyes wide with love, and just like that she has forgiven me.

'I love you, cookie. Eskimo kiss?'

We scrunch up our noses and rub them together. I'm aware of Mum watching from the top of the stairs, and just like that she has forgiven me too.

When we arrive at the sports centre, I tell Mum to run into the building with Clara, out of the pouring rain whilst I grab our bags from the boot, and it's there, right on cue. The black Audi parked in its regular spot right up the back of the car park. It knows my every move, my weekly schedule. It doesn't seem to care about being discreet anymore.

Arsehole.

Chandra has arrived first, standing at the reception in his Nike gym gear, large gym bag on the floor beside his feet, black sports cap hiding his normally sleek gelled hair. He took the memo seriously then; it makes me smile.

The centre is full of kids, all around Clara's age for their evening swim class. Not actually a swim class but toddlers that are splashing about in a pool while Mums and Dads drink coffee and wait for their kid's energy levels to burn out before bedtime. Mums went for a swim after getting Clara changed into her swimwear. Perfect, I can get my business with Chandra out of the way.

I head to the back of the cafeteria. I should just rename it Freya's office. Ann, the receptionist who never seems to have a day off, must notice something is going on. Maybe she thinks I'm a drug dealer and I do my business from here? I could have so much fun with that idea, wind her up, but it would just create some unwanted attention.

Chandra follows, sitting on the same seat as before. And like before, none of us follow through with the pleasantries.

He sits quietly for a few minutes, chewing the inside of his cheek, before asking, 'Are you sure you want to go through with this Freya?'

Please, he doesn't care. A token bit of concern half-heartedly executed.

'Yes, did you fill your end of our deal?'

He nods hesitantly. 'I need to know, Freya, before we sign the papers. Are you in some sort of trouble that could project onto me or the house?' he asks, leaning forward, I see the authority in him.

I had prepared for this question before meeting him tonight. 'I found out Nathan wasn't who I thought he was, and I need away from everything that belonged to him, our life. I need to start fresh.'

Lies, but also some truth. Fuck, it's all true, isn't it? 'Do you have the papers?' I ask.

Chandra takes them from the sports bag in an A4 brown envelope and hands them to me. I briskly scan the paperwork. Set price, £900,000... Friday, November 9... all looks fine. I don't have time to examine it in fine detail.

I sign my name at every X he points out. His facial expression never changes. I can't tell if he's happy, or still wary of what's going on.

'I've slid a locker key into that envelope with the signed paperwork. Locker 524, head down and transfer the money into the gym bag inside it. Leave the key in the lock. The pools shut off for swim classes tonight that are already in progress, so no one else will be in the locker rooms for another hour. I'll wait here until it's done. Then our business is complete,' I say, and I'm cool, surprising even myself.

We don't shake hands. He gives an appreciative nod, and in return, so do I. I remain seated, watching him leave the cafeteria, down the stairs into the locker room.

Five minutes later, I watch him leave. As does Ann, before cranking her neck from the reception desk to get a good look into the cafeteria at me. I stare at her, expressionless, making her flustered. She turns, lifting the reception phone which I expect wasn't even ringing.

I exhale in relief, tick another box on my mental to-do list and head to the spectator's box to watch Clara finish her swim lesson. I call Detective Collins on my way there and let him know the transaction with Chandra went smoothly with no hick-ups. He asks me if I'm prepared for tomorrow. I tell him yes.

A complete lie, I'm not ready for tomorrow, I don't think I ever will be.

Please, God, please give me the strength I need. And please forgive me at the same time.

Twenty-Four

Freya

Thursday, November 8, 2018

I went to the bank first thing this morning to deposit the money from Jai Chandra, for the house. I've left feeling even more confused than ever.

There is a balance of £456,155 already in the account, a small portion of it being interest as it has been sitting for a year. Nathan opened the new account with it.

What is that money? Where did it come from? More money that he stole? Was it the money he stole from Bryce? I hadn't thought it would be that much. It can't be the money Mum gave us to buy the house. How would he have paid for the house then?

My head hurts, bursting with questions and the one person who can answer them all, can't. I have no time to stop; I need to stick to my times, no distractions. Nothing can seem off, not with that black Audi sitting outside the sports centre, making sure it tracks my every move. Next stop, the hairdressers to transform my hair into the short caramel brown wig from my new passport pictures. This should be easy, compared to everything else.

I hope.

I return home in the afternoon, wearing the blond wig I had hidden in a locker at work. I need to look like myself until I leave the sports centre on Friday morning. I will walk into the centre Mrs Freya Lynn for the last time, I will leave as Miss Stephanie Shenton.

Mum doesn't notice any difference. Not even as we sit and eat dinner together. She knows I was at the hairdresser today and only remarked how nice I looked. When I say eat, I mean push my food around my plate.

When Mum takes Clara upstairs for her bath, I make my next phone call.

'Hi, it's Freya. Listen, are you free? I could do with a friend right now,' I say.

The phone is silent, making me instantly regret making the call. 'God, I'm sorry, you're busy. I'll speak to you later okay, sorry.'

'Freya wait, you threw me off that's all. I haven't heard from you since I dropped by the house last week. I thought maybe I had upset you?' Bryce asks.

You thought right then, didn't you?

Snake.

'No, of course not, I've just not been myself. That's why I thought it would be good to meet, catch up. If I've caught you at a bad time, I can call later.'

'I'm just tying up a meeting. I can be over in say an hour?'

'No!' I snap, my voice jumpy. Calm down, Freya, keep calm. 'Mum's here, I need out of the house. Can I come to your place?'

'Um sure, eight o'clock suit?' he asks.

'Perfect, I'll see you at eight.' I hang the phone up before my nerves break.

Nausea flows through my veins like a tidal wave, I need to do this. For those poor babies.

'Hey, sweetheart,' Mum says, appearing behind me, dumping Clara's dirty clothes on the worktop.

I try my best to hide the tears, pulling my sleeve over my hand and wiping my face. I can hold myself together around anyone, with Mum I crumble.

'Aw Fee, what's the matter, darling?' Mum takes me in her arms.

'Nothing, I… I'm going round to Bryce's tonight. I… I just need out for a little while. I...'

Mum squeezes me tighter, understandingly tight.

'Shh, it's okay, sweetheart, it's okay. No need to explain. You get yourself out.' She loosens her grip and looks at me. 'He's a good man, you know, Bryce. You're a young woman. Your life doesn't need to be over. It doesn't mean you're a bad person. That's what you need to do, continue to live, for yourself and for Clara.'

Voices scream from the inside so hard I tremble. They scream the truth at Mum; aching to be heard, but they fail. I ache to speak the truth to her. I know I can't. I want to tell her Bryce is not a good man, he's the Devil himself.

I smile, but my eyes are vacant.

After two meltdowns, three phone calls back and forward to Detective Collins, a large glass of wine and double gin, I make the drive over to the address Bryce texted me.

It's alarming how close it is to the supermarket I stopped at for the passport pictures. Secretly praying I get pulled over by police and breathalysed, throwing a spanner in the works of the plan for tonight, giving me my much-longed-for way out.

When did I get so weak? I can't quite put my finger on it. Maybe when I found out my husband was working for a psychopath who sells newborn babies who never asked to be born into this cruel world. Or when I let the psychopath into my life? My thoughts are unsettling, but the thoughts of those defenceless babies light a fire inside me, egging me to keep going.

I release my foot from the accelerator, coming to my senses.

I can't fuck this up, I can't fuck this up.

Everything depends on me, *me*, not Nathan, not Detective Collins.

Me.

I can't fuck up.

The sat nav squeaks I have reached my destination and I tell the polite woman's voice to fuck off. I seem to swear more than I ever have.

I glance at the newly built apartments. Why am I not surprised Bryce lives in one of them? My stomach muscles convulse at the thought of going inside. My car door swings open, startling me.

'I thought that was you.'

'Bryce!' I screech, my voice a pitch way too high.

'Who were you expecting? Santa?'

Ironic he would use a word that is an anagram of Satan. I try to laugh it off and even surprise myself how shifty I am.

'Everything okay, Freya?' Bryce asks, standing back from the car door.

Shit, if I don't calm down, he's going to suspect me. I've never acted one bit interested in him and then after all this time I call him out of the blue and ask if I can come to him.

'I'm... sorry, it's just you know, I've been on my own for a long time now and I'm trying to move on, sorry if I seem a little on edge.'

Bryce lets out a long sigh. I'm not sure I want to know his reply. He kneels at the side of the driver's door beside me, his eyes locked on mine. For a moment, we stare at one another.

Bryce looks genuinely sincere. 'I get it,' he says, putting his hand on mine and I'm instantly taken aback. 'You don't need to say anything. Come on up. I've made dinner.'

This is not what I was expecting. I step out from the car, straighten myself up and follow Bryce into the building.

The apartment is open plan. Walking in the door, I think I can see the full length of it. Its decor is simple, all light but cosy. Full of dark and light shades, but still warm. The floors a glossy black marble with flakes of glitter, all walls an eggshell white, matt finished with black furniture. Very classy for a single man. He must have had help designing the interior. Possibly from a girlfriend? He looks like he has the money to hire an interior designer though. Again, not what I was expecting at all.

'Would you like a glass of wine?' Bryce calls from the kitchen area.

'Um, I really shouldn't. I need to drive home.'

Bryce lets out a sarcastic laugh and asks, 'Do you normally use alcoholic breath mints when you're visiting a friend?' He strolls over to me, two glasses of white wine in hand, sporting a stupid grin.

Shit. 'Nerves,' I say, the word rolling off my tongue.

I put the glass to my lips and take a sip; I close my eyes and enjoy the sweet taste of expensive wine.

'So, you want to tell me what's going on with you, Fee?' Bryce makes his way over to the large leather sofa in the open plan living area.

The sofa faces out over the city lights; the views are stunning from six levels up. He sits on the sofa and I follow him. *Showtime, Freya, hold your nerve*. This will all be worth it. This *needs* done. I must do this.

I sit, relaxing back against the leather, the sofa smells like new, and close my eyes. I take another sip of the wine, it's lush, I almost forget where I am and why I'm here. If only I were here with someone else. The thought upsets me.

'I've just been struggling these past few weeks and realise I've been a horrible friend,' I say, lying.

Friend, I will never be your friend.

'I understand, it's tough. I meant it when I said we miss him. He was a good guy.' Bryce takes a long drink of his wine.

How can you call an employee who stole from you a good guy? If I had an explanation for all that money in the account Nathan opened, I'd be certain Bryce was lying.

'I can't comment on what kind of man he was. I really didn't know him all that well, remember? Life is cruel.'

Just like you.

Bryce fidgets, and for a moment he looks vulnerable, nervous perhaps. 'I just want to thank you for coming tonight, Freya. I thought the day would never come when you would phone and ask me if you could come over,' Bryce tells me.

Shit, he's being serious. I don't know how to respond. I take another drink of wine and realise I've drunk the whole glass.

'I... I just needed time,' I say.

'I think you know how I feel about you.'

My mouth drops, and for a moment, I feel out of body. Has he fallen for me and I haven't noticed it? How could he ever think I would be interested in someone like him? He's handsome, yes, but that handsome stature hides an evil persona.

'You have no idea, do you? How I feel about you? Your face says it all,' he says, watching me, waiting for an answer. I hear the weight of him gulping in anticipation.

This isn't going to plan.

I quickly realise I came here with no plan. I came here with one task in mind, to retrieve the book, I haven't thought the rest of it through.

'I had no idea, I… I just thought you were trying to get your money back. I'm so sorry, I didn't know.'

I don't want to know because I don't care.

'You must have had some idea. If you didn't, then why did you come?' Bryce asks.

'I just needed a friend.'

'So, you came here for a shoulder to cry on?'

Shit, he looks like he's getting mad, this isn't going well. 'I knew, I just think I wasn't admitting it to myself. I didn't think I was ready for anything. How about another drink and some of that dinner?' I give the best smile I can and pat him on his knee.

'Dinner and wine, now that I can do,' he says, standing and walking across to the kitchen. His mood seems to have picked up as he saunters around the kitchen.

I lift my wine glass, now refilled, and have a wander around the apartment, looking for any sign of the safe. Of course, it won't be in full view, but where? Bryce watches me as I drift over the floor, a smug smile on his face.

'Your apartment is beautiful. You definitely must have a cleaner to keep it looking so pristine.'

Bryce laughs from the kitchen island and says, 'Guilty.'

Guilty, I imagine him saying that somewhere else. I welcome the thought.

'You must have had some help decorating it?' I ask.

'None, well, my personal assistant helped with the decor for this apartment I must admit.'

'Really?' I ask, a little shocked he has more than one.

How many are there? The wine must make me feel brave because I ask that very thought.

Again, he laughs, and answers, 'I travel a lot so never really set up home anywhere. I'm not getting any younger. I'd like to settle, make an actual home, start a family.' He lifts his head and watches me as I take in his last statement.

'Sounds like a good idea, Bryce.'

The thought of a family with this creep makes me shudder inside, and I turn away from him to hide my disgust.

Bryce serves two plates of pasta on the dining table overlooking the balcony. If this night was with anyone else, it would be perfect.

'I couldn't think of a more perfect night to spend with you before I go away. Hopefully, we can do it again when I get back.'

I gulp, 'I would really like that. Where are you heading?' I force a smile.

The more this night drags on, the more uncomfortable I get.

'I'm going to Berlin. I'm meeting with a potential new client who is looking to have his mansion completely renovated, I'll be away four days. I'll be leaving early tomorrow morning for travelling. But dinner will have to do for now. Next time we'll have more time.'

He's planning on sending me home after dinner. It must be tonight. It has to be. It will be too late after that, then this entire week would've been for nothing. My heart is picking up pace, I can't see any other way. I feared this is what I would need to do, to get close to him. I pray to God for forgiveness for what I'm about to say. My body seems to have toughened up; my mind has toughened up.

'I don't think I can wait until next time,' I say, fixing my eyes on Bryce, making sure I have his attention.

'Are you saying you, you want to spend the night, Freya?' he asks, shocked.

'Yes.' No, I don't want to, no, no, no. This is a terrible idea, no, no I don't want to. I swallow hard, 'Maybe it's too soon, maybe it's better if we wait.'

Bryce pushes his chair out on my last word, stands and begins walking over to me. He grabs me by my arms, pulling me to my feet, and I'm instantly terrified. He can see right through me; he knows what I'm trying to do. I want to scream, but I freeze. Fear is ripping through my body at 100mph and I'm unable to react.

He holds me tight, inspecting my face, and I stare into his eyes as they soften. He leans into me, slowly his lips touch mine. My body weakens when his grip on my arms loosens and he kisses me hard, fast. I kiss him back against my will.

I want to be sick.

I want to hit him.

I want to scream.

I need to give in. A tear drips from my cheek and I tell myself it's the only emotion I will give him.

His hands move down, gripping my thighs, swiftly lifting me, and I wrap my legs around his waist. He carries me to a bedroom, his bedroom, kissing my neck as he walks. I scan the room, looking for the safe. I can't see it, he's moving me so fast, then throws me onto the bed. His roughness growing, I return it; I bite his ear. I grab his hair in my hand and tug. He breathes heavily in return. I close my eyes, trying to picture someone else, anyone else, not Nathan. He smells nothing like Nathan.

He runs his hand up inside my inner thigh and I shut off; I close my eyes and wait for it all to be over.

Twenty-Five

Freya

Friday, November 9, 2018

My body lies frozen, weighed down by a sleeping arm resting over my waist. Bryce is tight up against me, making me a prisoner in his bed.

Last night has played on repeat in my head. Unable to sleep, I watch every minute appear and disappear on the bedside clock; the numbers burning my eyes as I stare at them. The alarm finally sounds, 05:00, beeping low but stern.

Bryce's arm stiffens, then his body follows. He's stretching, his body waking, and I squeeze my eyes tightly shut, pretending I'm still fast asleep. Bryce reaches over me, giving the alarm a swift hit to silence it. His hand catches my shoulder, gently pulling me onto my back. I can still feel his naked body against me.

I try to keep my eyes shut. I just want him to go. My skin itches to be washed, to wash him off me.

'Morning beautiful,' he says in a soft tone.

I give a sleepy *mmm* in reply.

'I need to get ready, as much as I wish I didn't. You sleep on. I don't want you driving home to early with all that wine you drank last night. I want you in one piece for me getting home next week,' he says and leans into my face, planting a gentle kiss on my lips.

He's being a gentleman. It makes me want to be sick. I shock myself at how much I've kept it together to get this far. I suppose once you're broken, there's nothing else to break.

My body broken, my emotions broken, my life broken.

I lay absent, lifeless, waiting for him to leave.

I hear the front door opening, then closing softly and a gush of air releases from my lungs as though I've been held underwater since last night. The relief is fuel on a fire, nausea explodes, and I swallow it back down, hard. The shame is overbearing; I take a few minutes to compose myself, and I'm thankful no tears make an appearance.

I watch the alarm clock and wait fifteen minutes before I make a move. I sit up slowly, my body achy, I feel sick. I'm not sure if I feel sick because of all the wine or because I shamed myself last night. I quickly snap out of it. I need to remember why I came here. I need to find the safe. A flush of nausea rains over me and I rush to the bathroom, throwing up right into the sink.

Get it together, Freya, get it together. You've brought up the wine, clear your head, focus. Find the safe, get out and go home.

I rinse my mouth out in the sink with warm water, ignoring the bottle of spearmint mouthwash resting at the side of the sink, watching me. I close my eyes and remember the taste of spearmint and wine when Bryce kissed me. I shake off the thought and give myself a half-arsed attempt at smacking my face.

Right, find the safe.

Where the hell would Bryce hide it in here? It wouldn't be on show, not when it holds so much crucial information, he's too smart.

I try to think back to last night. There wasn't anything that stuck out, nothing that looked out of place. Then, from nowhere, it comes to me. The model of the red haulage truck, it must have been about a metre long and was the only thing of colour amongst all the shades of black and white. Bryce's words enter my head when I tried, but failed, to push it.

'It's stuck down, so no one steals it, it's my big boy toy.'

I go to the living room and examine the truck. It sits proudly on top of a charcoal-stained sideboard. I try again to push the truck along the sideboard, but its wheels stick to the glossy wood, then I see it, the license plate on the back tailgate slightly raised.

I pull it back further to reveal a combination pad. I memorised the code. I couldn't chance bringing it written or saved into my phone.

110762.

My hands shake as my fingers punch in the digits. To my relief, the back doors of the truck release. Two black leather-bound books stare back at me.

You've got to give it to Bryce, hides all the information in a toy truck when he uses a life-sized one to do all his dirty work.

No laptop. I noticed a laptop bag resting on top of a small travel case beside the front door of the apartment last night, Bryce must have taken it with him to Berlin.

I grab the notebooks out and a flood of passports land on the floor. Every one of them with Bryce's picture, but all different names.

One sticks out, Benedict Hewitt. I know that name. Where have I... It can't be? My stomach churns and sick fires up my throat again, burning, choking me.

Benedict Hewitt was Cassandra Chesterfield's partner. Bryce was her partner. My house was their house. Her baby was Bryce's... Benedict's.

I pick the passports up, taking a picture of the three of them on my iPhone, my hands shaking. I gather my belongings, flee the apartment as quickly as my legs will take me, closing the truck doors and clearing the code before I go.

Mum's awake with Clara when I arrive home.

'Freya, is that you sweetheart?' Mum calls from the kitchen.

I was hoping they would still be asleep, I'm not ready to face Mum, I'm not ready to face myself.

'It's me, Mum, I'll be there in a minute.'

The chirpy laughter of a toddler is a welcomed sound as I enter the house, but my legs take me right up the stairs and into the bathroom. I strip off my clothes as quickly as my hands let me, step into the bathtub and turn on the shower.

The water is scolding. I sit in the bath, my arms cradling my knees, and I allow the scorching water to console me whilst a flood of emotions spasm my body, shaking me so hard I feel every nerve react.

You did it. You got the notebooks. You've done the hardest part. The voice in my head cries with me.

I need to wash him off me. My mind snaps and my tears halt. I grab the mesh sponge and begin scrubbing my skin, ripping it over and over. The pain I deserve. I deserve punishment. I scrub every inch of my body, trying to wash him from my soul. My skin bleeds. I sit back, watching him swirl down the drain amid my blood and my shame.

My last day with Mum goes in a flash. Day? Morning really.

I've packed everything into her car I've saved from the house. My gut still clenches when I think of the disappointment Mum will feel when I don't return home like I promised. I shake off the thought. No time to cave in now.

'Granny loves you, my darling, and I'll see you real soon,' Mum tells Clara as she stands at the side of her car, squeezing and showering Clara with kisses. 'Granny loves you both so, so much.'

She looks to me, and my eyes swell. 'We both love you too, Mum, you're our glue. You always have been.'

I wipe away the flowing tears and hand Mum the gift I've wrapped for her birthday next week. Nathan was right. She will love it. Unknown to Detective Collins, I've hidden a note inside her birthday card, taped to the front. He'll be so angry when he finds out, if he finds out. But I didn't have a choice. If I had to disappear saying nothing to Mum, she would have herself on every news channel with a missing person's statement, and then the entire world would be looking for Clara and me. That was the attention we didn't need. I couldn't tell her the full extent of everything that's happened, that would put her in danger. The less she knew, the better. I agreed with Detective Collins on that aspect. But I did, however, explain about Bryce falsifying the criminal records and that Nathan wasn't a criminal. I told her in little detail that the police were after Bryce and that I was helping, and that's why Clara and I had to leave. I pray she understands.

'Freya,' Mum begins, handing me Clara. 'Whatever has gotten

into you these past two weeks...'

Oh shit, she knows. She knows what I let Bryce do to me, she knows.

She continues, 'Keep chasing it, sweetheart. It's like you've had a new lease of life and I've seen sparks of the old Freya. You've had your moments, yes, but whatever happened, it has been good for you. It's given you focus, a new purpose.' Mum hugs us both, and I never want it to end, for I know it will be my last.

I watch Mum climb into the car and wave with a happy, see-you-soon smile. I walk down the driveway to the junction of the main road and watch as she drives off. Unaware it will be our last goodbye.

There it is. The black Audi. Sneakily parked up the road in a lay-by, surrounded by trees, not hidden enough that I can't see the matrix headlights peering out.

Game time, asshole.

09:08. I walk back up the drive, strap Clara into her car seat and drive to the sports centre, a twelve-minute drive away. I check my rear-view mirror and see the black Audi following a few cars behind.

Twenty-Six

Stephanie

We strolled out of the building, Clara in the pushchair, a cabin bag pulled beside us, and no one batted an eyelid. We walked to the taxi rank, and now here we are. Standing impatiently waiting in the check-in queue at the airport, holding Clara... Ava, and her scruffy Peter Rabbit in my arms. I look at the masses of people hovering around beside me, scanning their faces for the slightest glimpse of familiarity. I don't think anyone followed us.

I changed in the sports centre, and binned both wigs and my old clothes in a bin outside the changing rooms. A pushchair was delivered to work for Clara—*Ava*, and a small cabin bag for the journey. I packed everything we needed into my gym hold all and transferred it all into the cabin bag before we left the sports centre. As much of our lives as I could squeeze in. All I have to remind me of my life now is a gold crucifix necklace that my Grandparents got me for my 18th birthday around my neck and Nathan's platinum wedding band.

I fought with myself to throw it away, to dispose of it, but I couldn't. I need to remember he was still Clara's father. She deserves to know who he was when she's old enough.

The necklace, I've never taken off since my Papa passed away five years ago. He always hangs close to my heart. I wish he were still here. He's been my lucky charm through everything, but there is so much left behind, so many memories. I wish I could have taken everything with me, but I know it's not possible. Mum has the most important things with her, so I know they will be safe.

The check-in stewardess finally calls us forward.

About bloody time.

She holds out her hand and with a forced smile, asks for our passports. My heart leaps into my throat. I gulp trying to clear it and pass them over to her hesitantly. Becoming more anxious with every passing second as her eyes roll over me, judging me.

Can she tell the passports aren't real? My psyche asking me over and over, looking for reassurance, but I have none to give, wishing she would just shut up.

'Do you have any cases to check in, Ms Shenton?' she asks, looking slanted from the left side of her tall desk at the one small cabin bag, resting against the pushchair.

Is this woman being serious or just plain stupid? Maybe it's because her ponytail is that tight, it's cutting the circulation off to her brain. She can see there aren't more bags, I snap silently into myself, fighting the urge to grit my teeth, intolerant to the fact check-in is moving too slowly for me.

'Just one carry on case,' I answer, my voice rough but frank, gulping again with my heart travelling even further up my throat.

Cold sweat layers my face and neck and descends my top lip. The politeness I keep for special occasions is non-existent today, terror is bullying it to get past this over analysing woman and through the airport.

A stranger now lives on my passport, a person I barely recognised sporting shoulder-length hair, brunette with tones of caramel and copper and dull hazel eyes. Every inch of me is feeling out of place in skinny jeans, an oversized black parka, and a pair of black baseball Converse. Most definitely not my normal style.

Well, that is the whole point of it, is it not?

My nipping eyes are trying to indulge the coloured contact lenses. The stewardess tilts her head forward for a clearer view. Her eyes peering over her glasses that have slipped down the bridge of her nose. Is she suspecting us? She saw from the tickets we are going to Los Angeles. She's probably thinking how odd it is just one small carry-on case for a grown woman and a small child going such a long distance. Her eyes fix on me for a minute before moving over to Clara... *Ava*, shit. I wish she would hurry the fuck up. My nerves can't take this, the feeling we're going to get caught is pounding in my head.

'Ava Rose Shenton is a pretty name for a cutie pie,' she comments, her smile now looking sincere.

Ava is balancing on my right hip, her head timidly resting on my shoulder along with Peter Rabbit, her hands clinging onto my jacket. The woman looks concerned. I don't blame her. I have runaway written all over me.

'Are you girls going on holiday?'

The forced smile I've been wearing on my face since we got called forward now hurting my cheeks.

'Visiting family,' I answer.

That was the quickest answer that sprung into my mind. My threshold to lie weakening, I've never been good at it.

Giving one last forced smile, she reluctantly hands back our passports and tickets, wishing us a pleasant flight. From the tone of her voice and dimmed eyes, I know she isn't sincere, well towards me anyway.

At that moment, walking away from check-in, my legs turn to jelly. Struggling to keep a grip on Ava and handle the pushchair, I march through the crowds of passengers. I examine every face that drifts past us, their eyes on me, reading my every move. Thinking the same as the nosey check-in stewardess, I bet.

I know it's my imagination; I know my nerves will settle down when we are on the aeroplane. Our first destination is Los Angeles, over eleven hours to get there. I have to hold it together. I'm falling apart a lot earlier than expected.

My phone bursts into loud rings, and I jump, my nerves on edge. Layla's name flashes on the screen. Shit, I forgot to bin my iPhone at the sports centre with the rest of my old stuff. I've ignored her calls and texts all week. I owe it to her to say goodbye, even if she doesn't know it's goodbye.

I sit down on the nearest chair and wrestle the phone from my jacket pocket.

'Hey you,' I answer, a burst of confidence thrown in for good measure but mostly apologetic.

'Fee, what the fuck, I've been so worried about you. I've been going out of my mind. Why haven't you texted or answered my phone calls? I'm outside your door, where are you?'

Layla sounds concerned and pissed, swapping my confidence for guilt.

'I've not been good, I just needed to be alone.'

'Fee. I know you. I've been with you every step of the way. Why didn't you just call me? Two heads are better than one.' Layla's voice is reassuring.

I wish I could tell her; my heart screams to tell her like it did for Mum, my head making me see sense, I can't put her in danger too.

'Where are you? I'll come get you. I came round last night too, but no one answered the door?'

Fuck. I can at least tell her what I did, that's allowed, isn't it? I need to get the shame off me, Layla will tell me it's all right.

'Fee, are you okay, honey? Speak to me, it's me for fuck's sake.'

'I did something horrible last night, Layla. I...' If I say it, then it will make it even more real.

'Come on Freya, whatever it is, I'll help.'

'I'm beyond help. I slept with Bryce,' I say.

The confession spills from me, laid bare in front of me for all to see. I'm ruined goods. The phone goes quiet, she's judging me. No, she wouldn't, she's always been there to dry my tears and pick me up. She's just composing an answer that will take away the sick feeling that sticks to the memory.

A laugh crackles down the phone, Layla's laugh sounds different, sardonic. 'You stupid cow, you utterly stupid cow. What? Do you think he loves you?' her laugh continues.

I can't fathom what's going on. This isn't Layla.

'Cow! You deserve everything that's coming to you, and I'll be first in line to witness it all. Where the fuck are you?' she snaps.

'Layla, why are you being like this?'

'Oh, poor little delicate Freya, always gets what she wants. You've wanted him all along, haven't you? You must have taken me for a fool, telling me you want nothing more than friendship with him, that you owe him, you bitch! Were you paying him back in sex?'

The penny drops. She knows Bryce. She's jealous.

'How do you even know him? You've met him once.'

'That's what he wanted you to think. Bryce and I are together.

He asked me to keep an eye on you, and I did.'

'What?' I snap. 'You are the reason Bryce knew everything? Where I would be? What I was doing? Why would you do that?'

'Because I love him, I'd do anything for him, even put you out your misery!' Layla's voice is threatening. I can't listen to her anymore.

I hear her voice raise, asking where I am again, and I quickly hang up the phone, throwing it in the dustbin beside me. How could I be so stupid?

I grab Ava and the pushchair again, and head for the departure gate as quickly as possible. Still a long way to go before I can breathe easy, thousands of miles to be exact. All I want right now is to watch the ground disappearing from beneath us as we take off, away from this hell we've been living in.

Twenty-Seven

Stephanie

Dusk broke on our short forty-five-minute flight from Anchorage. The view is breath-taking, tranquillity setting all over my weary body, watching the land below me grow closer. Spectacular views of the coastal Chugach Mountains, vast glacial ice fields and heavenly pristine snow.

I had the luck of sitting with a kind elderly lady, a resident of Valdez who educated me on the scenery. No words fill my mind except a simple wow. I've instantly fallen in love in a way I never thought was possible. I've never visited Valdez in my life, but for a split second, a shock of familiarity buzzes through me as though I was almost home from a long break.

A taxi was waiting to pick us up at the airport, kindly booked by our new landlady. I noted the wary face of the driver when he only had one small cabin bag to lift into the back of his car.

'Luggage got lost in LA,' I explained.

He didn't ask, but I felt I had to give him some sort of explanation.

Ava's exhausted, her head hits my knee as soon as the car moves, the way she's spent most of the journey. Safe to say, it relieved me. I hate crying in front of her. Tears streamed down my face as soon as we landed in Valdez. They also streamed down my face when we landed in LA and Anchorage too. It had become a celebratory habit every time we touched ground. Tears of joy for coming so far. Possibly tears for leaving Mum the way I did, my potential downfall of letting the man who steals precious babies, put his hands on me. Tears for letting Detective Collins down and betraying him with what I've done, I suspect he will know now, but I needed too.

Goddamn you, Nathan!

If I had just trusted my gut the minute I met him, we wouldn't be in all of this mess. A sharp pain protrudes my heart at the thought of not having my little sidekick, she's all I have now. My mind quickly changes, they're tears of relief knowing we're safe, or for the time being at least. We will find out soon enough.

I used to be one who liked change, a challenge at new things. I once welcomed the diversity, always comfortable enough to go it alone, that's why I used to travel so much. Now, the thought of starting over again terrifies me more than I could have imagined. Three flights and 4,431 miles later, we're finally here. Every broken part of me waking in recognition of the tremendous achievement.

The town was busy for Friday evening. Passing so many unknown faces seems so daunting but exhilarating all at once. No one knows us, exactly what we need.

The taxi comes to a slow stop beside a white Jeep Cherokee parked outside a cabin. I wipe away the salty tears from my wet cheeks, trying to straighten my blurry vision, and put a smile on my face as best as I can with what little energy I have left in me.

'Ava sweetheart, wake up,' I say and shake her gently.

Her eyes still not open yet, but I know she hears me. She stretches her arms out and gives a little cheeky grin in recognition of my voice. Her little body is drained. Trying her hardest to sit up, using the last of her energy to swing her short arms around my neck and squeeze me. My little darling gives the best cuddles, just when I need them.

I had little input about where we were going to be living, all done discretely by Detective Collins' witness protection team, which included him, Mr Leighton and no one else. Albert had arranged everything, although the only request I made was to make it as far away as physically possible. The further away, the safer we are from harm.

Fuck, I hope that's true.

As I step out from the taxi, standing in hushed awe of our

new surroundings, my eyes sprint to the most stunning cabin I have ever seen. Pitched up a level off the ground, wrapped around an old tree, like every adult's inner child's dream treehouse. Constructed of glorious caramel timber under a steeply pitched slate roof with gables. And best of all, it's covered in a blanket of freshly fallen bright white flawless snow. Full of character and promise, and just waiting to make fresh memories.

The envelope Detective Collins gave to me on Friday morning before we left the sports centre, contained a letter with all the details about where we would be living. The landlord will watch our flight details and wait for us at the house with the keys. Maybe to show us around. Her name, Olivia Wyper. Sounds like an old name, I expect she's older than me. I have an image of her constructed in my head. Grey, short and frail.

I lift Ava and glance around, noticing a small light beaming out through the front window. Mrs Wyper must be inside waiting for us. The taxi driver kindly takes my small case and Ava's folded pushchair up the wooden steps to the door before leaving. I follow, my legs about to buckle with exhaustion, carrying us both up the stairs. I think I counted ten? Maybe I counted wrong because it felt like fifty.

I give the door a knock, taking deep breaths in of crisp fresh evening air, patiently waiting for the door to open. The heavy wooden door springs open quickly, banging off the wall inside, startling both Ava and me. A man, maybe late twenties, tries to catch the door as it bounces back from the wall. Who the hell is he? For a moment, I pause, wondering if the taxi has brought us to the wrong address.

'Stephanie Shenton?' he asks, a grin on his face.

My defences build—his grin instantly makes my skin crawl. His eyes run from my head to my feet and then back to my face. He looks overly impressed with himself, arrogantly.

'Yes, I'm supposed to be meeting Mrs Wyper?' I say cautiously, pulling Ava closer to my body.

Ava takes after me. She tends to run away from the male species; she isn't overly fond of them. Probably because she wasn't around many, not a lot of men left in our family.

'I'm her nephew, Billy. Something came up, and she asked me to meet you here. I hope that's not a problem for you?' he asks with a slight snap in his voice, his grin disappearing.

Wow, what's his problem? He answers me like I've offended him in some manner. He's average height, maybe on the short side. Rough looking, mousey brown hair tucked behind both ears, wearing a black and red plaid shirt tucked into dirty denim jeans. A look I usually melt for on the opposite sex, apart from being short that is, but his attitude is letting off a foul stench. He's a stranger to me, but I'm discouraged by him. First impressions in the past have been long-standing with me. Under the circumstances, I'm willing to start over.

'Please excuse me, Billy, we're exhausted and just want settled, it's been a very long journey.'

He raises his hand gesturing to come in but doesn't speak, sulking quietly into himself no doubt.

In a flash, I forget the stranger as the eye-catching interior steals my attention, it's just as stunning as the exterior. The walls clad with caramel covered wood panels, the same as the outside. Hardwood floors covered with vibrant red trellis rugs branching into every room. Walking to the door on the left, I enter a large reception room hosting a chocolate leather sofa and one matching armchair at the far end of the room. A beautiful wicker chair takes place in front of the long window, draped with chocolate coloured velvet curtains and pelmet. I run my hands along the solid oak sideboard in the living room, a light layer of dust gathers on my fingers. I don't think anyone has lived here for some time. The cabin was dated in fashionable status, but I'm in love. A feeling inside telling me this cabin had been waiting a long time for us.

The moody stranger disappears to the back of the cabin, I follow with Ava and find him in the kitchen leaning against an old-style Rayburn cooker, beautifully preserved like an ornament not to be touched. Ava's made herself and Peter comfortable on one of four chairs perched around an oval-shaped, pine dining table positioned centre of the room.

'Mummy, I hungry,' she tells me.

Shit, food. I didn't even think.

Fuck.

Billy opens a cupboard above his head, pulling out a bag of chocolate chip cookies. The cupboards stocked with tins of food, biscuits, pasta; the list goes on. Enough to see us through for at least a week, I don't believe it.

'My Aunt was gave instructions by your Uncle. Albert, was it? To stock up on a few essentials you and your kid would need, should keep you going for now. Refrigerator's full too, you'll find everything yourself,' Billy explains.

Wow, Detective Collins thought of everything. For a moment, I forget Billy's snappiness when we first arrived. He seems quite normal now.

'Here, this is everything you need to know about all the financial stuff like the rent,' he says and hands me a colt blue folder full of paperwork.

'Thanks, how do I contact your Aunt if I have questions?'

'You don't. Read the paperwork.' He cuts me short, and my capacity to deal with him wears thin. 'Before I forget, your jeep keys on the keychain with the cabin keys.'

My what? I have a car?

'What jeep?' I ask.

Billy rolls his eyes at the question. He's not shy in hiding his boredom.

'You blind? The ride sitting out front. Your Uncle said you would need a ride. My Aunt was selling hers, 'cause it sits in the drive and doesn't get used now, so they worked out a deal.'

Detective Collins bought me a car! Why the hell would he use his own money to buy me something so expensive? I don't understand. My head is buzzing with the lack of sleep.

I can't even bring myself to call him Albert now, I feel I've lost that right. He'll know by now I've betrayed him. An invisible knife of guilt stabs right into the pit of my stomach.

'How about I get the kid some milk, I'll make us some coffee, and we can get better acquainted?' Billy asks, winking at me, and I'm sure he sticks out his tongue in a suggestive manner.

Is this guy bipolar or what? A wave of uneasiness rolls over me, I get the impression he's trying to be more than just friendly. He's so rude it infuriates me. I don't even know how to tell him to piss off anymore.

My eyes are stinging from the coloured contacts. I just want him to leave so I can get them out.

'Sorry, but I'm exhausted. I need to get my daughter something to eat and then into bed. We've been travelling for over eighteen hours. Thank you for your help, though.' I raise my hand in his direction and gesture to shake his.

His smile drops. He shakes his head and chews his bottom lip. Turning his back, he ignores my gesture, then promptly leaves the kitchen. This arsehole doesn't enjoy being told no. I put my hand back down in embarrassment.

I follow him down the hall to the door, keeping a safe distance. He opens it to leave but stops, turning his head back to me.

'Oh, and just so you know, the shopping was a one-off. My Aunt ain't your servant.' His moody attitude makes a return as he leaves, slamming the door shut.

I stand, stunned. What's his problem? I'm not letting that piece of shit bother me. Hopefully, I won't have any more dealings with him, and by God do I hope he doesn't get his attitude from his Aunt.

I make sure the door's locked before I turn and take in the beautiful interior once again. My eyes filling with fresh tears of contentment. We made it, we're safe.

The nine-hour time difference has thrown us off. My body drained, Ava's tiny body running on empty.

Cuddled into my unfamiliar bed, I ask her once again before we drift off to sleep, 'What's your name, sweetheart?'

She tilts her head to the side, giving me her thinking look, screwing up her nose, one eye squinting. I've said Ava at every opportunity, hoping she remembers. She'll be so confused.

'Va,' she replies hesitantly in her soft, innocent voice.

I give her a cheeky smile back. 'That's right, clever girl, Ava Rose. Your secret princess name.'

She puts her hand up to her mouth in shock and then giggles. She's pretty smart for a fourteen-month-old, like she has been here one too many times before. She absorbs everything you tell her, her brain like a sponge. I sometimes wonder if it's a good or a bad thing. Part of me always thinks I don't deserve her. She's the only good I have left of my existence.

My eyes open, I don't know this place. Silence fills my ears, and I sit up. A clock pinned to the wall ticks loudly above the dressing table at the far side of the bedroom. 04:05. The ticking sound switches to a hammer banging on the wall, everything else so quiet.

We're in Valdez.

A tidal wave of the last few days hits me. Just a few short hours ago, Detective Collins would have handed what evidence I gave him into his superior, taking everything out of my hands. There will be no way for him to contact me, to tell me if everything went to plan or fell apart, or to tell me he's disappointed in what I've done to him. He made me promise not to contact him. We couldn't risk anyone finding out where Ava and I went. Trust no one, he told me repeatedly. He had a lot of doubts about people in authority, and only one he knew who he could trust. I had twenty-four hours to leave the country before he would go to his old friend, a friend he trusted with his life. Now a friend he trusted with our lives. The shit will now have majorly hit the fan. God, I could throw up thinking about it.

I'm now officially a dead woman.

Twenty-Eight

Stephanie

I spit the last of my fingernails from my left hand over the hardwood floor under me. My fingers ache from the nervous chewing that kept me from sleeping. My once perfectly nurtured, long nails are now bitten to the quick.

I find myself curled into the wicker rocking chair in the living room, looking for solace, wrapped in a thick fleece blanket, my body still trembling with the cold. The window overlooks a serene forest in front of the cabin, and I sit tentatively watching the dawn appearing from above the trees whilst I move on to my fingernails on my right hand, my anxiety spiking with my dark thoughts.

I hate that wretched feeling of being in the dark and not knowing what's going on in England. As time goes on, I'm being tortured by my psyche reminding me constantly of what's happened, and possibly happening now that I don't know about. Reminding myself I'm a prisoner of my actions, and my punishment is not being able to know the consequences of the chaos I helped set alight.

It's not that I'm not proud of what I did, I am, immensely. If it helps find any of those poor babies, then I have served my purpose. I'm disappointed in myself for what I have done to Detective Collins. I think about his face, his dismay at me.

Why did I ever doubt him? Fucking idiot that I am.

I debate back and forth with myself to contact him, to apologise, but my one-sided argument has gotten me nowhere. He would be so angry if I had to contact him. I mustn't as much as my head pleads with me to do so. The switch in my head feels like it is about to trip, setting me off on one of my episodes that Mum is usually at the ready to intervene with and calm me down. The fear I'm tipping over the edge of a breakdown with no one here to save me from myself is unbearable.

Christ, the tips of my fingers ache. Every nail bit down as far as I could. I miss my beautifully manicured nails, showcasing a different vibrant colour every month to match my vibrantly blissful persona. I haven't felt that persona since I met Nathan.

My mood drops to a lower level now thinking about it, and I start a light nibble at the skin lining the inside of my cheeks.

I stand from the wicker chair, making my way to the bedroom to check on Ava, who's still sound asleep, in the same sleeping position I left her in. Her sleeping habits have come a long way from when she was first born, the little distraction vacuum.

My attention goes to the oak ottoman at the end of my bed. Reaching inside, I pull out a large grey marl T-shirt. It still smells of him, Nathan. When I put it on, I imagine him wrapped around me, and we're in our bed, in our beautiful bedroom, in our own home in England. His hands running gently over my skin, my heart tingling at the bittersweet memory. Surrounded by our possessions, our comforts and everything that made our lives perfect.

I kept one of his T-shirts, only one, unwashed. When he first died, it was my comfort going to bed, but now it doesn't have the same feel, the same effect on me anymore. Lies have extinguished my love for him. It makes me wonder if I ever did truly love him if it's this easy to hate?

The T-shirt slides from my hand and crumbles lifeless on the floor.

The vague aching of a migraine is forming behind my eyes. I gently slide into bed beside Ava, curling up into a ball. Dare I attempt to sleep? I'm exhausted. Bryce's face lives in my nightmares, he's there waiting to grab me as soon as I close my eyes. Every night I dream he puts his hands around my neck and squeezes tighter and tighter until I'm unconscious, my mind screaming for Nathan to save me, but he never answers my pleas for help.

I try not to be so angry at Nathan for everything that he's caused. How was he to know he was working for a psychopath? I'm angry at myself for not sticking my ground when he gave me the ultimatum of moving to England with him or ending our relationship. I'm partly to blame for this too.

For the first time since reading the files Bryce gave me, my heart breaks when I think of him. As much as I hate him for what he's done, there will always be a place in my heart for him. A small place as Ava's Father.

He's standing over me, smiling happily as my body succumbs to the tightening in my throat. I try to scream, but I'm fading away. My grip on his brawny arms weakening and I'm unable to fight him off any longer.

The gasps for air die to a halt, and I'm on the cold hard ground, lifeless, dead.

Clara is in her basket in front of the fire, crying inconsolably as the basket swiftly swings from side to side. Her crying echoes to every corner of my dream. My psyche is still alive, screaming for him to leave her alone. Screaming for me to move, to get up off the floor, but I don't respond.

He lifts her roughly from her basket with patches of words I can't hear clearly. He turns with her in his arms, stepping over my motionless body.

I hear the words, 'New home, little one,' his voice deep, tedious as it fades when he walks away from me.

My eyes open rapidly, sweat thick on my forehead. I try to adjust my watering sight. What was that dream?

Lying still, my body in shock, trying to grip onto the fragments of it that quickly dissolve in my awake reality.

For all the dreams I've had, he has never once got his hands on Ava. The nightmares are getting worse. I can't live like this. It's going to kill me.

Depression has hit me hard in the face, the regret of leaving my Mum behind playing heavily on my mind. Christmas is three weeks away. She must be beside herself with worry. I know she'll be missing Ava terribly.

I lift the telephone that's perched on a cradle and run my fingers over the raised buttons, making a pattern over Mum's telephone number. If I could just hear her voice, let her know we're both okay. The aching in my heart consumes me. I'm going crazy, yet I'm still scared stiff to set foot out of the cabin.

I miss Emma. She would set me straight.

Get yourself together, you bloody idiot, you're not dead, get a grip.

I hear her voice at the back of my mind. She's right; I need to get a grip. I know I can't keep us locked away forever; the phrase cabin fever comes to mind. The only time I've unlocked the door was to grab packages off the front porch since I've become a recluse and fan of online shopping. Clothing, food, toys—the cabin is full with every basic homeware essential that we need, yet it still isn't home. My focus now set on making it as homely as possible, to retrieve the feelings I had when I first stepped into the cabin.

Delivery drivers come and go a few times a week, as does Bipolar Billy. He's visited occasionally in the last three weeks. After our first meeting, I didn't feel like speaking to him. Can't say he's a person I wish to have in my life, and it's completely put me off meeting his Aunt too, who has also visited occasionally.

A note takes up residence on the door saying; *Out for the day, leave deliveries on the porch, thanks.* So, to Mrs Wyper and her creep of a nephew, it looked like we were living it up in Valdez, when in reality Ava and I were hiding upstairs in our very own treehouse attic.

I would peer out from behind the curtain like an insane loner, waiting for them to leave before unlocking the door. I grab the packages as soon as they disappear out of sight and then sprint back inside.

Ava's behaviour has been shocking since we arrived, even though she was always so well behaved. This change is affecting her in the wrong way. I know she's bored being locked indoors. Poor kid, why should she suffer because of me. I need to try going out.

Last week springs to mind and how terrifying it was driving for the first time in a new country. My anxiety attack in front of Ava, driving through town with her in the car scared me half to death, and we ended up parked in a forest until I stopped shaking enough to drive back to the cabin. No driving this time, time to try walking into town.

Give yourself a fucking shake, Stephanie.

We are living in a beautiful town full of stunningly mesmerising history, wildlife, and so much more. Surrounded by calming Mother Nature, maybe the medicine I need. We both need.

'Ava, how would you like to go out and pick a Christmas tree?'

Ava springs to her feet with excitement, clapping her hands and shouting yes. Her innocent, enthusiastic laugh is intoxicating, just hearing it fills my body with sparks of happiness. Poor baby has only seen Christmas in films. She was too young to remember her first Christmas.

My mood cranks up a level. We get dressed quickly and head outside before I change my mind.

Twenty-Nine

Stephanie

The fresh winter air smells pure, refreshing. I take a deep breath in, preparing myself for my second public venture since the first was wretchedly unsuccessful.

Ava jumps in the snow with her new purple glitter wellies and fur hooded winter coat. Her mousey brown hair peers out from the side of the hood, catching drops of the light drizzling rain. My confidence grows with each step we make.

We stick out like sore thumbs, though. The faces some people are making at us, clearly already branded as odd, only because we're unknown to them. My eyes meet passers-by, giving each unknown face the same wide smile as the last, most of them don't reciprocate. I don't let it bother me, they're strangers to me. Like my Mum used to say, strangers are just flashes in life that you shouldn't waste time on.

Ava grabs my hand, and I think it's her way of reassuring me. We skip down the sidewalk in our own little bubble, mesmerised by the illuminated displays of Christmas lights hanging from one building to the next. My little angel is back to her smiling, happy self. Maybe after we find a Christmas tree, I could brave going food shopping in the actual world instead of via the internet. How hard could it possibly be?

Across the street, a little store seems to stick out from the rest. There's a large window display full of all sorts and decorated with glorious flashing fairy lights. Outside, the window framed by helical stripes of festive reds and greens. I lift Ava in my arms and cross the street. Winter, Christmas, it's all me. My best time of the year.

My mood cranks up another level at the thought and back down two when I think it's the first one we'll spend alone.

In the window, a beautiful handcrafted vintage doll's house takes pride of place on full display. Ava's hands press up against the window, admiring it closely.

'Mummy, ook!' she says, her voice a squeak higher.

It's identical to the doll's house I had as a child that Mum still has in the attic. Forever telling me, she kept it only to pass onto her Granddaughter one day if she was lucky enough to have one. My mood dips again.

Come on, you're doing so well. Chin back up!

We have to have it, I think as Ava steers me inside. I picture her face on Christmas morning. Toys fill the store just as stunningly kept as the doll's house. A sign above the front desk reads; *Refurbished and extremely cared for toys. We hope you love them as much as the love we have given to them.*

It's crammed full, but neat with a smell of varnish and paint. I tighten my grip on Ava's hand as I approach the older man at the desk to enquire about the doll's house.

'Gee Gee!' Ava lets out a yelp and runs to the back of the store.

I turn my head in shock and go after her. Standing at the back of the store is a smart, well-dressed lady with greying blonde hair. Her fringe swept sidewards, and the rest in a perfect bun pinned to the crown of her head. She's taking reading books from her bag and placing them onto a bookshelf. Ava reaches her, wrapping her arms around her legs, almost knocking her off her feet.

'Oh, hell, I'm so sorry!' My face turning flushed red as I try to prise Ava from her.

I can see why Ava thought she had seen Gee Gee, her Great-Grandmother, my Gran. I was forever showing Ava photographs of her and Papa. They're very alike, although Gee Gee must have been at least twenty years older. The well-mannered lady seems quite taken with the situation. I would even say she doesn't want Ava to let go.

'That's alright dear, she's just a vision of perfect. I've been looking forward to meeting you both, but it seems you don't enjoy answering the door?'

She's wearing such a kind smile on her face when she speaks, making me smile. 'You must be Mrs Wyper?' I ask.

'Olivia, my dear, please.'

She's so kind, pleasant. I wonder for a moment if they adopted her nephew into the family or someone dropped him on his head as a child?

'Thank you so much for all the arrangements you made for Ava and me, and um... I'm sorry for not answering the door.'

I can't even bring myself to make eye contact to apologise. I realise just how embarrassing hiding from visitors is when I say it out loud.

'It was the least I could do for your Uncle Albert, he's quite the gentleman, always has been.'

Always has been? Does this lady know Albert? Detective Collins? How the hell does she know him? He said no one would know us here; I feel very uncomfortable now knowing she knows him.

Fuck!

'You know Uncle Albert? He never mentioned you?' I think that's subtle enough.

Olivia, still smiling at Ava while she sits on the shop floor flicking through a book about unicorn's answers, 'Well that's probably because I first met him and your Aunt Alice before you were born. I would guess you're about thirty?'

This is getting weirder by the minute. My Aunt Alice, so Detective Collins' wife I take it? If they both visited here together, I know it wasn't for his job. Anger peers its ugly head, thinking he's sent me to someplace he's been, with people who know him, a place where he has connections. Fuck. I'm not stupid enough to believe this was a random place chosen at the last minute. It's becoming obvious he has done all this by himself. He must have paid for all the travel by himself too. But why? I'm not an idiot, I knew this move wasn't official, but it's just smacked me full force across my face. Fury is building up, which makes me think again about contacting him to ask what the hell is going on. It seems he's kept me in the dark about certain details, important details that could endanger us even more than we already are.

'Nearly a perfect guess. I'll be thirty next May,' I answer, trying to keep the smile from shielding my utter annoyance.

'Ah, a spring birthday, my husband was May seventeenth. What date are you, dear?'

'The seventh.'

'I shall have to remember that. Why don't you come to the house for some tea whilst we get to know each other, and I can see this little darling again? It's only about a ten-minute drive from the cabin.'

I find it hard to say no to Olivia. What harm could it do to visit her? I feel like I've known her my entire life with her easing aura. She has all the stillness and grace of a lady with a beautiful soul. Her posture is completely perfect, but there is a hint of strictness about her when she moves, even when she speaks. I want to find out everything she knows about Detective Collins and figure out what he was thinking.

Olivia and I speak for several more minutes before she offers her nephew to deliver the doll's house back to the cabin for me. Billy the creep. I feel uneasy just thinking about being in his company again, but I don't decline her offer.

Thirty

Stephanie

My head has been in overdrive since meeting with Olivia this afternoon. I can't understand why Detective Collins intervened by himself and chose here of all places to send us. From my perspective, I can't see it being very safe sending us here when he has connections. But what connections? I need to take Olivia up on her offer for tea. I have a few questions for her, and I need to find out what she knows, sooner rather than later. A spark of purpose flurries in my belly now I have something to set my mind to.

A rough knock sounds from the door, startling me from my chain of thought. It's 19:45.

For all the times the door has knocked, I've never once answered it. I know it will be the tree we picked in town today being delivered, but I shudder at the thought of answering the door in case it's Billy. I'm too tired to deal with his mood swings tonight. I must open the door though; I need to. Ava will be sorely disappointed if she wakes tomorrow to find we still don't have a Christmas tree, all because her nerve bag of a Mummy is too much of a wimp to answer the door again.

Bracing myself behind the door, I take a deep breath in and unlock it. Opening it only slightly enough to see who it is. A gasp of relief exhales from my mouth when I see it's not Billy. Although in some weird way it looks like him, only taller with dirty blond hair. Spiky and messed up. And if I was honest with myself, a lot better looking.

'Hey, Stephanie?' he asks, and he sounds better looking than Billy.

'Yes, and you're here with our tree?' I ask cautiously.

He looks confused. 'No, sorry, my Aunt Olivia asked me to pick up a doll's house from Seb's and drop it to you? Sorry, it's so late, I had a few deliveries to do myself and thought I would catch you on the way home.'

That explains it. Olivia has two nephews. Least one of them doesn't seem like he has anger issues and terrible people skills, AKA, a dick.

'Actually, it's worked out great. Ava fell asleep earlier tonight. Our adventures today knackered her so I can hide the house until Christmas morning easier now,' I say.

He smiles, and I can't help but smile back.

I hold out my hand and wait with anticipation to see if he reacts the same as his brother.

'I'm Stephanie.'

Stephanie, it still sounds alien.

Heavy breathing laughter releases from his mouth.

He already knows that, idiot.

What the hell is happening to me, one smile and my senses are evaporating out from my head. 'Noah,' he replies and shakes my hand.

His hand is warm and rough. He doesn't have a desk job with hands like that. 'Where are my manners, please come in?'

'I'll just grab the doll's house from the back of the truck first.'

'No problem,' I say, and watch him saunter to his truck, his body screams tired.

His jeans hanging loosely on him, tucked into his tan-coloured rigger boots. With one swoop he lifts the solid wooden house, cradling it in his arms, making it look the weight of a feather. I'm not sure what's going on in my head, but I have a strange sensation that I can't seem to fight. 'Would you like a coffee?' I ask as he ascends the stairs.

Adult company with a sane person is in reach, and I snatch it with both hands. Inside, I'm waiting in an excitable manner for a response. Outside, I'm as cool as I can be.

'Sure,' Noah answers, but I'm sure he screws his face up at

this.

Sure? Does that mean yeah sure, I'm just answering to be polite and I really just want to go home or is he good at playing calm like I am? 'Milk and sugar?' I mumble.

'Both please.'

He's not much of a talker, or do I just think this because I'm dying for some conversation?

He takes a seat on the brown leather sofa, looking uncomfortable but slightly at home in the dull sitting room. It's his Aunt's cabin, after all, he must have been in here before.

I saunter into the kitchen and boil the kettle, still conflicted over his cool *sure* reply. And then it finally dawns on me. Maybe he hates coffee, maybe he is the complete opposite of his brother and said sure, just to be polite. I could offer him a beer if I had any.

Again, idiot.

I've done my best to avoid human interaction for nearly an entire month, then one day outside the cabin, and I've found a new lease of confidence. Christ, I'm even trying my best to get this stranger to stay. Adult conversation and stimulation are what I've been needing. I've been left with my thoughts for too long, it's completely unhealthy.

'You've changed the place a bit, looks good,' his voice is politely attractive.

'I tried to make the place a little more like home for Ava, help her settle better.'

He reaches his hand out and takes the hot coffee mug from me. I can't help but find it amusing how completely different to his brother he is, although they may be very alike, and Noah is a master of disguising it.

'What's so funny?' he asks before taking a sip of coffee.

I can't help but be honest. 'Not being rude, but you're completely different from your brother.' Maybe that is a bit rude.

'I get that a lot, would you believe? I hope he hasn't been rude to you?' he asks, looking annoyed.

God, I hope I haven't offended him, and he's setting himself up to defend his brother.

'Doesn't take kindly to the word no, does he?'

'Billy doesn't take kindly to much. I'll have a word with him.'

Well done, Steph! Already causing problems and I've only

lived here for five minutes. I don't think I'm liking this Stephanie that much yet.

'God no, please. I wasn't trying to cause trouble. I just got the impression he was, um…' What's a kind word for bipolar?

'Moody? Forward? Pain in the ass?' he says, laughing lightly.

Fuck, he knows him well; I hold my laugh back.

'Yes, all the above,' I say, then I laugh lightly back, unable to control it.

Our eyes meet, locked onto one another, neither one of us looking away. I see a sadness in his beautiful wide eyes. For a moment, I feel calm, lost in his glare, just as though there is no badness hanging over me. I want to lose myself in there forever, it's surreal. I have never had a feeling come over me like this when anyone has looked at me, not even Nathan.

'Bang!'

There's a loud clatter at the front door, and it sucks away the feeling of calmness. I jump to my feet, frozen to the wooden floor with worry. Noah stands up, taking in my reaction, and walks to the door, signalling me to sit back down. Quiet words exchange between him and another man. I still can't move from where I'm standing.

The door quietly closes with a gentle thud. Noah appears at the entrance to the living room, holding the top of a fresh green fir tree, the rest trailing on the ground behind him. Thank God Ava has grown out of being a light sleeper or she would've woken up by now, not sure I'm ready for her to meet anyone else.

'Where's it going?'

'Um, the back of the room, maybe?'

As he drags the tree through the door and sits it upright against the back wall, a low voice murmurs hello. Ava is standing in the doorway, cuddling Peter Rabbit and watching Noah handle the tree. I expect her to run to me, scared of the strange man in the cabin, but to my surprise, she bypasses me and saunters to Noah. Curious of who he is.

I don't speak, I'm too shocked.

She stops beside him and looks up, her eyes inquisitive. Noah crouches down, one knee bent to the ground, supporting him. 'Hello princess, you must be Ava,' he says.

She doesn't move for a second, drinking Noah in, sizing him

up. Her feet slowly shuffle forward, and she leans into him, resting her head on his chest. Noah looks to me, his eyes asking for help, and I nod. I still can't believe it. Emotions swirl all over my being, I have never seen Ava like that with anyone she doesn't know, especially a man.

Noah places his hands under her arms and lifts her. She looks so content resting against him. He must be freaking out. Poor guy came to deliver a doll's house, and a sleepy toddler attacks him.

'Here, I'll put her back to bed.' I lift her from his arms.

I notice how good he smells, amazingly good, when I'm close to him. No wonder she was happy to cuddle him.

'Listen, I could come back tomorrow if you like, give you a hand putting up the tree. That tree's solid, might take both of us to get it secure into a pot?' Noah asks.

Yes, screams through my body, and I want to scream it out loud. 'That would be great, thank you, but only if you're not busy?'

I pray he's not busy.

'Great, I'll come round about noon?'

I nod and walk him to the door. My gut tells me what you see is what you get with Noah, and that is just what I'm needing.

Thirty-One

Stephanie

I'm not sure how long I've been lying here awake, Ava's head tucked into the small valley between my arm and stomach, snoring away. Did I even dream last night?

No, I don't think I did?

I slept all night, didn't have any nightmares that reminded me of the evil that's now searching the world for me, (most probably but entirely unsure,) and have woken up feeling, well, I'm just not sure because this is a new experience for me.

Do I like it? Yes, I do like it.

The relatable routine of falling asleep and waking up with the notion there is zero of the old me left inside, almost like I wasn't an actual person and just someone I had memories of meeting in a previous life, have all taken the day off. The terrible heartbreak of realising I had entirely lost myself somewhere along the road a long time ago has finally hit a point in my life where I'm learning it's okay not to be okay. I'm still figuring things out, and you know what, that's perfectly okay too. There is no quick fix to being happy. And to be honest, after last night, I went to bed with the glimmer of hope that Ava and I really could live a normal life here given half the chance, with both of us being blissfully happy.

I went to bed thinking about Ava's encounter with Noah and how beautiful it was to watch her with him, even if it was only for a few brief minutes. Reminiscing of all that happened yesterday makes my mood lighten today. There is the minor detail of visiting Olivia though and doing some detective work of my own. If she knows Detective Collins, then surely she'll know how to contact him?

Noah could turn up any minute, and I'm still lying in bed. I better get a shower. I hotfoot out from bed, carefully though, so I don't wake Ava. Impulsive motivation, welcome back.

The shower feels good today. I would even say it was amazing like the first shower I had after a hiking holiday in Skåne, Sweden, when I was twenty-two. Just one of the many adventures my fallen, confident comrade embarked on, fearless and hungry for adventure.

The wonders of a great night's sleep really do work miracles. I switch off the shower and wrap my towel around myself. A flash of low crying swiftly brushes past my ears, making me stop motionless.

Nothing but silence.

My mind is playing tricks on me. I continue to dry my revitalised body, tones of coconut glide in the air from the waving towel. Thoughts of Noah drifting in my mind. I've never noticed how attractive a man is when he's good with children, I've never really had the pleasure of that experience. I need to stop thinking like that.

Another flash of crying buzzes in my ear, this time louder. Ava!

I pull the bathroom door open and run to my room, her screams loud, crying out for me. My heart sinks with worry thinking what's happened. I find her in the middle of the bed, her face bright red and wet with tears. 'What's wrong, Ava? Mummy's here!'

I scan the room for anything out of sorts, thinking the worst. Someone has scared her, her crying turning to a controlled sob.

'Oou wen away,' her quirky voice upset with me.

She jumps and swings her arms around my neck. Since we got here, we have always slept in my bed together. Not even taking the chance of letting her sleep in another room. She must have gotten a fright waking up to find me gone. I forget Ava's still adjusting to life here; it's only been a few short weeks.

I squeeze her tight. 'I'm sorry cookie, Mummy will never ever leave you. I pinkie promise to the shiny moon and back.'

She lifts her hand for me to link pinkies with her. 'I think I owe you pancakes for being a bad mummy.'

She instantly forgives me. I imagine what my life would be like if pancakes would solve everything. What a glorious life that would be.

The door raps, and I stop dead. My heart murmurs over a beat. I walk down the hall, sorely cracking my knuckles with apprehension kicking in. Out of nowhere, Ava rapidly flies passed me like a gust of wind steaming through an open window, heading to the door. I thought he had forgotten about his offer; the time hitting 12:30. Shit, best open the door now, he's probably heard Ava's charge of yelping from the other side.

My shaky hand grabs the handle, and I straighten myself up.

'Hey,' Noah begins. And there is that attractive voice greeting me.

Looking robust in semi-tight fitting jeans and hoody, a thick woollen beanie hat covering his hair, showcasing his stunningly inviting green eyes. He looks skittish, standing with his hands behind his back. On first glance, I think his hands are tucked away in his back pockets; on second glance, I see something is hiding behind there.

'Hey,' I whisper, I can't say anything more looking into those wide beautiful eyes.

There's an awkward but nice silence.

'Hallo,' Ava's voice sounds cuter today, or maybe I just haven't noticed how beautifully innocent her voice is for a long time.

'Would you like to come in? We're just making pancakes for breakfast. Mummy was bad.' Before he thinks I'm a terrible Mum, I explain, 'Apology pancakes.' I shrug.

His lips widen, parting ever so slightly with a smile, 'Sure.'

There's that sure again, he seems to like that word. Doesn't give much away, it's bothersome. His mannerisms project nerves, but his words tone it down coolly. His brother won't shut up around me, but I can hardly get him to string a full sentence together.

Ava shadows his every step into the living room, springing up beside him as he sits himself down on the sofa. She's curious of him, not scared like her normal response would be towards men. She watches him tentatively; he watches her tentatively too, getting to know one another visually.

Ava points her little finger to a box in his hand.

'Oh, this box?' Noah holds the box in front of him.

She nods her head excitedly in response; her elbows fall onto his thigh, waiting patiently for him to answer.

'Well, when I was young, me and my little brother used to help Mom decorate the Christmas tree. She always made sure lights covered every branch. My Mom used to say the lights were a symbol of how well behaved me and my brother had been all year so Santa would know how many presents to leave us, so she covered every inch of the tree in lights so we would get lots of presents. This is a box of special lights I got for you to put on the tree because I'm guessing you've been a really good girl this year helping your Mommy in the new house and we need to let Santa know.'

If I didn't find him attractive before, I sure as hell do now. My veins are pulsing with ecstasy watching them from the door, his beautiful words storing in my mind, so I never forget them. I wonder where his Mum is? Least I know he can string a sentence together now.

I can't take my eyes off him no matter how hard I try to; we hardly know him, and yet Ava's infatuated with him. I think I'm a little infatuated too. He's so good with her, why hasn't he been snatched up and married now? He could be a psycho for all I know. Good excuse to keep a close eye on him. He looks up from the sofa and catches me looking at him, smiling like a complete idiot.

'Coffee with your pancakes?' I ask, trying to get the smile on my face under control.

'Sounds good thanks.'

'Wow, no sure? Progress.'

Holy fuck, did I just say that out loud?

Oh, shit, I did. My face feels hot and probably turning beetroot red. He looks shocked, please for the love of God let the ground open up and swallow me now. To my amazement, he bursts out laughing.

'Noted,' he says, his eye's narrowing at me, I feel that means game on.

I take to my heels and walk to the kitchen, my face projecting heat and embarrassment.

Ava's giggle's glide through the cabin, it's infectious. A smile widens on my face as I enter the living room, trying to balance a tray of pancakes and hot coffee in my hands. A memory of Clara running through the house, shouting for Mum to chase her, her infectious giggle's making Mum and I laugh. I really miss her. I fight with myself to stay upbeat.

Noah's crouched down at the log fire, the flames cracking over the logs. The smell of cosy heat fills the room. I suddenly feel a blanket of comfort wrapping around my shoulders. There's that feeling again, normality.

'Hope you don't mind,' Noah asks, pointing into the fire.

I shake my head and smile. 'I hadn't got around to lighting it yet,' I say.

Ava's spread out on the floor beside the tree, pulling decorations from shopping bags and eagerly waiting to start the festive launch. Noah stands to his feet and looks to Ava. 'Will we get this tree sorted then?'

Ava jumps to her feet with an *about time* look on her face.

'How you liking Valdez?' Noah mutters as he sorts through a long string of fairy lights.

'Um, I haven't really seen much of it. We've only been out once, into town and then back to the cabin.'

I don't disclose the real first time we went out, when I had a flake out in the car and found ourselves parked in a forest.

'Once?' Noah sounds shocked. 'There's so much to do here. You've been here about a month now, yeah?'

'Yes, almost a month, it's scary, you know. A new place, not knowing anyone,' I whisper.

'Think we'll have to fix that then. I could show you about if you like?'

He wants to take us out. Why do I feel like I should say no when I really want to say yes? Something is holding me back. Or is it someone? Maybe seeing the town with Noah will be less scary than it just being Ava and myself? Don't suppose I'll know unless I try it.

'I think Ava would like that.'

'And how about you?' he asks, his eyes fixed on me.

'I think I would like it too.'

'Good, we can get something arranged.'

Clearly, he hasn't been snatched up. It rolls off my tongue before I can stop myself. My tongue doesn't seem to have a filter around him.

'So, you're not married then?' A bit forward? 'Sorry, that's none of my business.'

His eyes force back to the fairy lights and answers, 'Nope.'

Nope. That brief answer meant nope, not a subject for discussion. Interesting.

'How about you?' His eyes fix back on me again.

For a moment, I'm thrown off guard. Searching for an answer, I'm Stephanie, the girl who got knocked up after a one-night stand. Christ, I can't say that. I may as well just get a name tag saying Stephanie the whore. Actually, I've never really thought about it. Am I still married? Are you classed as single if your spouse dies? I don't suppose it really matters now, does it? Freya's gone.

'I'm so sorry, Stephanie,' he says before I can answer, his face solemn, our eyes locked again. 'That's none of my business.'

That's the first time someone has called me Stephanie, and it's felt real. I'm a proper person. The past few weeks completely lost, completely out of place and I meet this stranger once and I'm settling back into a normal way of life. Why does he have this effect on me?

'No need to be sorry. Ava wasn't planned. Me and her Father were really early in our relationship when I fell pregnant, and he didn't hang about when he found out. We do fine as a duo, though,' I say with a smile and a loud sigh exhales from my mouth, that's my nope, not a subject for further discussion.

The mood has taken a dip; I need to break the atmosphere. 'So, I think we're ready for these decorations to go on the tree now cookie.'

It's shortly after 2 pm, Ava has crashed out on the sofa between Noah and me. All the excitement this morning has worn her out. The Christmas tree looks practically imperfect and messily stunning, lighting up the back corner of the room with a misty glow of magic. A sweet piece of heaven admiring it beside the log fire, crackling as the logs burn to ashes, our joint effort masterpiece.

Nathan enters my mind. A veil of sadness drops, thinking if this is how our Christmas's would've been in our old home. But the thought doesn't stick, Nathan's out of place, he doesn't fit in when I try to picture it.

'Thank you for today, it was... really needed,' I say with a grin, my emotions a jumble of happiness and sadness.

'Likewise. We haven't celebrated Christmas like a normal family for a long time. I think on some level I needed it too.'

'Why? I thought your Aunt Olivia would be very traditional, she's quite the lady,' I say that with sincerity.

'My Aunt Liv's heart is full of love, for everyone else. Always puts others before herself. But Christmas died a death a long time ago for us when my parents died, and Billy lost the plot.'

My face screws up at his name, Billy, the creep.

'Not fond of my little brother, are you? What did he do?' Noah seems irritated asking me this.

Well, they always say honesty is the best policy. 'Olivia had him meet me here the day we arrived. I think he was trying to come onto me and got a bit of an attitude when I turned him down. I've been trying to avoid him ever since; I know it's very impolite, but I hide when he comes to the cabin.'

Noah's head twists sharply in my direction. 'How many times has he been here?'

My voice lowers as I say, 'A few times.'

The last thing I want is to cause any trouble, but my senses tell me there's tension on Noah's part towards his brother.

'I'll speak to him. Billy's too forward for his own good. I'll leave you my number. If he turns up again, I want you to phone me. Don't open the door to him,' he tells me, his tone is stern, and a wave of uneasiness ripples over me.

I came here to get away from one psycho and I end up meeting another. Fan-fucking-tastic.

'Can he be dangerous, Noah?'

'He can be stupid, as experience has taught me.'

Doesn't exactly answer my question. My nosiness gets the better of me. I would ask what Billy did, but I think we've shared enough information for one day.

'Do you have any plans for dinner?' he asks.

An uncontrolled nervous laugh escapes my mouth, Noah's face remains serious.

'I haven't had plans for a very long time,' I answer with my now serious face.

'I was wondering if I could ask Ava if she would like to come to Aunt Liv's and help with our tree? I could make dinner as a thank you, to you both.'

'But I thought you didn't celebrate Christmas?'

'It's not that we don't, it's that we've never had reason to for so long. Aunt Liv doesn't stop speaking about meeting you both. I know she would love it. But it's only if you want to. You can say no.'

I hesitate, wary, but I don't want to say no. I don't want him to leave, or this feeling to disappear. When he's around, all the bad thoughts are dormant.

'Sure,' I smile.

We drive to Olivia's house in Noah's truck, stopping to pick out a real Christmas tree on the way. Ava has been hyper since Noah turned up at the cabin today, her cheerful spirit projecting onto both Noah and me. I can't help but feel we knew each other in a previous life. The thought of him being an old friend is calming.

We spend the afternoon decorating Olivia's house, and she made the most amazing home-cooked meal of beef stew and dumplings. Memories ignite in me from my childhood, an air of nostalgia. She's old school and I love it.

This afternoon I found out Noah and Billy are Adeline's children, Olivia's baby sister. She died in a house fire when Noah and Billy were just young boys. Olivia and her husband took on the role of caregivers, as Olivia put it.

I wonder if that's why Billy is so angry all the time—so messed up in the head?

Olivia was a teacher, an old school headmistress at Valdez

elementary school. When Adeline died, she gave up work to care for the boy's full time. Jacob, Olivia's husband, built the log cabin as a way of income, renting the cabin out to holidaymakers over the years. That's how they met Albert. He and his wife Alice used to rent the cabin for holidays.

Olivia spoke fondly of Uncle Albert and Aunt Alice. She told me they had twins, a boy and a girl that died at birth. She was quite shocked that Uncle Albert had never spoken of her to me, so naturally, I had to lie a little.

Uncle Albert and I never saw much of one another, he was my Father's brother, who had left my Mother for her accountant. A little lie and a little sprinkle of the truth, quite like what Albert had done to get me here.

It isn't until Noah drives me home that night that I realise I haven't had one bad thought all day, not one. Normality is healthy.

Driving back to the cabin, Billy's attitude plays on my mind. He wasn't best pleased that Ava and I were there. It worries me how angry he can get at the slightest inconvenience, the less I need to see of him the better, although after tonight I know I will find it hard to stay away from Olivia and Noah. They have both made me more welcome than I could've imagined. My mind doesn't have time to reminisce when I'm in their company, I like it. I can tell Ava does too. They seem to have a way of saving me from myself.

We both sit in silence, Noah and I, Ava asleep in the back. I'm not surprised her eyes shut as soon as the truck took off, she's normally in bed for 7 pm, she's done well staying awake until 9 pm.

The cabin is only a ten-minute drive from Olivia's, but it feels as though I've only just blinked and we're home.

Home.

That's the first time I've felt the cabin is home. It's home, thanks to Noah. I find myself stuck for words; I know what I want to say. I want to say thank you for a perfectly normal day. I want to say you silence my bad thoughts when you're around me, but how do I say that without him thinking I'm insane? I opt not to say anything. Freya would have him grovelling at her feet by now. But Freya has gone. Stephanie doesn't treat men like they're beneath her, and I kind of like it that way, it's different. I like different.

I sit still in the truck, waiting for Noah to speak, but it seems he's frozen, just like me, just like the air outside. I smile, I seem to do that a lot around him.

My head turns to look out of the truck window. My eyes fix on the bedroom window, something's different. A sense of worry flusters over me. Am I automatically imagining the worst again? I examine the window again, my smile disperses.

'What's up?' Noah asks, his voice low, noticing the worry on my face.

'I'm positive I put three candles at every window, look at the front bedroom.'

Two burning candles are glowing, the wick dancing erotically in the cabin's darkness.

Noah turns his head towards the window and then back to me. 'You did. Maybe the batteries have burnt out already.'

'Maybe,' I answer but I'm not convinced.

I know I over analyse everything with my nervous wreck of a brain now, or what's left of it, but something is telling me it's not the batteries. My instinct for disaster seems to have grown into a fully formed beacon, active around the clock in my mind that now detects the worst in every situation, every possibility from every angle, preparing me for tribulation.

'Um, Noah, could you walk us in, please? If you're not in a rush? I'm still settling in here and I'm a bit nervy, you know,' I say, my voice timid.

'Yeah, 'course,' he answers.

I love his voice, his accent, American English, manly and protective. His face reflects ringing alarm bells, telling him I'm a little more insane than a bit nervy and to keep back. He's curious about me, about my tendency to jump out of my skin. Even my shadow scares me. It's only a matter of time before he queries my past. The heavy burden of secrets I have weighing me down sinks me a little more each day. I wish I could tell someone.

Noah takes the cabin keys from my hand. I follow, carrying Ava up the steps close behind him, scouting the dark forest around me. It's beautiful in daylight but eerily peaceful at night, ominous.

'I'll check your room,' Noah says, unlocking the door and sliding inside, slowly, cautiously.

I shadow him, preparing myself to discover the worst, someone hiding in my room waiting to pounce on me. I daren't think his name... him waiting on me, he's found us already.

Noah switches the light on. Every nerve in my body sparks with horror when I see the pillar candle lying in the middle of the bed. 'Someone's been in here!' I shout.

My heart palpitates and I hold Ava tighter to me. I'm comfortably confident I'm not overreacting.

'Stay here and close the door behind me. I'll check the house.'

Noah disappears into the hall, I close the door, sit on the bed, pulling Ava tight into my chest, fearing someone has found us. We need to leave as soon as possible. I need to pack. I'm freaking out internally, trying to calm my breathing, scared I wake Ava.

The bedroom door swings open, Noah's face is red with anger. 'No one's in here. The back door's locked, and no windows are open, so it hasn't been a break-in,' he spits.

'But someone's definitely been in here, Noah!' I snap, springing heavy to my feet in fear.

'Yeah, I can guess exactly who the hell it's been.'

His face, the setting, it is serene at its finest. I'm watching from above, as we stand side by side, our hands entwined in a tangle of fingers, in the greenest field.

Our guests hold their breaths around us, waiting for the 'do I,' and then the next, 'I do.'

Butterflies remind me how alive we are. I can feel your butterflies too, there's no place I'd rather be.

You give my hand a gentle squeeze to say hello. I'm not watching from above anymore, I'm standing, face to face with you. Alone, in a haze of white clouds, just you and me. I see your beautiful smile through my veil, butterflies in a frenzy waiting for you to lift my veil and kiss me. You raise your hands towards my face, I close my eyes taking in the moment, waiting to feel your lips on mine. You plant the first kiss, gently caressing my lips with yours. You pull back slightly, but I keep my eyes closed.

I feel your lips again. They're different, moist, rough. Your hands drop from mines and grab my shoulders, forcing your tongue into my mouth, I don't like it. Your taste, it's different, it's...

it's not you.

I open my eyes, horror.

Bryce!

Bryce stands beside me at the altar. Everyone applauses the new bride and groom. I scream, but they're silenced. I can't speak, can't make a sound with the tight grip he has on me.

'Nathan,' I scream.

I'm crying, screaming for help, to free myself from him. No one can see it. They see Nathan, but it's Bryce.

He drags me into the forest at the side of the field. Mum sits in the crowd, the proudest smile on her face, as I'm being dragged along the grass, kicking for my life, terror freezing my body.

'Please,' I shout, I don't want his hands on my body again, please.

I see Nathan at the opening of the forest as we approach the trees. 'Nathan,' I scream. 'Help me, God please help me!'

But he doesn't, he stands lifeless, all but a crooked smile on his face, he's in on it. He takes my legs, and they both lift me from the ground, carrying me into the dark trees, into the darkness.

I wake, screaming, sweat dripping from me. My chest rising and falling, trying to keep up with my erratic breathing. My chest hurts, the pain, the heartache, that nightmare. I'm crying hard, so hard my whole being aches from the emotional workout.

Please God, I can't do this anymore, please let it stop. I plead with all that I have. I wrap my arms around my knees, bringing them close to my chest as I rock myself, consoling myself, calming myself. It was just a dream, a horrible, horrible dream. My mind still doing overtime from earlier events.

I need Mum; I need her so much.

I need her badly.

Thirty-Two

Billy

The door slams behind me, and the thud echoes in the house. When the echo dies, chatter projects from the kitchen.

A kid? No fucking way, it better not be.

Well, well, well, surprise, surprise.

It fucking is.

My temper rises from my feet, burning up my legs, watching them sitting there, playing happy families with a complete stranger. Noah's head lifts to look in my direction when I walk into the kitchen, his eyes scream, *that will be Billy, brace yourselves*.

I notice Aunt Liv's strict shrug of her shoulders at him, at me.

'Hello, darling. Have you had dinner?' she asks, trying to play peacekeeper.

'What's going on? Looks like the North Pole threw up in here!' I snap, my tone sharp.

I'm not joking. The place looks like we're hosting Christmas for the Claus's this year.

Aunt Liv stares at me, not embarrassed, yet. More of her behave yourself look, and I know my shitty attitude is on show.

Fuck it.

The kid scurries over to her, the bitch who blew me off, flinging her arms around her waist. Clinging onto her top, trying to pull herself onto her knee. Looks like I scare her, good.

'You finally gave in and came to see me then?' I laugh.

I know all too well who she's here to see. Noah, my big brother, the one who gets everything, everyone.

'Stephanie and young Ava came to help decorate the house with Noah after they decorated the cabin. Doesn't it look wonderful, darling?' Aunt Liv's face is beaming.

I'm not amused. I know my face reflects it; I don't care. I turn my focus to Noah and shake my head. That dick helped them decorate the cabin? Is that the reason she's been ignoring me when I visit? The bitch won't even open the door, but she invites him in with open arms and lets him decorate a fucking tree? My temper is now rising past my waist.

'It does, Aunt Liv, it looks great. So glad you're all playing happy families together.' I force a smile, fuelled with sarcasm.

I don't even try to hide my annoyance with Noah. What's his deal? I decide I've had enough, that bitch can't even meet me eye to eye. I turn and leave the kitchen.

I hear Aunt Liv sigh as I go. 'Where are you going, Billy?' she asks, disappointment sounds in her voice, and if I'm not mistaken, a tone of relief.

'Out!' I snap back.

Modesty was never one of my strong points. Neither was hiding my shitty attitude. What's the point in always having to put a face on? To save upsetting Noah?

Pussy.

Storming down the hall to the front door, my irritation level high, I grab the handle and swing the door open. The row of hanging keys on the wall catches my eye. I wonder... I'm sure Aunt Liv used to keep a spare set of keys for the cabin; I search through them, trying not to make a sound.

Bingo.

Two keys linked to a keychain reading *Adeline*. Mom. Olivia named the cabin after her. Now time to see what the happy family have been up to?

Jealousy fuels my thoughts, and I'm not afraid to admit it. Why does he always land on his feet? Every fucking time.

I jump in my ride and head towards the cabin. She was mine.

Now he's got in the way, again. History repeats itself it seems, not this time. I punch the steering wheel hard at the thought.

'Dickhead,' I mutter, my temper now as high as it could be.

The cabin looks peaceful from a distance; the windows glowing with pillar candles placed along the inside ledges. It almost looks like it has come back to life; the way it used to be when Aunt Liv's heart was still in it. When I hadn't given her so much hassle.

I remember when it was first built, how me and Noah used to play in it. Seems like ten lifetimes ago, I feel my heart sink at the thought and swiftly shake it off.

Get it together, wimp.

The truck door swings open. I've stopped the Mustang in the lay by down from the cabin, out of sight so no one can see. I step outside, look around and make my way up the road, around the back. It isn't breaking in if you use a key and your family own the place, right? *Course not*.

The back door unlocks with ease, and I step inside cautiously. What's the smell? Spiced apples and cinnamon. How fucking lovely. That glorious smell used to live in Aunt Liv's at Christmas time. The thought makes my irritation grow even more with Noah. Why does he get to experience all of this and I don't? How come Christmas sucks for me, and this stranger and her kid turn up and get it?

Two coffee cups sit on a tray beside the sink, and three plates holding some left-over pancakes on each. 'How nice,' I snap to myself.

The bitch wouldn't take me up on my offer of coffee, but she makes him pancakes. Noah fucking hates coffee!

I stroll from the kitchen towards the living room until the curiosity of what her bedroom looks like enters my mind, when I see her door open. I wonder if Noah, the God, has seen it yet, or stepped foot in it. Or her bed? The thought sets my temper through the roof.

I push the door open, hard, hard enough that it slams back at me when it makes contact with the wall behind. It's still the same pine framed double bed that's always been there. Dressed in a silver tartan, festive red faux fur throw-over covering half the bed and scatter cushions to match.

Very fucking cosy.

Didn't look this cosy when I brought Isabella here, then we weren't here to check out the interior, all we needed was the bed. I wonder if Noah knows I brought her here? I'm sure I may have brought it up to rub his face in it. Might do it again soon.

I walk around the bed, past the window to check no one is outside. Unconsciously lifting a pillar candle from the window ledge, I throw it onto the bed. Fake candles. Fancy bitch.

My eyes fix on the small case resting on the pine ottoman at the bottom of the bed. Wonder what's in there?

I open the case. A grey T-shirt, smells of fusty, men's after-shave maybe?

'What the fuck is this?'

I lift it, a man's, bet it's her old man's. I wonder if she did a runner? I drop the T-shirt back into the case and rummage through the small, zipped pocket on the front. Jackpot, passports.

Stephanie Marie Shenton, born July 5, 1989, British citizen.

Ava Rose Shenton, born August 24, 2017, British citizen.

'I knew her fucking eyes were different tonight!' I mutter.

Sneaky cow. What's she up to? When she arrived, her eyes were dark, just like on her passport, and tonight they were blue, the brightest blue I can safely say I have ever seen. And July? I'm sure Aunt Liv said she was a Taurus like Uncle Jacob. May seventh, if I remember?

Lying cow.

What the fuck did this bitch run away from? I think I'll keep this to myself, for now, have a little fun with our new guest.

Lights grow inside the bedroom, then die. A truck has stopped outside, it's Noah's truck. Always there to ruin my fun.

Shit.

I tuck the passport back into the case, sprint up the hall, leaving out through the kitchen door.

Thirty-Three

Stephanie

Christmas Day, 2018

Walking into Olivia's house, the most fantastically smelling turkey greeted us with all the trimmings. I felt like I had walked back in time, back home into my Grandmother's kitchen on a Sunday afternoon with all my family when I was just a child.

Her stunning stone dining table fully set. Pristine white tablecloth showcasing a festive red table runner and matching napkins. A white china dinner set that looks as though it should be on display and not used, rests beside freshly polished stainless-steel cutlery, surrounded by red candles in silver candelabras and elegant novelty crackers. Each item placed perfectly on their marks. It was elegant and orderly.

Olivia was standing at her oven, dressed in a gold A-line skirt, pristine white blouse, flawlessly ironed apron on top, glowing with happiness. Completely in her comfort zone. For the very few times I've met her, I never seen Olivia anything other than happy, but today, her smile shines, lighting up the entire room. It's infectious. I realise I've been smiling so much that my cheeks are hurting.

It's truly amazing to feel part of a family again. I feel selfish now, not wanting my guilt of trying not to miss Mum overshadow how perfect today is. I really miss Mum, she will be lost, her first Christmas without us. My smile falters, I need a distraction.

We sit at the table, sharing stories, laughing, enjoying being alive. Ava sits on Noah's knee, feeding him mashed potato and gravy, which he subsequently ended up wearing most of rather than eating but didn't seem to bother him one bit. I can see what type of Mother Olivia was to the boys when they were growing up, and why Noah turned out to be polite. Doesn't quite explain what happened to Billy, though, and my curiosity grows.

There was a place set for him at the table, but he never turned up. I can't help but think that's why the atmosphere is so relaxed, why everyone is getting along so well.

I wonder what happened between Noah and Billy? There was a very noticeable divide between them. A divide so bad that if they weren't brothers, or both connected to Olivia, then they would never keep in contact. The dinner table is most definitely not the place to ask, I don't want to darken the mood.

Olivia offers for Ava and me to stay over. Ava has fallen asleep on the sofa beside Noah, who overindulged in Aunt Olivia's chocolate fudge cake earlier and also fell asleep like an overgrown child. I feel like I could sleep too. I have eaten little in past months; I haven't been eating much at all. My clothes becoming slack on me, I know Olivia must notice it, and the dark circles under my eyes. It's hard to keep a good appetite when you're struggling to survive. Surviving daily somewhere that isn't my life with people who don't know us, know the truth.

It worries me though; how attached Ava is becoming with Noah. Watching them together tonight, my heart cracked thinking about what her relationship with Nathan would have been. A small balloon of anger bounces in my stomach, reminding me of everything he put us through and reminding me Ava deserves better.

I can see why she loves him, though. He's everything you would want in a partner—in a Father. I find myself attracted to him. He's tall, over six feet, and well-built because of his job—

a stonemason with his own company. Olivia tells me he is doing extremely well for himself. Wholehearted, kind personality, not one fragment of selfishness in him, and not to forget the most delicious eyes. I'm just not ready to be with anyone, I can't let myself fall for him. I find him extremely hard to read though; I don't think he's attracted to me. He treats everyone the same, always so kind and helpful. He would do anything he could for anyone.

I realise I'm overthinking everything once again and squeeze my eyes shut until the thoughts pass.

Olivia opened a couple of bottles of wine with dinner, gradually making my confidence spike. I finally ask her about the relationship between Noah and Billy before I can stop myself. Fuck. My filter is not doing its job again, must stop drinking.

She takes a sip of her coffee, and I notice the smile slowly disappear from her face.

Top marks for ruining the mood, idiot.

I sit quietly, letting Olivia take the lead. 'Noah fell hard in love at a young age, to his high school best friend. He loved her from the minute he met her. He was fifteen, she was fourteen. However, she didn't feel the same way at first. Well, for the first seven years of knowing one another. She saw Noah as one of her best friends. The poor dear was distraught. He was an overly sensitive, tall, skinny teenager. He watched her over the years chop and change boyfriends, she was quite the popular little hussy... sorry I mean, lady. Slip of the tongue.' Olivia gives a cheeky wink.

Well, well, Miss Olivia, someone you don't like, interesting. I listen with anticipation.

She continues, 'He would never look at other girls, not the way he looked at her. I was having doubts it was girls he even liked. An observation I kept to myself. One day something must have just snapped inside him. It was Isabella's 21st birthday, they were out celebrating with a large group of friends, and her then-boyfriend. Noah caught him getting overly friendly with another girl. It set off a fire inside him. He attacked the boy. Well, attacked is a bit of a strong word. He made him pay for cheating on Isabella. He had filled out by then, grew into his height. And it really opened her eyes. She saw Noah freshly after that, in a non-friendly way. They were inseparable afterwards. They married two years later; it was a whirlwind romance. Nothing stopped them,' Olivia stops, her eyes glazed over, she looks sad.

She continues after a long drink of her coffee, 'I saw what was in store for them though, a heart-breaking disaster of a marriage, on Noah's part. Noah was besotted with her; blinded to what was in front of him. However, I wasn't. I watched it unravel scene by scene. I pride myself on being an excellent judge of character. Never once have my instincts proved me wrong.'

Shit, I wonder what her instincts tell her about me?

'Isabella loved Noah, no doubt about that, but the way her body language changed when Billy was in the room was something else. Billy thrived on it. He didn't play it down or ignore her. He encouraged it, feeding her thirst for him more and more. Flirting back with her when Noah wasn't looking, but I was. I witnessed everything. I made a tough decision to keep it from Noah and approach Billy. Noah was headstrong, but not heart strong. His wife was his life, a wish that he finally got after years of patiently waiting. I would not let Billy, who took great pleasure in winding Noah up, ruin his brother's marriage. I took Billy for lunch. I'm the one person in his life he hates to let down, the only person who can ever get through to him.'

I wonder how Olivia would react knowing Billy broke into the cabin? Key or not, it's still breaking in. The guy makes my skin crawl.

'I started the conversation first, of course. I told him to stand down and stop whatever it was between him and Isabella. I have always fought Billy's corner, stood behind him no matter how many times he messed up in life, no matter how much trouble he got himself into, but that goes beyond any boundaries. He tried to look like he had no idea what I was talking about, of course, but I cut him off before he could explain himself.'

I realise I'm listening with my mouth wide open, eyes wide open, shocked. I thought Billy was just a creep, I now know he's vicious. How could he do that to his brother? His blood? Poor Noah, his life sounds like it has been just as fucked up as mine. I glance through to the sofa and watch him sleep; I soften more for him.

I turn back to Olivia. Dare I ask? 'Did it stop? What was going on between Billy and Isabella?'

'I paid a visit to the little hussy, and it stopped.'

Wow, Olivia is badass, I can see she has a power of authority, perfected by years of teaching. I raise my glass to my mouth and take a sip.

'For a little while,' Olivia continues.

My eyes fire up to meet hers. It didn't stop them? My mouth falls open again.

'Or I thought it did. Noah and Isabella tried for a baby with no success. He had no idea her decision to have a baby was because her relationship with Billy ended. They tried for over a year. They had visited a doctor for fertility testing. Then one day out of nowhere he moved home, no explanation, just moved all his things back into the house. I didn't question it at first, I didn't want to push him, so I gave him a little time to get his head together. Then, she turned up at the house a few months later, with a growing bump. It then became clear she had fallen pregnant with someone else's baby.'

I'm sure the thud was my chin hitting the floor. Billy?

'She told me everything. That the baby could have been Billy's, or the man she slept with on a trip to Florida she had with her girlfriends.'

'And Noah hasn't murdered Billy?' The words spill from me before I can control it, I don't care.

Why is he still alive?

Olivia laughs slightly and answers, 'No darling, Noah has always been the bigger man. He wouldn't dream of leaving a child without a Father. We still aren't sure the boy is Billy's. Isabella disappeared. Florida, we think. You can guess why.'

Poor Noah. I want to wake him, hold him, look after him. Billy, I want to kill. If I wasn't keeping my distance before, I will be now.

Creep. Major creep.

'I see something in you, Stephanie. The same as I see in Noah. A brick wall, guarding you from emotion, from further hurt. Although you have something Noah doesn't,' she says, tilting her head to look at me.

My heart beats, thumping through my chest. Am I that transparent to Olivia?

'I see your battle scars, every one of them,' she tells me, leaning over to me, placing her hand on mine. 'You don't have to survive the aftermath alone. I'll be here waiting when you're ready.'

Her features are soft, safe. I don't want to survive alone, not anymore.

I nod in return and turn my eyes back to Noah. I still have to thank him for my gift he left under our tree. A Nikon D6 digital camera, which must have cost an absolute fortune. I told him I was a professional photographer, and how much I missed it. He must have remembered. The gift is too extravagant, but I can't wait to get out and explore Valdez, with his help, and use it.

This day couldn't be any more perfect.

We spend Boxing Day together, Olivia, Noah, Ava and me. A morning of building snowmen, playing with toys, then dining at The Wheelhouse in town, like a proper family. We eat dinner overlooking the harbour and the mountains.

I got the chance to try out my new Nikon. Just holding it in my hands, looking through the lens, I felt familiarity. A limb that has been numb for too long now regained all sensation. Every snap I took, I could already see its beauty developed in my head.

Olivia opts to go home after dinner, exhausted, she tells us, but I sense she wants to leave Noah and me alone. I'd forgotten what it felt like, living. My body exhilarated with life. And it's because of him.

Noah sits beside me on the sofa, his legs resting on Ava's beanbag on the floor, my feet resting on his thighs as I lay stretched out. I fear I may slip into a food coma at any minute.

Coldplay's the Scientist plays gently from the radio, sparks of flames from the burning logs crack in the background. Ava's sound asleep in her bed after the action-filled day we've had. The first time she's slept in her own room.

Is this what a normal family does? I hope so because I love it. But it also fills me with fear. What if everything slips through my fingers again? I wouldn't survive the heartbreak. I was barely surviving until now. Until he saved me, he pulled me out of the darkness I had become so accustomed to.

I watch Noah, the way he moves, the way he breathes. His profile glows from the light of the fire, projecting all that is good in him. I study him as he lifts the bottle of beer to his mouth, gently pressing his lips against the rim. Those lips. I wonder what they taste like, what they would feel like on mine. He swallows as though it's his first-ever taste of beer and savours it like it's the last time he ever will, then rests the bottle down on my legs and turns to look at me.

My stomach flutters.

There was so much pain in his eyes when we first met, but tonight, I see the same light that's sparking in me. I try to catch my breath. He doesn't take his eyes from me and it's there again, that surge, making my heart palpitate. Nerves are tugging at my stomach, begging for him to move closer. I never really believed in soul mates, I used to think it was a lot of rubbish, people's judgement of love clouded with lust, but I'm not torn anymore. I believe it, and I know he does too.

The Scientist ends as the radio presenter wishes his listeners goodnight and plays one last song. The music begins. Purple Rain, Prince. A request from Melody, ironically, for her lover.

Noah turns away, his eyes fixed on the radio. Shit, he doesn't like this song? My feet slide from his legs as he stands up and makes his way to the radio. He's going to turn it off.

No, please don't turn it off. Maybe he has bad memories of this song, maybe the hussy has invaded his head, invaded our night.

The song grows a little louder. He's turned it up, not off. Noah turns to face me and raises his hand to me, waiting for me to accept his invitation with a little wink and cheeky grin. My hand slides into his and he gently tugs me to my feet. Noah's left hand slips gently around my waist, his right-hand cups mines, guiding me closer to him. My head tucks under his chin, he smells deliciously sweet. His left-hand squeezes around me a little tighter as Prince begins his lyrics, and we sway lightly over the floor.

I hope it's the extended version; I don't want this to stop.

My breathing has never been so calm. His heart is in sync with mine, and for the first time in a long time, my thoughts are silent. I don't want this moment to end.

Noah pulls backs slightly, I lift my chin, my eyes meeting his, wide with want. His head lowers, and his lips brush over mine ever so lightly, like the touch of a feather. I taste him, his beer, it leaves me wanting more. He pulls back again, taking in my reaction. My heartbeat speeds up, my breathing pitches, so does his.

He holds his gaze. Sensual twitches reach every part of my body.

I want him; I crave him.

I run my tongue over my bottom lip to taste him again, biting it. I feel his heart jump. He leans back in again, our lips lock, his tongue wrestles through to find my own, I melt. We stop kissing, Noah scoops me up in his arms, easily, and I'm as light as air.

He whispers, 'Bed?'

And I whisper, 'Yes,' into his ear, kissing his neck as he walks.

Thirty-Four

Stephanie

Noah stayed true to his word. He showed me Valdez in its authentic form, and it stole my heart, as did Noah. Spending more and more time together, life would be unimaginable without him. My guilt slowly evaporating, allowing room for me to forgive myself and make a normal life, or try.

Olivia's offered to look after Ava a few times to allow Noah and me time alone. There were only so many times I could graciously decline her offer without looking ungrateful like I didn't trust her. I undoubtedly trusted Olivia, Billy, though, I didn't.

There was always an air of sleaze when I was around him. His presence would make my skin crawl. Brief comments here and there such as did I know the bible lied? There wasn't just Adam and Eve in the garden of Eden. There were multiple Adams and multiple Eves, never created to be faithful, only to procreate. Created to create, it was our human duty.

Then the comment that I wouldn't dare repeat to Noah; did I want to be with someone who couldn't create?

Hate is a strong word, not a word I have used a lot in my life, but it's the only emotion I have for the snake.

Venomous scheming snake.

Billy was smart, though. His whole demeanour would change around me when Olivia or Noah was there. We were very rarely alone; I made sure of that, but I couldn't bring myself to let Noah know how he made me feel. How differently he acted when we were alone. I sure as hell wanted to tell Noah I was smarter than his ex-wife, that I would never go near Billy.

The thought enters my mind that Olivia never mentioned if their separation was made final? Did they divorce? My mind over-works, I'm jealous. I don't like the idea of him still being married to that slut. Harsh, I know, but she is. I talk myself out of asking him; it's none of my business.

One comment from Billy bothers me more that I'd like to admit to myself, it's like he knows something. I thought at first it was paranoia, then I wrote it off as him trying to get a reaction out of me, and if I didn't know better, I would have said he was trying to blackmail me.

'I don't mind used goods, the more miles, the better. You have secrets, and I'm good at keeping secrets for the right reasons.'

His voice was chilling. His hand ran down my back. I wanted to smack him, scream at him, but Olivia came back into the room, and he quickly stepped away from me.

'I was just speaking to Stephanie about the bible Aunt Liv, teaching her what you taught us about good deeds, do you remember?' he told her.

Olivia looked happy at this. 'I am so glad to see you both getting along, it makes me so happy,' she said.

I couldn't tell her, I kept my mouth tightly shut, guarding Olivia against the truth that her nephew was a creep, a creep who prayed on women he couldn't have. It was the chase that frilled him, gave him his sick kicks. I decided there and then to stay away from him as much as possible and keep myself out of situations where we would be alone. He stopped dropping by the cabin, so I knew I was safe from him there.

I plan on surprising Noah today, treating him to show him how much I care about him. Ever since we met, he's started taking time away from work, which is a good thing Olivia reports since he used to work seven days a week and the rest.

I phoned Olivia and asked if her offer to watch Ava was still open. I could feel her grinning from ear to ear through the phone.

'Yes, oh, Stephanie, I would love that. Yes, please,' she beamed.

It's a bonus Billy is out of town for the weekend, which makes me more relaxed. Maybe he won't ever come back? Maybe he will be in a terrible accident or piss off the wrong person who will murder him?

Ha, I wish.

First plan of action is to make sure Noah won't be home for a couple of hours so I can go to Olivia's and pick up a few things. I've booked a shoreside chalet overnight, made up a picnic basket of some local delicacies and champagne. The butterflies in my stomach have been doing somersaults all day with excitement. We've spent a lot of time together, but always with Ava. I love it when we all spend time together, but I feel I need to get to know Noah alone; I sense he holds a lot back and I'm hoping this trip will help him open up.

'Hello gorgeous, how you doing today?' Noah answers and the butterflies go into a frenzy.

That deep voice, full of masculinity and desire.

'I'm good, thank you, when are you going to be home today?'

'Um, I have a few things left to do, maybe around 6:30?'

Shit.

That's much later than I had planned, he's usually finished around three o'clock on a Friday afternoon. I can work around it. 'Great, I have a little something planned for us, I'll pick you up around seven tonight,' I tell him, trying not to sound too disappointed.

'Sounds interesting. Sure, can't wait to see you,' he says, his voice sounding huskier on the phone, and I don't want the conversation to end. 'Catch you soon, gorgeous.'

The phone call ends.

Ever since I've arrived here, I've worn jeans, jumpers, UGG boots. They suffocate me. I've bought a dress for tonight. Nothing fancy, but it's more me. A black check corduroy mini dress and tights, something I can breathe in, something familiar. When I'm dressed, I feel a spark of confidence in myself, enough to face the world today.

I load the jeep, strap Ava into her seat and drive to Olivia's. It's only five o'clock, so plenty of time to settle my nerves before Noah is home.

I blink, once, twice, ten times to clear my vision. Surely, I'm imagining what I see? Noah wouldn't lie to me.

Would Noah lie to me?

As I turn the jeep into the drive, Noah's standing on the door-step of Olivia's house, holding a baby-seat. A baby inside, wrapped in a blue shawl. From behind him, a blonde girl appears, buttoning up a knee-length coat. Once she's finished, she wraps her arms around Noah from the back.

Very fucking cosy.

He looks uncomfortable. Yeah, probably because he's noticed me pulling into the driveway. After lying to me he wouldn't be home until later. Makes sense now, he's never home this late on a Friday. He lied to keep me away.

The butterflies disperse to make room for the spike of fury in the pit of my stomach. I can feel the heat radiate from my cheeks.

Turn the car around Steph and go back to the cabin.

Cheating snake, just like his brother. I think I would rather put the car into drive and hit her. The slut for stealing him back.

Would he allow that? No.

I know the answer to my question is no. Why would he take her back with another man's son? He wouldn't. The son of a man she cheated on him with.

Noah raises his hand, waving at me to join them, and I'm aware I seem like a psychopath sitting in the car, staring at them. I'd rather stab myself in the eye than join them.

How could he?

I shake my head, preparing to turn the jeep around and drive back to the cabin, leaving them to continue their cosy little re-union. Has my gut failed me once again?

I freeze. Freya would challenge them. Swagger up full of con-fidence, one hand held out to shake the hand of the slut that hurt him, that foolishly let him go. Freya would give her a look, a look that only women knew meant, 'He's mine'. But where was Freya?

Dead, buried.

Stephanie, the coward, had it built in her to turn away. Shame. I'm not sure I like me all that much. I'm dressed like Freya, though, may as well try to act like her.

What was that I heard about the Mona Lisa? From afar it's stunning, but up close it's just a big old mess? Seems to sum up this situation when I see the slut closer. There's that stabbing sensation again, jealousy.

Please piss off.

I wonder how many times she's hugged him like that, and he's welcomed it wholeheartedly? Never once was I jealous of Nathan with any other woman, well, maybe once. Even the time we were on our honeymoon in the south of France and the petite tanned server took every opportunity to touch him like I wasn't even there. I found it amusing. I do not find this amusing.

'Hey you,' Noah says, shifty.

Hey you? No, *hello gorgeous*? I narrow my eyes at him; I'll deal with you later.

'Stephanie, this is Isabella, Isabella, this is Stephanie,' Noah's voice remains the same.

The slut extends her hand; there is nothing friendly about her demeanour. She's as nervous as me, but shit at hiding it, unlike me. I could have a little fun here.

'Ah, Noah's ex-wife?' I say and reach out, shaking her hand, wearing my best good girl smile.

'Well, not legally,' she answers with a smirk. 'I don't believe Noah has mentioned you?'

'Very soon, though,' Noah interjects.

I can tell by her face that hit her harder than a runaway train. Good.

'He's mentioned quite a bit about you,' I say and hold my gaze on her.

I feel the weight of her gulp, the heat of her cheeks flushing down her neck, and I'm sure I see Noah trying to hide his amusement.

Noah hands her back the car seat. 'My lawyer will be in contact.'

Her eyes shift quickly back to him, shocked by Noah's quick dismissal of her. She takes the car seat and walks to her car, her head hanging in shame.

Small lanterns cover the shore, glowing in the dark like fireflies, just enough to see silhouettes of the surrounding trees. The water is peaceful, still, a sheet of dark glass between us and the far away embankment on the other side of the lake. Only occupied by the mirroring reflection of the moon. Looking at it calms me, and I quickly forget how furious I was seeing Noah with his ex-wife, for him lying to me.

'Tell me three things about yourself I don't know?' Noah asks.

I'm taken aback because as much as I sit here as Stephanie, does she like the same things as Freya. I've never thought about it much. All I know about Stephanie is she's much more placid, nervier, and a lot friendlier than Freya. Apart from that, I'm still getting to know her.

'Like what?' I ask, trying to delay me having to answer.

Noah gives a soft laugh. 'You're a tough cookie to read, Stephanie. Like, what music do you like? What's your worst habit? No, no, scrap that, I don't think you have any,' he says, winking at me, and I laugh out loud in return.

If only he knew.

'What was your childhood like?'

Stephanie's childhood? This is it, Stephanie was born just a few short months ago.

'Well, I'm a bit of a jumble with music,' I say.

I smile because it's true, whatever my name is, our tastes are the same.

I continue, 'I love the Foo fighters, loud. I love Kings of Leon. I love lots of random songs from different artists but don't like the artist singing. I love old songs, Simon and Garfunkel, Nat King Cole,' my voice chokes, the last one makes me pause.

I haven't thought about my Papa for so long. I squeeze my eyes together, a warning to the tears building up they're not welcome right now. I open my eyes to find Noah watching me, and for some reason, I want to tell him about my childhood, Freya's childhood, our childhood.

'I grew up in Scotland. My Mum and I lived in a big house with my Gran and Papa, my Aunt and my Uncle. It was brilliant. The house was always full of family and friends. Sunday roast and Nat King Cole were my Papa's thing. He would sit in the living room, a massive cooking pot at his feet, pulling tatties from a bag and peeling them.'

I see Noah squint at the word tatties. It makes me laugh.

'Sorry, potatoes for the less cultured,' I say, winking and stick my tongue out at him.

He scrunches his nose up, pretending to be insulted.

'My Dad wasn't around after I was about four or five, I can't remember, he wasn't very present as a Dad when he was there. In my eyes, my Papa was my Dad. Between him and my Uncle, they never let me down. The only men in my life who haven't.'

'Why are you here, Steph? You sound like you have a family who love you very much, and who could miss you equally the same?' Noah asks.

I think about this for a minute, gripping the right words I want to say.

'My Papa was the healthiest man you would ever meet, used to carry me around on his shoulders. My Gran didn't keep very well, and my Papa cared for her. They diagnosed my Papa with bladder cancer, would you believe? Healthiest man alive, survived the war, could walk for miles every day and then gets taken down by cancer. My Uncle helped with my Papa's care. He was old school, a gentleman, so he wouldn't let any of the women help him. I never once in all the years I lived with my Papa saw him in his pyjamas, he was always dressed when I got up. Shirt, tie and sweater, very handsome. My Uncle went to work one day, and died of a heart attack, killed him outright. After that my Papa gave up, cancer spread into his bones, and he passed away at home with my Mum, my Aunt and Gran beside him six weeks later.'

Tears run from my face, and I feel the hurt like it was yesterday. 'My Aunt Margaret, Mum's twin, married into money and told my Mum that Gran and Papa's house was hers, so we lived there, caring for my Gran until she passed away in her sleep of a broken heart. They had been together since my Gran was sixteen. My Gran told me she came from a time where if your marriage was broken, you fixed it; you didn't throw it away like the young folk do these days. That's what I wanted, a marriage where I would grow old with my husband.'

'Wanted?' Noah asks, 'you don't anymore?'

I've never really thought about getting married again. I don't think you can even call my marriage to Nathan real. Maybe on a piece of paper, yes, but in heart, no.

'Never say never,' I say, I don't want to say no because that just opens another path of questioning.

'That's two,' he says, confusing me.

I lift my eyes from the water and focus them to Noah. 'Two?'

'I said tell me three things, you told me what music you like and about your childhood. What's the third?'

He gives an encouraging smile. I think about this for a second. 'I'm almost thirty-years-old and I was losing hope of ever finding true love.'

This makes Noah's smile widen. 'I still can't believe you arranged all this. It's amazing. I don't think anyone has ever planned anything like this for me,' he tells me.

It makes me sad, thinking no one has ever treated Noah like this before. He's so kind; I'm pretty sure his heart is one hundred times bigger than my own. It seems we've both had the short end of the straw in love. I smile at him, then turn my gaze back over the water.

'I'm sorry, Stephanie, for lying to you. I didn't intend for it to be a bad lie. I just,' he pauses with a painful sigh. 'I just need her out of my life.'

I'm not worried he sounds pained thinking of her out of his life, because I know what she did to him.

'I need her out of my life because I realise her being in it was toxic from the start. Thanks to you.'

My head spins to face him. I search his face looking for an answer to his last statement.

'I thought I was in love. I thought I was being loved back. When I met you, the very first time I met you, I knew I had never been in love with Isabella, I mean I loved her, but not in the way I should have. I didn't feel things for her, I feel for you.'

He doesn't tell me he loves me, or he's in love with me, he slides his hand into mine, entwining our fingers together and that's enough for me, because I know he feels the same about me as I do about him.

I haven't even asked him three things about himself. 'Your turn,' I say, giving his hand a gentle squeeze.

'Oh, where to start? So many to choose from,' he laughs playfully, and then his smile fades as though a dark memory has presented itself.

'My Mom and Dad died when I was young. My Dad was tough,

a real man's man. It was clear for as long as I can remember, he expected us to be the same. When he wasn't around, Mom would let us eat pink cupcakes and have bubbles in our bath. Stupid, I know. When I started getting older, I wondered why Mom married him. I think it's because she was his anchor. He was a bit of a loose cannon, and she kept him grounded. My Dad wasn't a bad guy, but no one messed with him. I'm more than sure he was the gangster type, offered people protection for money. And I'm also pretty sure that's what got him, and my Mom killed. Aunt Liv doesn't say much about it, but I think the fire was meant for Billy and me too.'

Noah shrugs his shoulders, defeated at the fact he will never fully know the truth if he was meant to die alongside his parents.

'Okay, so second fact. William, my kid brother has screwed me over more times than I can count, but I still can't find it in me to hate him,' he says.

I lean over to him and rest my head on his shoulder. I don't press him to continue, but I sense there are things he needs to get off his chest.

'Billy was a good kid, really sensitive. He used to follow me everywhere, and I loved it. I loved that he depended on me so much, even when Mom and Dad were around. He feared Dad, and I protected him. He wouldn't beat us or stuff like that, but he would make us skin rabbits, gut fish, shoot deer. Billy hated it. Wouldn't think it now, would you? I would do it for him, then tell Dad we both did. When they died, it was like Dad's soul transferred to Billy, and he became a little prick. Pretty sure Aunt Liv's filled you in on Isabella?' he asks.

I nod my head on his shoulder, and he feels it.

'Truth is, I'm not even angry about that anymore. Billy did me a favour before it got too late. God knows how many other guys she was with. She loved a girl's weekend, and every time she returned home, she wouldn't look at me for a week. Billy just helped confirm it. Inside I know he's still a good kid, I just need to be there for him until he comes good again.'

As much as I like Noah being open with me, the mood has dipped, and I don't want to ruin this night. I try to lighten the subject. 'Wow, we really are a pair of miserable shits,' I say, and we both burst into laughter. 'But you're not getting away with number three.'

Noah slides his shoulder away from underneath my head, repositioning himself to face me. The way he looks right into my eyes, deep inside me, makes every part of me melt away, and I can't help staring at his lips.

'I'm thirty-years-old, and I was losing hope of ever finding true love,' he pauses and gulps, hard. 'Until now.'

Thirty-Five

Stephanie

Anxiety spikes, for the first time in months, I don't know why. Guilt at being happy, possibly? Maybe it's a sly reminder that I don't deserve happiness. Life has been great the last few months, and it makes me sad that I can't phone Mum to tell her how things are, that we're okay. I want to tell her about Noah, about how amazing he is, with Ava, with me, how he looks after us.

The thought has crossed my mind, almost every day, to call her. Just hearing her voice, knowing she is safe, is all I need to know. But what if she isn't? She should be if Bryce got arrested.

I try to shake off the sickening thought that something happened to Mum; it eats at me to the point it makes me act. I grab my MacBook, open it wide, type in my password and watch the screen wake, waiting for my command.

I try arrests in Edenbridge, nothing of relevance appears. I try arrests in the London area. Again, nothing of relevance appears. My gut bugs me; it's not enough to settle my nerves.

I type in Bryce Holmes. Nothing but business advertisements and pictures of haulage vehicles and a lot of other crap that people believe about him, Mr Perfect.

I try it again.

Arrests, murders, Edenbridge, London. Enter.

The search engine gets to work, and a mass of information greets me. It highlights three of the search words in a paragraph halfway down the scrolling page. I click to reveal the full story.

My throat drops to my stomach. I jump back from the laptop screen onto my feet. My chair fires backwards and slams down dead onto the floor as I lean myself against the wall, trying desperately to stop my legs crumbling from under me. Breathing heavily, I edge forward, slowly steering towards the screen, and once more, I'm met by her face. Her smiling, happy face.

I pick the chair up from the floor, perch myself on the edge of it and read the news report dated November 2018.

The body of thirty-one-year-old Layla Whitmore was discovered at seven o'clock this morning by an early morning jogger. Miss Whitmore was said to have been wearing sportswear and running shoes and seemed to have drowned in what police are calling a freak accident, after sliding on an icy pathway into the River Thames. Chief Superintendent Mathews stated no suspicious circumstances are surrounding Miss Whitmore's death. Her family has been informed.

My head is blank. I still shed a tear for Layla, regardless of how we parted. Did Bryce have her killed? Never once did I see Layla in sportswear, nor do I remember her love of running. Come to think of it, I didn't know Layla at all. Our friendship was a relationship of convenience for Bryce.

He had her killed, why? She said she had to keep an eye on me, maybe Bryce punished her when I disappeared. He took it out on her.

Oh my God, Mum!

My fingers tremble as I try to type Moira Anderson, Stirling. I'm amazed at the amount of Moira Anderson's that appear, but only one stands out, and my heart skips a beat. A picture of Mum, beaming, standing outside her gallery. She went ahead with the gallery opening. I'm so glad she did. I begged her in my letter, not to let me going away stop her from her plans. The name is beautiful, Clarafee Originals. I love it. I know she is safe, the date of the article by Stirling Observer, February 2019. I want to tell her I'm proud of her.

I press her number into my phone before I can stop myself. My heart is thumping, listening to the rings, and then… 'Hello there.'

Mum, it's me, Freya, I want to say. Clara and I, we're safe, and we miss you, but I can't. I inhale deeply, and it hurts.

'Hello, is anyone there?' Mum asks.

I exhale, and it hurts even more.

'Freya? Petal, I know it's you,' she says, pausing. 'I love you, sweetheart, and Clara. I miss you both so much. I wish you could speak to me.'

I hear her; she's sobbing. A crushing pain attacks my chest.

'We love you too, Mum. I'm proud of you,' I whisper, quietly and hang up the phone.

I feel more vulnerable than ever. I check the time on my phone, 23:50 and text Noah. He replies instantly to my request for him to come over. At night when we're not together, it's too much time I'm left inside my head.

I can't be alone. I can't do it anymore.

I can't sleep, my head in a whirlwind of thoughts once more. I watch Noah sleeping, his perfect chiselled jawline, the peacefulness of his breathing, I want to watch that every night.

The sudden thought doesn't shock me. I don't doubt it; I want him beside me every night. I need him beside me every night.

I whisper in his ear, 'Live with us.'

His body reacts in return, rolling onto his side, facing me, his sleepy eyes erotic with an answer. 'Yes,' he breathes deeply and pulls me tightly against him.

When I wake in the morning, and Noah has left for work, I throw Nathan's old T-shirt in the rubbish bin. I think it's time to throw him away for good.

Olivia has told me it's time for me to make my mark on this town, and she's right. I have all that money sitting in my bank account, screaming to be used. When I see her and Noah later for dinner, I'll lay out my plans, what I want to do.

Keeping myself mentally busy is all the therapy I need. My mood lifts from the pit it was in last night, and I've concluded whatever fate Layla came to, was her own doing.

Mum is safe. Ava is safe, that's all that matters.

Thirty-Six

Stephanie

Saturday, March 8, 2019

'So,' is all Olivia can say at first.

'So…'

'Here we are,' she says, swallowing hard.

'And here we are… it has been a long emotional journey; my mind is exhausted.'

I try to swallow a hard lump that has lodged itself in my throat. We both sit in silence. The sound of my knuckles cracking lingering between us as I fidget, waiting patiently for her response. I expect Olivia to say something, to comfort me, but she doesn't. It's out of character for her. Her eyes are silky with water. I realise she can't speak for fighting back the tears. Breaking her usually composed and subtle character.

A weight has lifted from me, a strange sensation I can't explain. It… it feels… good. Olivia was right. I needed to tell someone something, everything. Well, almost everything. I didn't go into the details of my sex life with her nephew.

That person I was, Freya, I'm sure is almost dead. It would take a spontaneously intense miracle to pull her back from the pit she was rotting away in, suffocating in fear, in remorse. I lost Freya the night I allowed Bryce into her most intimate parts. I need her strength; I need her to help me become me again.

'I miss the old me,' I whisper.

Suddenly, I have an urge to hold a minute's silence for my fallen self, grieving for the dead, confident me that would usually stick two fingers up to the world and move on. I hang my head in respect.

There are a few things I would change about her, though. Would Noah have liked Freya?

No.

Olivia wipes her eyes with a paper tissue, taking a deep breath in when she has finished. 'Stephanie sweetheart, none of what happened was your fault, none of it. You did what you did to protect your family.'

'Are you going to tell Noah?' I ask, and I find myself unable to look Olivia in the eye.

'No, I think that's up to you.'

I nod. She's right; I know she is. If Olivia doesn't think badly of me after all of that, maybe there is a chance Noah won't either?

'Noah loves you, Stephanie. He will, no matter what. You both found each other at the worst times of your lives. He will understand.'

I hope Olivia is right. I love him too. I love Noah. I need to tell him. I love him in a way I never have before.

It feels... real.

A wave of guilt ignites in my stomach, I loved Nathan, but it felt nothing like this. Is that even possible? Nathan's love was controlled, I see that now, on his terms. The feelings I have for Noah make me question if I was ever in love with Nathan. I'm in love with Noah; I know I am.

I tell Olivia thank you, for listening, for helping, for not judging and leave to pick Ava up.

It's peculiar how clear my thoughts are. The heavyweight that has been haunting me for so long has crossed over to where it should be. I'm confident it's finally time to move on.

I text Noah walking to my car, I'm calmer than when I first got here, telling him today went brilliant, that I will see him tonight. I can't wait to see him tonight. I love going to bed beside him, holding me. I love waking in the morning, and his face is the first thing I see. Well, that's if Ava hasn't crept in beside us during the night and claimed him to herself.

She calls him Daddy, no one told her to, no one suggested it, she calls him Daddy of her own free will and he has proudly taken on that role.

I'm proud of him for taking that role.

Ava is so excited about her new pink sparkly dress. We went shopping after I picked her up from playgroup, a little treat to spike both our moods. She can't wait for Noah to see her in it, the little lady has completely fallen for him. The worry I once felt about their bond is wearing off me. She's so happy around him. I couldn't take that away from her.

Skipping up the hall, singing with not a care in the world when we arrive back to the cabin, back to our home. What must go on in the beautiful mind of an eighteen-month-old, I wonder.

I close the door behind us and turn around. Ava is standing at the entrance to the lounge looking in. What is she up to now?

'Come on, sweetheart, in you go.'

She turns and looks at me confused, worry in her eyes. Shaking her head from side to side. 'What's wrong, Ava?' I ask, my heart picking up pace.

I drop the shopping bags at my feet and walk towards her, cautiously.

'Man,' she mutters and points inside the room.

Possibly another one of her imaginary friends, she has lots of them.

Walking up behind her, I freeze, fearing a ghost from the past has found us.

Thirty-Seven

Billy

I march through town, lost in my world of bitterness, and I don't fucking care. Noah stayed with that bitch and her brat again last night. What's he got that I haven't? Aunt Liv, the peacekeeper, trying to tell me Noah and Stephanie are just friends, to leave them both alone.

Yeah, just friends because she's nothing but a cock tease.

It's only noon, but never too early for a bottle of Jack Daniels. I march down the sidewalk, banging shoulders with anyone who doesn't move out my way.

Thump.

I fire backwards, stumbling on my feet, trying to get my balance back. 'What the fuck, dude?' I snap.

A man I've never seen before stands before me. I can tell straight away I shouldn't mess with him. He's tall, well built, could probably crush me with one blow.

'Watch where the bloody hell you're going, mate!' the stranger snaps with a broad English accent.

Holding my hands up to apologise, I take a step back.

The man drops something at his feet, a photo. His eyes still locked on me as he bends to pick it up from the sidewalk. 'You local here?' he asks, still frowning at me.

'Yip the last time I checked.'

Who does this dick think he is, some sort of lawman?

'I'm looking for someone who may have moved here. Her

name's Freya, distinctive blue eyes. Has a daughter.'

Well, isn't this fucking interesting? In a small place like Valdez, it's hard to miss someone new moving here and not to notice. I know exactly who he's looking for.

'That a picture?' I ask, pointing at the man's hand.

I'm telling this dick nothing until I know what's in it for me. Without hesitation, he hands it to me.

Holy cow, bingo! Would you look at that, a picture of Steph and the kid? The brats a lot younger and that scheming bitch has blonde hair, but it's them alright. 'And who are you?' I ask, raising my chin undaunted, folding my arms over my chest.

'I'm her husband, and by your stance, I'll take it you know her.'

This guy doesn't just look the business in his expensive-looking suit, his body language screams business, serious business. Fireworks explode inside me, the sheer pleasure of thinking I hold every card on this bitch now. I could do Stephanie a favour and say I don't know her, but this could be my chance of payback for all those pathetic rejections, playing little miss sweet and innocent. I could get rid of her and the brat, and happily watch Noah suffer, again. It's a straightforward decision.

'She did a runner, with my daughter and a chunk of my money. The money I can live without, but my daughter is my life. I'm not leaving here without her,' he tells me.

God, I almost feel sorry for the jerk, but just a little because he seems like a total dick. I silently observe, but Mr English holds his eyes on me like he wants to kill me.

'I can tell you where she lives, but it's my Aunt's place, so I don't want any hassle.'

The guy dips his head, screwing up his face, but agrees.

'What you gonna do to her?' I ask.

'Nothing she doesn't deserve for what she's done. I'm not a violent man. I just want my daughter.'

Not convinced he's not violent, but the bitch's domestic situation ain't anything to do with me. He hands me a pen from the inside pocket of his suit, and I write the address down on the back of the photograph. I'm even surprising myself with how easy I find it to hand the photo back to him.

I walk away, smug and satisfied. I still feel the guy's eyes watching me walk away. A commotion of horn's blast a few metres down the street. Some dumb brunette has just run in front of some cars driving down the street, idiot. Nothing that concerns me.

I think a visit to my brother is on the cards. Mr Jack Daniels can wait until later.

When was the last time I felt this happy?

Fuck, I don't know.

Oh, wait, I do. When I opened the door to the bitch when she arrived here. She should've been mine. I saw her first. I'm doing my brother a favour, I got a lucky escape, but that poor bastard's caught hook, line and sinker.

I turn into the gravel driveway, Noah's pickup truck's parked at the side of the house.

Bingo. I'm going to enjoy this.

Noah's sitting at the stone dining table with Aunt Liv, a fresh pot of tea beside them. She got the good stuff out. She must have known I was coming in a good... no, a great mood.

I know I've given her a lot of trouble over the years, well, all the trouble over the years, but this is my chance to redeem myself. She will be so proud of me after this, saving Noah. Showing them what that bitch is, who she really is.

Aunt Liv and Noah look up from the table at me. I take my time, savouring the moment. I want to enjoy it. Like the time I found his dog dead, drowned in the river out back, I couldn't wait to tell him. He loved that fucking mutt more than he loved me, his kid brother.

'Hello darling, how are you today?' Aunt Liv asks.

'Oh, I'm great today,' I answer, struggling to hide the smile widening with every breath. I also notice the smile dropping away from Noah's face.

Dick.

Give me a chance to wipe that smile completely off your face.

'What's up, Billy? Something going on?' Noah asks, sighing. He's losing patience already.

'I was in town today, noticed a guy in a suit showing folks a piece of paper. And you know me, I like to help when I can.'

Noah jumps in, slurring the words, 'Stick your nose in, you mean?'

I laugh, shaking my head in disappointment. 'I asked him if he was lost, he told me he'd just arrived in town and was looking for his wife and daughter. Then he showed me the photo he was holding.' I pause, observing Noah's face. Waiting for him to react.

Aunt Liv's eyes are wide, watching me.

'And? Is this story going anywhere, Billy? Or you just wasting our time with a pointless story that has nothing to do with us?' Noah asks, bored.

I unfold my arms, place my hands flat on the stone dining table and lean forward towards Noah. 'Oh brother, you have no idea just how much this has got to do with you, with all of us. It was a photo of Steph and Ava,' I explain, staring at Noah, he remains silent. 'The guy's her husband.'

I look at Aunt Liv. She's crying, tears dripping from her pale cheeks. She stands to her feet. A spike of guilt stabs at my gut.

'We need to find Stephanie quickly! She came here today in hysteria as she thought she saw him at her lunch meeting with Eliza. Oh, goodness. I told her she imagined it!'

My mouth drops open. What the fuck is she talking about? I focus on Noah. 'So, you see big brother, your little miss prim and fucking proper is nothing but a lying sack of shit.'

Noah's hand is around my throat before I can react or defend myself. Aunt Liv screams and pleads for him to stop. All I can do is smirk at him. It's clear she knows what's going on, and he's the only one who doesn't.

'Aunt Liv, you cannot seriously believe him?' Noah is growing angrier, his hand getting tighter on my throat.

'Noah, please, we have to find her. That man is not Stephanie's husband. We need to find her before he does!' Aunt Liv pleads with Noah, and I realise how terrified she is, the colour drained from her face. I've never seen her scared before.

'How do you know it's not her husband?' I ask, gasping for air, as Noah removes his hand from my throat and picks up his mobile phone from the table.

'Because William, Stephanie's husband, Nathan, died outright in a terrible car accident when Ava was only one-month-old. Noah, witness protection moved them here,' Aunt Liv says, trembling.

Fuck. What have I done?

A wave of sick blows up onto my tongue, I've never felt guilt like this before.

'She's not answering her phone or the cabin line,' Noah spits at me, and sprints from the kitchen to the hall and grabs his truck keys.

Aunt Liv follows him, shaky on her feet, I did this to her, me.

Fuck Billy, fucking idiot!

'This guy said his name was Bryce,' I tell them as though his name is going to make the situation any better.

I watch as Aunt Liv loses her balance and stumbles towards the wall, her hand swings up to her mouth in shock.

I watch what I've done, *me.*

'We need to find her now, Noah, please. If anything happens to her or little Ava, I will never forgive myself.' She raises her hand, ushering Noah from the house.

Noah nods and leaves through the front door, I hear the truck fire up, the gravel spitting as the truck wheels spin down the drive.

My heart races. 'Aunt Liv, I'm sorry, I don't understand. I thought I was helping,' I explain, and I can feel her fury towards me as I help her back to her feet.

'Helping? You've done a lot of bad things in your life, William James, but this! You might not know it yet, but you have just signed Stephanie's death warrant. Hers and little Ava's!' she shouts, and shrugs me from her, as though my touch repulses her.

'William, as much as it kills my soul to do this, I'm cutting all ties with you. I have done everything in my power to bring you up to be a decent, well-mannered young man, but you have done nothing but kick it all back in my face like I mean nothing to you. I cannot bear to see you like this. Your Mother... she would be very disappointed in you. I never want to see your face ever again. Leave.'

I haven't cried since I watched Mom and Dad being buried, so the sensation of my chest tightening and tears flooding my eyes is grim. I let out a gasp of air, trying to catch my breath between sobs.

I care about you, Aunt Liv, I do. I want to scream it at her; her look stops me. My shoulders droop. All I can do now is leave.

I turn and head for the door.

Thirty-Eight

Stephanie

The lounge is in darkness, the light from the streetlamp outside beams in the windows, casting shadows around the room. A silhouette of a figure sits in the armchair at the back corner of the room. I adjust my eyes to see it against the dimming backdrop. I see the fiery tip of a cigarette move slightly, smoke gliding up into the air. Neither Billy nor Noah are smokers; I know it isn't either of them. My grip on Ava's shoulders grows tighter, pulling her closer to me.

'Well, well, would you look at you, you've changed your hair. Looks good on you. Sexier. Almost didn't recognise you.'

I know that voice.

The tone has changed a bit, a wicked sarcasm sounding through it. I've never heard that side to him before. I don't like it.

Growing scared, I gulp. 'Bryce?' I ask, my voice shaking, my body shaking.

He stands to his feet, slowly walking nearer to the window. 'The one and only, baby.'

Everything about him has changed. I can't see his face clearly, and I'm too afraid to move to switch the light on. His stance, his attitude, his body language all alarms me. He moves more loosely, more mischievously. It's Bryce, but not the Bryce I remember.

'You have no idea how great it is to see you after all this time, Freya, and I mean that heartfelt. You and little Clara. She has grown so much. A beautiful little girl.'

My heart beats rapidly, finding it difficult to act calm. How did he find us? It doesn't make any sense that he's here. I stand in the doorway clinging onto Ava, my arms wrapped around her, trying to think what to do. My head telling me to lift her and run, but I'm paralysed with shock. I can see something in his hand, a dark object. I can't make out what it is in the darkness. He changes direction and turns around, walking towards us. Terrified beyond all belief, but I can't let it show in front of Ava.

He crouches down to Ava to speak to her. 'You won't remember me, Clara, but I was friends with your Mummy, and we have a lot of catching up to do princess, so would you go play in your room for me while your Mummy and I catch up?' he says, followed by a crooked smile.

Ava quickly turns and grabs my legs, looking up to me for reassurance. I give her the best smile I can and tell her to go play. She instantly runs to her room.

Bryce grabs me by the arm and pulls me to the sofa. He tells me to have a seat and throws me down. I know he means business; he switches the light on beside the fire surround, and the dark object comes to life.

It's a gun; he's holding a gun.

My head is filling with screams for help, no one can hear, I know no one can help.

'I've waited a long time to find you, Freya. I had almost given up hope until one of my associates called me one day with the best news like Christmas had arrived early, and I was buzzing. I had the excellent sense to have a little trace put on your Mum's phone. I knew you wouldn't be daft enough to phone any of your friends and blow your cover, but I knew you couldn't stay away from the lovely Moira. That's right, your little silent phone call to her last Sunday night done it. You held on the line just long enough for the trace to track you. So, thank you for the favour and your absolute stupidity.'

'You better not have been near my Mum; this has nothing to do with her!' I jump to my feet with rage, my body trembling.

'Relax, you silly woman, I haven't been near her. I have people doing all of that for me. Your Mum is fine. I have no need for her,' he says, then laughs. 'At the moment anyway.'

When he talks, I see his evil mind coming to light.

'I don't understand. Detective Collins...'

He stops me as soon as I have mentioned his name. 'Ah yes, good old Detective Collins, such a shame and a blessing what happened to the poor old boy,' he says with a smirk.

What has he done to Detective Collins? I don't dare ask, but I need to know. I can tell he's loving this, getting a thrill from terrifying me.

Ava's gentle voice echoes from her room, talking to her dolls, not one bit wise to what's happening. My stomach is churning with terror, thinking of what Bryce is capable of. I need to keep him focused on me, so he leaves Ava alone.

A rage pulses through Bryce's body with each new word he speaks, I can't help but look at the gun as he swings it around with his hand, pacing back and forth in the living room. He was always so calm and collected. There wasn't one piece of calm about him now.

'What have you done to Albert?' I whisper over the lump in my throat.

He stops and sits beside me on the sofa, swings his arm over my shoulders with the gun hanging loosely in his hand. 'You really think you can handle the truth about the chaos you caused?'

He takes the last draw of his cigarette, and I feel a scorching pain at my left elbow. Burning like electric shocks, I want to scream, but I bite my lip to contain the pain.

He whispers in my ear to be quiet; his cigarette end has burned into my skin. 'Shh, you don't want your daughter to come in here. You never know what could happen if she gets too close to me, Freya.'

Thirty-Nine

Detective Albert Collins

Friday, November 9, 2018

The room fills with a tiresome silence. The house in complete darkness, all except the small spotlights underneath the wall-mounted kitchen cabinets. They shine a light beam over the dining table, throwing a shadow over the black leather-bound A5 sized book.

My fingers tap nervously on and off the solid crystal glass encasing whiskey and ice, feeling frustrated with myself that I can't find it in me to open the ledger.

How long have I waited to get my hands on this? It has the power to open a gateway of justice, to convict all those corrupt official bastards, to find out the truth of so many unknown crimes that have been committed and covered up. It holds the truth of what happened to those ill-fated newborns.

If it's the correct one, that is.

Freya only found one, Nathan said there were two, and a laptop. Bryce must have taken the other ledger and laptop on his business trip. I pray it's the right ledger.

I lift the glass; the whiskey disappears in one gulp, and I drop it with a bang back on to the table.

This little worn-down indispensable book has the power to

prove I wasn't going crazy like everyone previously thought. Chief Superintendent Mathews told me I was making up crimes in my head to shut off from the grief of losing Alice. No matter what was going on in life, I never neglected my duty of being a Detective, and a bloody good one at that.

A fluster of guilt trickles across my skin. I told Freya only what she needed to know. Knowing the full extent of events, how deep the lies ran, all parties involved, would have finished the poor girl off.

I slide the elastic band off the book. One finger lifting the front cover, showing just a glimpse of what secrets hide inside. Something stops me. The book falls closed, and I lift the half-empty whiskey bottle from the table and fill the glass again, fuller than before.

How can you be so thirsty for the truth, that you can taste it drowning you when you have it in your reach? Another large gulp of whiskey disappears down my throat, burning as it goes.

A loud knock at the door rattles through the house, and I don't flinch, only hesitate. I know that knock.

'Come on, Bertie, put the whiskey down and open the door, it's pissing down out here,' Chief Superintendent Mathews shouts, come to check I'm still alive, no doubt.

I drag my feet down the hall behind me and open the door. Mathews doesn't look shocked to see I'm a bit worse for wear. My old friend knows this has become a Friday night ritual, whiskey and sulking.

'Geez, you look like shit. What's happened?'

Of course, Mathews doesn't look shocked. He gave me the whiskey yesterday, a birthday gift. It was the only thing he knew I wouldn't refuse and try to return.

'Whiskey?' I ask, strolling back up the hall to the whiskey bottle.

'No thanks, Bertie, got the car and you know I can't stop at one. Lily would have my balls.' He pulls out a chair and sits at the dining table, and I sit across from him.

'So, what do I owe the pleasure at this time of night?'

'Do I need an excuse to check up on you?' He squints his head at me, as though just realising a bottle of Glenfiddich 21-year-old Reserva was a bad idea. Bloody fine it is too. I could act as though

I'm insulted, but I'm not.

'Okay, I just wanted to see how you were getting on with the newborn case, that case I asked you not to get involved in. One of the lads came to me and said you'd requested documents from the hospital again?' Mathews folds his hands on the table and leans closer and for a minute, I think I have picked him up wrong? I *hope* I have picked him up wrong. How could he have known that?

I keep my composure, trying to hide my wariness. I haven't discussed the case with anyone. I always follow my instincts, and my instincts told me there were rats in the department. I've been treading exceptionally well, or so I thought, even going in disguise to meet Freya.

Earlier that day, after making sure Freya and Clara got to the airport safely, I drove to Edenbridge and District War Memorial Hospital to make some enquiries and ruffle some feathers. Making sure to speak to a few different staff members and get it circulating that an old case had been reopened, and I was looking for some information on stillborn babies. My theory was to draw acquaintances of Bryce's out from the woodwork.

After handing a few cards out, I left. I knew that before the night was over, there would have been a knock on my door. To my misery, Mathews had taken the bait.

My oldest friend.

We graduated together for Christ's sake; he was my best man, and I was his. Never once did I suspect it would involve him; I trust him with my life. Or I did.

I swirl whiskey around in the glass, looking deep inside the golden liquid for answers. 'You know, Benji, I didn't request any help from the lads. Let's just cut the bullshit, shall we, old friend?' I say, looking him in the eye, shaking my head in disbelief.

The fact he can't look back at me, tells me everything I need to know. He never could make eye contact with me when he was in the wrong.

I take another gulp of whiskey and continue, 'How could you be any part of this? How could you do this to Lily?'

Mathews, becoming uncomfortable, stands to his feet. Walking speedily to the window, he puts his hand onto his face and runs it down his cheeks.

I can see how much he's aged, his brown hair turning grey around his ears, the wrinkles cover every part of his face and neck, somehow, he seems smaller. Smaller in stature, smaller in vain.

'You set this up? Going to the hospital was another one of your plans?' he asks, spinning around to face me.

'Yes, I did. I knew if I got it to circulate around as many people as I could, then whoever was involved at the hospital would phone the rat in the department to ask what the hell was going on. Throw the cat amongst the pigeons, so to speak. Then it would just be a matter of time before I knew who it was.'

Mathews is becoming more irritated. His hand reaches up to his forehead, resting his thumb on his left temple. His fingers harshly running over his forehead, rubbing back and forth faster, his cool stance dropping away from him with a heavy sigh.

'I have warned you off this case so many times now, Bert, to protect you, but you're that fucking hungry for the truth you don't know when to stop. I thought with what happened with Charlotte and Charlie,' Mathews pauses, not sure to go on, as if he knows he is treading on thin ice.

My eyes dim, watching him, curious.

He starts again, 'I thought when this case first started that you would find it too difficult to investigate and I could have some idiot on it instead of you, but you kept pressing more and more when there wasn't anything to press at. Then bloody Alice became obsessed.'

I spring to my feet, throwing the chair back. It smacks to the floor.

'I'm sorry, you know I loved Alice. I didn't mean to disrespect her like that,' Mathews says, dropping his head.

I see the hurt from his words soften him. Lifting the chair from the floor, my hands shaking in anger, I sit back down.

'I got myself into some trouble a few years back, gambling, I lost everything. Gambled our savings, the house, everything. Lily was ready to leave me. I was desperate. I borrowed more money from some dodgy guy that used to hang about the bookies and couldn't pay it back. He offered me a way out. I only meant it to be once. All I had to do was dismiss any allegations that came to the department and make sure everything was legitimate. It was just supposed to be a one-off.'

Mathews pity for himself slowly turns to reckless disregard for what he's done as though it justified it. He continues, 'It was easy money, hard to turn down after the first time. He wouldn't let me turn it down after the first time. Told everyone it was Dad's inheritance money, mind?'

My mind wanders back. I know the exact time he's talking about. I even remember him treating me to a weekend of fishing with that money. Rage burns inside me. I'm a master at keeping a calm front, though. I don't answer; I let him go on.

'This guy had got a girl pregnant. She wouldn't get a termination, no matter how much he tried to talk her into it. It became very nasty between them. She was going to take him for every penny she could get, even threatened with exposing him and his business. He wanted to be rid of her. After a bit of digging, he blackmailed a doctor at the hospital where she was going to have the baby and made sure he made some money off it in return. He had a lot of nasty connections, people with unconventional tastes. Experience taught him you could sell anything in this world for the perfect price if you found the right buyer. The doctor had an injection waiting when the girl went into labour to knock her out, and they took away the baby. When she woke up, the doctor told her the baby had been stillborn. Even used a dead baby from the morgue for her to see. It was too easy to cover up, a lot easier than everyone imagined, and the interest he was getting from underground buyers gave him a rush. He couldn't stop after the first. All I had to do was dismiss any claims, make it look like we were investigating, then take my cut.'

Mathews is like a runaway train. He's giving away too much, too easily. Why? A case of a guilty conscience?

That's not it. I sit, silenced.

'How many times did I warn you to stop trying to be the damn hero! There was only so much I could do to protect you, Bert. Ben doesn't like any loose ends.' Mathews sits back down across from me, his face saddened. 'I can only help you now if you help us, old chap. Where's the girl?' he asks.

I top up the whiskey glass again, still sitting silently. Amazing how after knowing someone closely for forty years, you sit looking at a stranger.

'Would you like to hear something funny, Benji?' I ask before taking another sip of whiskey. 'Alice suspected you. Right from the very beginning of all of this, she told me she thought it involved you. Sometimes I wonder if she should've been the detective and me the schoolteacher.'

Another sip of whiskey disappears down my throat. Two-thirds of the bottle washed down with years of truth. I continue, 'We had so many heated discussions about it. I told her that was completely unthinkable. Even thought it was Fat Larry after he told everyone he was bankrupt until I realised he didn't have the brains to pull it off.'

I take another sip of whiskey while Mathews spectates.

'I always took great pride in being a Detective, a good Detective at that.'

Mathews jumps in, 'Not just good, Bertie, one of the best. You somehow sent that girl and her daughter away with no one catching you. Without even using any of our witness protection contacts.'

I look up from the glass, my body filled with sorrow. 'Not that great to see right through you, though,' I say, and it makes me laugh.

I can see the guilt eating at Mathews. 'Please Bert, where did you send the girl? If you tell me I can help you, I promise. Ben is only looking for the ledgers back. He's promised not to hurt them; you have my word on that.'

Ledgers? Freya must have the other. I'm not shocked, I don't blame her for not trusting me, the vast amount of lies she's had to endure.

My eyes feel heavy; my vision blurring. 'Your word means nothing to me now,' my words slur.

Mathews hangs his head, letting out a heartfelt sigh, and says, 'Then you leave me no choice. You'll be asleep shortly. I injected a little sedative into your whiskey bottle yesterday. Enough to make sure you're comfortable and don't feel any pain. I truly am sorry, old friend. You can be with Alice and the twins, where you belong,' Mathews words are hazy.

I fight to stay awake; my legs won't allow me to stand.

Mathews takes a cloth handkerchief from his trouser pocket, wipes down the chair and table of his fingerprints before slipping on a pair of latex gloves. He searches around the kitchen. Pulling drawers and cupboards open, looking for the ledgers.

'Shit, Bertie, did you let her go with the ledgers?' He hangs his head, muttering that I left him no choice over and over.

I watch, helpless as Mathews releases gas from the cooker hobs and I close my heavy eyes.

Forty

Stephanie

Tears forcefully descend from my eyes, stinging my skin. I stay quiet, my heart is swallowing every word I want to say to him, to the monster in front of me, like it's trying to protect me.

'You know I've always feared women like you, women who think they're equal to men. The type of women who can cause a lot of trouble because their tiny minds can't process when to shut up and stop poking their noses in business that has nothing to do with them. You were a terrible choice for him. I told him that when he met you, that you were a risk,' Bryce speaks, rambling on in his world of hatred.

What is he talking about? Nathan? He didn't know Nathan when we met. He's lying.

Bryce's laugh is disturbing—wicked. The sick bastard is enjoying himself. How did I not see this side of him? He walks to the back of the room, swiftly grabbing the armchair, dragging it along the floor, stopping it right in front of me. He sits down with a thump, letting go of the gun, and rests it on his knee.

His clenched fist raises, slapping me across my face. My hands fly up in defence to shield myself. My left cheek stinging with an aching heat.

'That was to make sure you pay attention, cause I'm about to tell you all about your perfect little Nathan,' he spits, taking the gun from his lap, gripping it with his right hand again.

Squirming uncomfortably on the sofa, I fix my eyes on him. Hanging on his last words. My hands twitching over my chest, ready to shield me from another blow. He's breaking me down bit by bit, torturing me to see how far he can stretch me before I break. Breaking isn't an option whilst I have Ava to protect. I can still hear fragments of her innocent voice playing from her room, it's quiet, but she's there. I can't let him hear her. I need to keep him talking, focused on me.

'Don't you dare speak his name! You're not worthy of speaking his name.'

My eye's draw off him, my face stern. He laughs in return, loud and amused. My body jumps. Why does he find that so amusing?

'I'm not worthy of speaking prince perfects name?' he asks, laughing louder. 'That's a good one, you silly bitch. You have no idea.'

The laughing drowns to a halt, changing to a face of serious irritation. 'It's good to know I taught him well.' He sits back in the chair. 'If you didn't hate him before, you sure as hell will after this.'

I feel like I can ease my defences and breathe now he's sitting back; he can't hit me from there.

'Nathan was a fucked up little homeless thief when I met him, only seventeen years old. I was in London on business when the little dickhead tried to steal my wallet. Safe to say he robbed the wrong guy. I gave him a choice, work for me or go to jail. You're a bright girl, I think you know what one he decided on. I cleaned him up, got him a flat and I must admit he grew into a right looker.'

'NO!' I yell. 'You're lying!'

'Pipe down sweetheart, that version would have been the simple explanation, but you're right, I'm lying.' He leans forward again, and my body clams up. 'I had no desire to be a family man. I got a local girl knocked up when we were both fifteen. Fuck, I still feel the sting of the belt from the beating Mum gave me. Mum was old school, no sex before marriage, that kinda shit. When she finally calmed down, she took the kid in, brought it up as her own, brought it up as my baby brother. Didn't really give the poor girl or her family a choice, she paid them off. The girl and her family weren't the sorts Mother liked to mix with, and she wasn't having her blood brought up by them. And well, the rest is history,' Bryce says, pulling a packet of cigarettes and lighter from his pocket, he sits back again and lights one.

A look of sadness appears in his eyes. 'Nathan, or Nathaniel if we're telling the truth, was my son.'

My head goes blank.

Lies. It can't be true.

When he speaks, I could almost believe him, believe his lies, but that's all they are—lies.

Aren't they?

He pauses for a second, taking my reaction in. And I finally see it, the resemblance. The eyes, Bryce watches me with the same narrowed eyes Nathan used too. The same one-sided smile curled up the left side of his cheek. A deathly shiver sparks down my spine as I process the truth that's been tucked away inside me.

'I was fucking this girl. I say fucking, she would say relationship. Beautiful girl, body to die for. Probably the body you used to have before you let yourself go,' he laughs again and takes a draw of the cigarette.

'She was familiar to me, and she did what she was told. She knew who I was and how I made my living, we had the perfect setup. She was faithful to me, my business. Everything was going great until the stupid cow got knocked up. I don't know what it is with kids. Do you bitches get pregnant and automatically think you can boss us about? I soon put her in her place.'

'Cassandra,' I whisper.

Crazy old lady was Cassandra's Mother. She tried to warn me. The card from the flowers. *This house is full of tragedy.* It was her.

'You killed an innocent girl and made it look like suicide? Her poor Mum, you're an even worse monster than I thought. What did you do to her?'

'That, you will never know,' he says, and laughs loud, amused again. 'No Freya, I'm cutthroat, but not that bad. Actually, you'll be pleased to hear it was your husband that came up with a solution. His mind was fascinating. Once, I found out one of my employees was talking to the police and Nathaniel locked him in his house with wolves he caught in the country, he had been starving them for days. Slashed the poor guy so the wolves would go for the blood. Amazing, isn't it? He always had the best plans.'

'More lies,' I whisper, my eyes serious, I stare directly into his.

He pauses, then leans forward, his head almost touching mines. 'God, I love your eyes, your beautiful big blue fuck me eyes when you're serious. I could have you right here on this sofa. You know that don't you?'

I try to keep my face serious. He can fucking try. If he sees that scares me, he'll do it.

'Maybe later though, I have a story to tell,' he says, taking another draw of the cigarette and leans back into the chair.

'You'd be surprised at how money messes people up, people who apparently have money. And me being the gentleman I am, was always there to help. Nathaniel was having some trouble with a doctor at the hospital paying an enormous debt he owed, which was the hospital Cassandra was going to be having the baby. Nathan suggested getting the doctor to put the baby to sleep and his debt would be cleared off. It was a great idea, but it would leave me a lot of money down. I know a lot of dodgy businessmen and it just so happened you could sell anything for the right price. Even babies, would you believe?' He looks chuffed with this statement.

I remain quiet, still, I can't antagonise him any more than he already is.

'Nathaniel had words with the doctor, and he agreed. I mean, he owed me a six-figure sum that he couldn't pay, so of course, he was going to agree. Cassandra had the baby. The doctor made sure he was there to deliver it, and Nathaniel was there to pick it up. Cassandra was told the baby was stillborn, then the next day the baby was shipped in one of my haulage trucks driven by one of my employees. It had taken a lot of planning but went extremely well to my surprise.'

As much as it kills me, I know it's true. It all makes sense now. Nathan wasn't out to get Mum. The plan all along was for me to get pregnant. His ultimatum was move to England or end our relationship. He needed me in a place where his soldiers were, and Bryce was close. I don't know if I'm angry or heartbroken. Angry at myself that the truth has been inside me all along, and I've chosen to ignore it.

'You're upset, I knew you'd eventually snap. Look at me,' Bryce sneers.

I can't. I don't look up from the floor. I can't look at his monstrous face.

'Freya, look at me, I want to see your heart snapping, piece by piece. I want it to snap the way mines snapped when you stole Nathan from me.'

I don't move, I can't, my body in shock.

My head springs back and I yell in pain. Another cigarette stings my wrist, my skin burning. Tears consume me along with the pain.

'Now see what you made me do, you need to do what you're told.'

I hear footsteps in the hall, Ava!

'I think someone's coming to check on her Mummy. Hello, little one.'

'Don't you speak to her, don't you dare!'

Ava is standing crying at the door; I try to stand, but he pushes me back down.

'Ava, Mummy is fine, go back to your room.'

She stands still, crying for me. I ache so much to console her, but I'm restrained on the sofa with his hand on my neck. 'Ava, please, go back to your room. Mummy will be in soon.'

She quickly turns, running back to her room.

'She looks just like him, but with your eyes. My client will love her.'

'You won't get your disgusting hands on her, you pig!' I spit in his face.

He laughs again, wiping the spit.

'And what are you going to do to stop me? Huh? Nothing, so shut the fuck up. I don't like to be interrupted and I want you to know everything, so you suffer with the truth until you're begging me to kill you and put you out your misery. You were getting in the way, ruining everything and losing me a lot of money. I had to get rid of you. All it would take was a terrible accident, and you were out of the picture. Or you would have been if you weren't so lazy and it wasn't for that bloody kid. I lost a great man. He lost his nerve after he met you. That day you smashed up the hall, I meant what I said, I missed him. He was my son, I loved him. Always wondered what he saw in you, though. After you were dead, he would've caved in and gave me my investment back. I lost a lot of money because of you, but not to worry, I have another investor set up. And he's offering a lot more now.'

He stands and walks to the window and for a split second, I know he's telling the truth, he loved Nathan. I understand now that crash was meant for me. He wanted me dead.

'You would have honestly hated the real him. You know why? Because he was just like me,' he says and lets out another wicked bout of laughter.

My skin prickles as the sound rolls over me. 'Like father, like son, both a pair of pricks,' I mutter.

A blow to my left ear comes from nowhere. The impact in slow motion but the pain is instant. Buzzing firing around my ear, a stinging pain exploding, turning the intensity up. No sound but a piercing buzzing to match my cloudy vision.

He's still in front of me, he's angry. What did he hit me with? The pain is excruciating. The gun, he's cracked me on the side of my head with the gun.

Pain, throbbing pain travelling all over my head.

He cradles my cheeks with his hands, pressing his fingertips into my skin. 'Do you know what that was for? For being a cheeky little cow. Maybe now you'll learn to hold that dirty fucking tongue. You sold my house, my family home, for fuck sake! Nathaniel had to sign your name on the papers to make it look legit, but he died in your place, and then you go and fucking sell it right from under me! All part of the big plan, you see. He was going to try his luck with your Mum. Quite the hottie, or so Nathan told me. He was willing to give her a go, so she would release some money out of that big gorgeous Victorian house, but the genius that he was, got you pregnant and got the money out of your Mum, anyway. It was all going so smoothly until he fell in love and then went and hid the money he got from her. Fucking tragic.'

He lights another cigarette.

Forty-One

Billy

Appearing through the dark straight ahead, I see the glow of red. My foot weighs down on the accelerator to catch up. Its Noah, firing through the drenched slush road to the cabin. The truck swerves hastily to the side of the road, coming to an abrupt halt.

What the fuck is the crazy bastard doing?

I slam on the breaks to stop and pull in behind him. The driver's door swings open. Noah jumps out onto his feet and walks to the back of the truck. His hand raised to his face, shielding his eyes from the headlights of my truck. I swing the driver's door open, jumping out onto the road. The wet mix of mud and snow rains over my jeans as I walk towards him.

'What the fuck are you doing stopping here?' I snap.

He looks pissed, his eyes glazed with anger. A look I haven't seen on Noah. Has my big bro finally manned up? Did it take me going too far to do it? I take a step back.

'If I pull up right outside the cabin and the guys in there it will spook him, then fuck knows what he could do. I need to get in there without him knowing,' Noah spits.

He rummages through the back of his truck, his hands working furiously, throwing objects around. He pauses, turning slowly to face me, holding something covered in a leather sheath.

No way, bro, no fucking way. Dad's old hunting knife.

A seven-inch Damascus-steel blade handcrafted for his thirtieth birthday. His initials engraved into the handle. His gift from Mom. I remember Dad using it on our camping trips. I remember Noah's arm around me as we sat on the stone shore beside the lake, watching Dad skin rabbits. I chose a long time ago to bury those memories.

Why? What the fuck happened to me.

'Turn around and go home, Billy,' Noah tells me, he can't even look at me.

'No way, we do this together.'

'Together!' Noah's voice is harsh, anger fuelled. 'You know nothing about doing things together! You're nothing but a selfish little bastard. Christ knows what he's done to her by now! And Ava!'

I swallow hard at the thought of the brat being hurt.

Noah tucks the knife into the back of his jeans, pulling his sweater down over it. Noah's temper is at a level I never knew was in him, I'm not ashamed to admit he terrifies me. He has Dad's look right before he would head out on business.

'I mean, Christ, what the hell were you thinking Billy! A kid, for fuck's sake! You're that jealous you would see a kid harmed!'

Chills pulse through my veins. Shit, he's right. What the fuck have I done; a fucking kid could be dead because of me. 'I can help fix this, brother. Please, you need me.'

'I stopped needing you a long time ago, little brother. Now turn round, go home, cause as soon as I'm done with him, I'm coming for you.'

Noah turns away from me and sprints for the cabin. What the fuck do I do?

Fuck.

I follow him.

Noah stops, hiding behind the branches of a tree from the side of the road, watching the cabin. I don't stop beside him; I edge forward.

Noah roughly grabs me back. 'Where do you think you're going?' he snaps at me.

I ignore him at first, trying to think of a plan.

'I say we go round back and go into the kitchen,' I tell him.

I can tell from his face he agrees. He won't admit it though; we're both as stubborn as Dad too.

He nods.

Travelling forward, we stick to unlit areas of the road, moving hastily but with caution. Fear is pushing me forward, fear what the dick will do to Stephanie and Ava if we're seen.

Our footsteps silent, springing quickly on and off the ground until we reach the cabin. Dad's hunting training is showing with our movements, and it's like we're kids again. The lights on in the kid's room. Noah stops beneath it.

'Billy boy, here, give me a hand up,' he tells me and points up to the window.

Billy boy, it's been a while since he's called me that.

I crouch down, linking my fingers, cradling Noah's foot, he boosts up to the window. A sigh of relief evaporates from his mouth. In a low voice, he whispers, 'Ava's in her room.'

A sigh of relief releases from my mouth too, I can't believe how relieved I am.

Come on, Billy, stop being a pussy.

'Noah, tap the window, see if she can go to the kitchen,' I whisper.

Noah gives the window a gentle knock, lighting his face up with his phone. 'Go into the kitchen, Ava,' he quietly mouths through her window, then gestures for me to put him down, and he jumps to the ground.

'Quick man, she's gone round back,' Noah says, running as quickly as he can to the back door.

Using the spare keys to the cabin, Noah puts the key to the lock. I can hear Ava behind the door. Noah opens it, puts his hand around and grabs Ava out and into his arms. He squeezes her, kissing her forehead.

I want to do the same. I'm turning into a pussy.

'Where's Mummy, Ava?' Noah asks her, now holding her at arms-length, checking her over. 'We need to get you to Aunt Liv's.'

She's upset, her lips pressed together, her nose scrunched up. The poor kid's petrified.

I need to fix this; I caused it all, it's all on me.

I slip my body inside the door, into the kitchen.

Forty-Two

Stephanie

Bryce's head turns swiftly; his eyes fixed on the doorway. 'Well, if it isn't my new friend,' he says.

What is he talking about?

His hand is guiding my head to look at the doorway he has curiously fixed his eyes on. Billy. My sinking heart has never been so happy to see him. If Billy's here, maybe it means Noah is too, but I don't see him?

'Freya meet my new friend. Billy, wasn't it?' Bryce drops his hand from my face.

Wait a minute, what? They know one another?

My ear feels wet; something is dripping from my ear. I run my fingers over it. It's blood. I feel sleepy. My body desperately wants to shut down and sleep. I try my hardest to fight it.

'I don't understand. Billy, what's going on?' I ask, my hands trying to support my head.

Billy doesn't answer; his face turned away from me. He can't even look at me. What has he done? Is he in on this? I try to focus my eyes back on Bryce.

'Ah, don't you know, Freya? Billy was the one who kindly told me where you were staying after I bumped into him today in town.'

My head hastily turns back to Billy, his eyes now locked on mine. 'What? Why would you do that?' I ask angered.

Billy knows nothing of my past, but to tell a complete stranger where I was is just nasty. That fucking nasty bastard. He's that bitter towards me he's put Ava and me in this position.

Ava! Oh God, I can't hear her anymore.

My heart flutters, missing beats with fear. He shrugs his shoulders non-apologetically. He's brought his shitty attitude with him.

'Noah is going to fucking kill you,' I tell him, anger boiling my blood. 'You piece of shit!'

'Now, now, is that any way for a lady to speak? After the things we did, I know you ain't no lady though,' Bryce says. His hand running up the inside of my leg, my legs shrugging him off in defence. 'So, tell me, Billy, what the fuck are you doing here? And who's Noah?'

Billy enters the room, cautiously straddling over to the log fire. 'Just wanted to check you got the bitch, okay?' Billy answers, stopping to turn around, rubbing his palms together as though thinking of his next move. 'And no, before you ask, Noah doesn't know I'm here.'

He turns to face Bryce and tells him, 'Noah, her boyfriend, is my arsehole brother who she blew me off for. Been waiting on payback.'

Bryce's smile widens, and he laughs, 'I see some things never change, making enemies wherever you go. Tell me, Billy, as a thank you for your help today, would you like a job? I like your I don't give a fuck about anyone attitude. Could do with a few more men like you.'

This offer seems to grab Billy's attention. 'Hm, what kinda work?' he asks.

'The work where you make more money in one trip than you would in a lifetime. And you'd be away from this hellhole.'

Billy's eyes narrow, and he rubs his palms together again. That piece of shit is seriously considering Bryce's offer.

Why is the pain in my head so intense, I can barely keep focus?

'Billy, do me a favour and watch the bitch 'til I check on the kid.'

OH GOD PLEASE NO!

'The brat's asleep, I saw her when I came in,' Billy answers.

Is she really asleep? I can't believe a word that comes out of his mouth; he's scum. My heart can't relax until I know for sure she's safe.

'Well, I suppose she can wait until I've dealt with you.' Bryce stands to his feet and lets out a sigh, his arms folded over his chest. 'What do you suggest I do with her?'

Billy rests against the fire surround, looking at me. His face is creeping with badness.

'I'm up for anything, man, what did you have in mind?' Billy asks, his eyes lighting up, he's enjoying this too. He's just like Bryce!

I'm going to die here, failing majorly with my promise to protect Ava. I can't think straight; the side of my face is pulsing with pain. I'm going to die in this cabin alone, and they'll take my child away to sell to the highest bidder. All thanks to him, that bastard Nathan! My wonderful fucking husband!

I hate him! I'm glad he's dead. Bastard!

My eyelids are so heavy; maybe if I close them for a few minutes, it will help.

'I've just had a fantastic idea!' Bryce chirps up, excited. 'Billy, my friend, come here. We'll call this your unofficial interview.'

Billy strides towards him, smirking and full of uncertain confidence.

'Take this,' Bryce tells him and throws his left arm around his shoulders, stretching out his right hand holding the gun. Gesturing for Billy to take it from him.

Billy freezes, staring at the gun.

'How much did it piss you off when she picked your brother over you?' Bryce teases him.

Billy's eyes widen, focusing on Bryce's words.

'Doesn't it infuriate you he gets to fuck her whenever he wants, and you don't?'

Billy glances back down to the gun, without hesitating he slides his hands over it and lifts it from Bryce.

'Don't you think she deserves punishment for thinking she's too good for us?' Bryce keeps going.

Billy's voice low, full of complete certainty, he answers, 'She does.'

My body's exhausted, fighting off the pain.

I'm going to die.

Forty-Three

Noah

Ava's safe with Aunt Liv, but my heart pounds and my legs shake as I creep inside the back door as quietly as possible. I reach into the back of my jeans, gripping the hunting knife, removing the leather sheath. My back presses up against the wall of the hall as I slide down it towards the front room. I can see the living room window, the end of the couch.

Low-pitched voices, male voices mix between the air, but I can't hear Steph. My body aches with panic.

Another slow step forward, Stephanie's slumped on the couch, she's not moving. The beating of my heart thumping in an erratic rhythm.

Fuck.

Another slow step forward. Billy is standing with a gun pointed at Stephanie. I press back against the wall, searching for a solution.

Think, man, think!

Aunt Liv phoned the sheriff, Garett should be on his way, I don't have time to wait.

'Pull the trigger, Billy, she deserves it. You know she does,' the guy is still coaxing Billy.

I know my brother doesn't need a lot of coaxing.

I peer inside the room again. Billy throws the guy's arm off his shoulder, and swings the gun in his direction, pointing it in his face. The guy's arms fire into the air in defence.

That's it, Billy boy, doing well, bro.

'What the fuck are you doing, Billy?' the guy scoffs.

'Did you think you could stand and fill my head with shit and then hand me a gun and I would actually shoot? My heads all fucked up on its own without you spitting bullshit at me.' Billy's got the guy nervous. 'Big mistake man, I came here to distract you while my brother got the brat out,' Billy laughs. 'That's right, while you were talking complete shit, my brother was taking her away. Probably called the sheriff on your ass too.'

Hold your nerve, Bill.

I glance again at Steph; she's still in the same position, her face covered in blood.

Shit. Please be okay, please God, let her be okay.

'Pay back's a bitch, ain't it? And I ain't your friend,' Billy spits.

The floor creaks under my foot, drawing everyone's attention to the door. The guy pounces on Billy, the gun goes off, and they fall to the floor. Both wrapped in one another.

'Drop the fucking gun!' I shout, noticing the weapon in the guy's hand. I try to grab the guy off Billy, but the gun goes off again. Billy's movements slow, he stops fighting back.

He's hit!

'Billy!'

I smash the knife into the guy, his arm, but I'm not sure. He screams in pain, throwing himself onto his back, something in me snaps, every bit of repressed anger.

I drop the knife and punch him, again, then again. Blood splatters across the room, there's something animal in me that even I can't control.

Dull sirens sound in the background, growing louder and louder. The gun in Bryce's hand swings at my head, I duck, sending me tumbling to the ground. Bryce stands, aims the gun towards Stephanie and fires, I try to block him, try to get the gun, but someone's arms wrap around my waist, pulling me to my feet.

'Noah, I got you, son. I got you,' Sheriff Payne yells, holding me, trying to calm me.

'Billy's hit, he's hit!' I fight until Garett releases me and I fall to the floor beside Billy.

A pool of blood circles the floor under his motionless body, his eyes open, staring up at me. A paramedic falls to his knees beside

Billy, ripping his shirt open. I watch anxiously as he works on him, trying with all his power to save him.

He stops and falls back onto his legs, looking across at me, sorrow in his eyes. 'He's gone, he's taken a shot in his heart. There's nothing I can do. He's gone.'

'No. He can't be, no!' I snap back at the paramedic.

I don't believe it. I refuse to. A swarm of emotions possessing me.

The other paramedic shouts in the background, 'This one's still alive.'

Stephanie!

I slide over to the sofa, she's unconscious, but she's breathing. The side of her face is badly marked, congealed blood mixed in her hair, but she's alive.

'He fired at her, but I think he missed?' My hands work furiously over her body, trembling. Checking for wounds.

'Open gunshot wound to her right thigh,' the paramedics confer between one another, whispering as they help her.

She's alive, thank fuck man, she's alive.

'Fuck, that's some crap news,' Bryce says, laughing, as he's pulled by his hands, bound by cuffs from the living room.

His face disguised with blood, his white shirt now brazen red.

'What the fuck did you say?' I jump to my feet. I want to kill this guy. I want my knife to rip him from neck to navel, gut him like the beast he is.

He laughs sardonically as he disappears from the cabin.

Forty-Four

Stephanie

'So, Freya huh?' Noah asks.

He hasn't left my side, his face was the first thing I saw when I woke up, and yet I can't look at him.

'In a life that's long gone, yes,' I answer.

Noah drops his head, focusing on his feet as though his next words were going to jump up from them. My eyes fixed on the ceiling of the hospital room, as they have been since I woke up from surgery. Not so easy to move around with a full leg plaster cast on.

The bullet bypassed my arteries, hitting some soft flesh and muscle. The surgeon said we won't know how much nerve damage it's caused until I get back on my feet. Said I was really lucky, could have lost my leg, apparently?

That would have been a small consolation considering Billy lost his life. He lost his life because I came here to live, I put him and his family in danger. He was a dick, yes, but didn't deserve to die.

'What's happened to Bryce?' I ask, my voice hoarse, my neck bruised, from him choking me.

'He's being treated for a stab wound in a secure ward here. Garett said they're holding him until the FBI get here and take over.'

FBI? Fuck. I wonder if I should... no, I can't even think about that right now.

'Did you know?' he murmurs, his eyes still focused on the hospital floor.

I don't answer him. I'm not entirely sure I know what he's asking about? If I knew my dead husband was a stranger? A son to a psychopath? If I knew I was part of their vulgar plan? If I knew how much danger I was in? Or if I knew about the tiny creature that has been growing inside me?

No is the answer to them all.

He lifts his head, and his eyes meet mines, he asks, 'About the baby?'

Our baby, the tiny creature growing inside me, our baby. I can't process all this, I'm not ready to talk about it.

I shake my head and lean back against the soft pillow. Noah stands to his feet. He doesn't stand tall with his head high above his broad shoulders. His body slumps in grief and sorrow, I badly want to hold him, to tell him I'm sorry but again I can't find the words.

'I'll let you get some rest. I'll come back later with Ava.'

As I watch him walk from the room, I lie still, empty with sadness. My heart is telling me to make him come back, but my head won't let me. I want to be alone, including away from Ava. I've done enough damage here. She'd be better off without me. Noah would have been better off if I had kept my distance. He wouldn't have lost his brother. He's angry with me, I know he is. His stature tells me everything I need to know.

I've made this mistake before. I let Nathan walk out once without telling him how I felt, and I never saw him again. I can't afford to make the same mistake. I loved Nathan. Or at least I thought I did. I loved a person who didn't exist. Noah's real, he's been the realest thing in my life. I can't let him go.

'Noah please, please don't go,' I plead with him to come back. 'Please don't leave me, please.'

He hurries back to my side, his arms wrap around me, tenderly. I know he's scared he'll hurt me.

'I'm so sorry about Billy, please Noah, please forgive me. I know you're angry at me, I'm so, so, sorry.'

It's hard to absorb that Billy died because of my past. The tears flow fiercely. There is not one part of my body that doesn't ache, but not as much as my heart.

'Shh, Billy died because he was a selfish fucking idiot. If anything happened to you, or Ava… if you had died…' He sits back down on the chair beside my bed, taking my hand in his.

He continues, 'I'm not angry for what happened, I'm angry I couldn't protect you. You make me happy, happier than I thought I deserved, and you drive me insane but keep my feet on the ground. You fill me with rage and fill me with love. I can't read you. I don't know what you're thinking, or what you've been through, but I know what you need, but you're too scared to ask for. I'm all over the place with you, but there is nowhere else I'd rather be. Just, please, cut the shit and tell me the truth, please.'

His eyes are pleading with me, he's hurting too. For the child he never thought he could have, for a brother that stopped being his brother a long time ago.

'Okay,' I whisper, I can't lie to him anymore.

I tell him everything. Every little detail. I try to look strong, confident, show him I'm not ashamed of what I had to do. Mentally I'm preparing myself for him to look at me in disgust, for him to stand up and leave me.

A couple of hours pass, Noah knows everything, and I wait for him to speak, but he remains silent.

So do I.

It's like I've just woken up, you know, like my life the last few years has been a dream. Only, I've not woken up as myself, on the outside, yes, but in my mind, the long journey of the dream has changed my soul. It's changed me back to the little girl I was before I realised how wicked men could be to women. Before my Father made me hate men, before I used them for nothing but meaningless sex.

Noah helped me wake up from that dream. I owe him a love I'm not worthy of offering or receiving.

'You have a past that isn't perfect and a person inside you, you've lost. Together we'll get her back,' Noah says, his cheeks wet, his eyes red and watery.

'I don't want the old Freya back. I want to start fresh. If you'll have me?'

His answer feels like it takes a lifetime to come and I'm begging him to say yes.

He nods, and that is good enough for me.

It's bright outside today, I lay on the sofa, watching the stillness of the weather from the window. The light icy breeze from outside creeps through the open window, gliding around the room. It blows through my hair, brushing my neck like the touch of someone's hand drifting over my skin.

'Steph, you okay?' Noah asks, standing in the lounge's doorway.

I can't face him. I killed his brother.

I've been living at Olivia's since I left hospital two weeks ago. It's best this way. I'm struggling to get around. My body still battered and bruised. I need help to look after Ava. Or that's what I'm telling everyone. I can't bring myself to set foot back in the cabin. Where Billy... where Billy died on the floor, because of me.

I should be the one who died.

My mood dies a little each day I wake up and realise it wasn't all a bad dream.

Do I even have the right to be dwelling on everything after Billy died from the trouble I brought here? He was the one who told Bryce where we were, after all, but still didn't deserve what happened. Olivia lost her nephew and Noah lost his brother. Regardless of how awful he was to everyone around him.

'Freya?'

I turn to look at him, shocked. That name rolling off his tongue is alien to me, like he's talking to another person in the room, not me?

'Please don't call me that, don't call me her.'

His eyes mirror my hurt, the damage to us both. We're more connected than ever.

'You know, one day you'll find yourself again and I hope that day you'll also forgive yourself.'

I watch him as he turns away from me.

Olivia's in the kitchen with Ava. Noah starts cooking breakfast. No one has an appetite, but I believe he's trying to keep things normal for Ava like it's the only thing he can do right now, and for that I'm appreciative.

'She's blaming herself for everything, Noah. I'm worried about her,' I hear Olivia whisper or try to, but I hear every word.

Noah doesn't answer straight away, but I know he feels the same.

'I can't remember the last time she ate anything. This isn't good for the baby,' she tells Noah.

The door between the lounge and the kitchen sits ajar, and I watch as Noah's body gently falls back, leaning against the work-top.

A sigh of sadness exhales from his mouth, 'None of this is her fault, she just needs time.'

'We all do sweetheart, but Stephanie has been through so much more than anyone. I fear she may never come back from this.' Olivia stops moving around, and I hear her say, 'Let me try speaking to her.'

She walks from the kitchen into the hall, and I tense, but she walks past the lounge and up the stairs. I wonder what she's doing?

A few moments later, the door creeks further open and Olivia peers her head in.

'Stephanie, could I come in for a moment? I have something for you.'

There's a brown envelope in her hand. I don't feel like speak-ing to her, I'm sickened at myself for thinking that way.

I can't face her. I haven't even said sorry to her for what's hap-pened. She's the one person I truly hate myself for letting down.

Olivia sits beside me on the sofa, careful not to disturb my leg, her gentle smile still the same as always, comforting.

'Why are you not angry with me, Olivia?' My eyes cloud with tears.

'Oh, sweetheart, I could never be angry with you. All that has happened, not one bit of it is your fault. I love you like a daughter, and Ava. I thank my blessings every day for having you both in my life.'

She places her hand around my shoulder, sitting me up and pulls me close to her. She holds me for a long time, and I know then she has needed this connection between us as much as I have. I wish with all my being I could believe her, but I've ripped everyone's lives apart.

'I have a letter from Albert. He sent it shortly after he called me and hired the cabin for you.'

I lie back down, shocked.

'He asked that I only gave it to you if anything bad were to happen. I hope now it gives you some comfort and helps you heal because you truly deserve to forgive yourself.'

She places a kiss on my head and leaves me with the envelope, heading back to the kitchen with Ava and Noah.

I don't think I want to open it. I've had enough of my past. I don't see how this will help me move on. Surely it can't be anything worse than what's happened, though?

I wipe the tears from my eyes and run my finger under the fold of the envelope, ripping it open. A flood of emotions takes over me when I see it's handwritten by Albert.

Hello Freya.

First, there will be no point in asking if you are well because if you were, then you wouldn't be reading this. I can't imagine what you think of me right now, but please believe me when I say I'm truly sorry for not telling you the truth. I wanted to protect you and I quickly realised it was the truth you needed protecting from. After our first meeting, I knew how vulnerable you were, I saw through the tough girl act straight away. There was no way I could have told you everything.

Your husband, Nathan, came to me for help like I explained to you, but there was a little more to it. He had known Bryce long before he met you; they were family. His job was meeting girls and long story short, conning them out of money, getting them pregnant and you know the rest. Bryce knew certain members of my department were becoming suspicious, so he sent Nathan further afield. That's when he met you. (I'm still not sure who his informant is in my department. I'm currently working on it but by the time you read this I guess that I will know.) He told me he could get every detail of business transactions and all employees in exchange for a new life for you, Clara and himself. He wanted out. He wasn't willing to give Clara up to Bryce. We had met a few times to make plans. I had contacts who could help give new identities. It was too risky asking anyone in the department for help. The morning he died was a few days before you were all due to be relocated. I recall him telling me don't send my wife anywhere hot because she only likes sunny places in brief spells, and she will spend the rest of our lives nagging me. Then I remembered Valdez. My wife Alice and I used to visit there every year since we were married, and like you, she hated hot places. When I first met you, it shocked me how similar you were to her. I saw a spark in you that my wife once had and if our daughter Charlotte hadn't of had such a short life, she would have been like you. Feisty. Through all my years as a Detective I never once grew personally attached to anyone; I was always professional. Olivia, landlady of the cabin, will look after you both extremely well. We have arranged everything you need and also a car. I don't have any family to leave my money to, so I hope you don't mind. I wanted to tell you about Nathan so many times, I just couldn't bring myself to do it. But Freya, he loved you more than you could have possibly imagined. He fell in love with you and was doing everything in his power to protect you both. Please forgive him, please forgive us both.

Also, one last thing, I need you to contact Lawrence Franklin; I have written his telephone number on the inside of the envelope. Tell him Bertie sent you for the favour he owes me. Tell him I'm cashing it in. Alice and I met him in Valdez and became good friends. He works for the FBI. You must phone him, Freya, and tell him everything. I know he will do his best to help. Otherwise, all the sacrifices were for nothing. It's one of the primary reasons I sent you to Valdez; he lives in Anchorage. Don't speak to anyone other than him, no one. I wish you both well, Freya and Clara. You are forever in my thoughts.

Albert.

Tears sting my eyes, and I blink furiously to clear my vision. My chest is expanding, and I feel like I'm suffocating.

My heart aches. All the times I thought I was heartbroken, I was wrong. This feeling is like no other I have felt before.

The kitchen has gone quiet, they're listening at the door. I need out of here; I need to get away. I can't chance hurting anyone else, they will all be better off without me.

I throw myself from the sofa, the thud of the floor sends shock waves of pain through my leg and I scream in pain.

Noah appears beside me, trying to lift me, and I try to push him away, but he scoops me into his arms, back onto the sofa.

'I need to get away, everything is my fault. I'm toxic, Noah, I'm venom. Everything I touch goes to shit,' I tell him, my voice choked, I'm crying, hard.

'And you thought trying to disappear would solve everything?' Noah snaps back.

He's angry, pacing the floor, his hand roughly running through his hair. I thought he was angry in the hospital, but now I realise it was sorrow in the hospital.

'You don't understand–'

'What? What don't I understand? What it's like to lose someone? What it's like to have something you thought you could never have dangled in front of you, then ripped away? You would really be that heartless that you could leave Ava behind?'

He's breathing hard, faster and faster with anger. 'I'm angry that you think you're in this shit alone!' Then his voice lowers as he drops to his knees beside me, 'I'm hurting because I'm painfully in love with you, and you're hurting and that's the worst because I know no matter what I say, or what I do, it won't make anything better for you. I just want everything to be better for you, but I, I just don't know how to.'

His head drops heavily into his hands as he exhales a crushing sigh, a sigh of defeat. I push myself forward towards the edge of the couch. Reaching out to Noah, I grab his hands from his face and pull him closer to me. Noah looks at me, really looks at me, the real me. Not the shell of the person I've become.

'I learned a lot about love over the years, and that was thanks to people who never really loved me. They showed me how someone shouldn't be loved. And that made my heart shrink. I learned the hard way I needed people around me who loved like I did. Someone who would love me for me. And you, you're the same. You need someone to show you how to be loved, even on your down days and not just the good. You need to realise you are not broken, Steph.'

'I feel there's nothing of the old me left inside Noah, almost like Freya wasn't a real person. Just someone I had memories of meeting in a previous life. It's horrible, you know, to realise I lost myself somewhere along the road a long time ago. And I can't even pinpoint when it happened. I'm lost, I don't know where to go. The one thing I know is I'm not okay. My heart has been crushed more times than any one person can live with. So, I'm broken, Noah, in mind, and my body. It's taken me a long time to settle knowing that there is no quick fix to being happy. A good starting point is to wake up every day and be thankful for being given the gift to live another day. Especially with someone you want to feel alive with. But I can't be thankful for living another day when someone lost their life because of me.'

Noah pulls himself closer to me, so close I can feel his heart beating heavy in his chest, the trembling of his arms, his warm breath on my head.

'You have more to live for than most, and she loves you unconditionally no matter who you are, or what you have been through because you're her mummy. She needs you more than you know. I need you both more than you know,' Noah tells me, spilling his heart out.

He's right. I need them both more than life too. I squeeze him tight and he squeezes back. My hands grip him violently. I don't want to let him go, ever. I don't want to let go of my real love.

'Noah, I love you. I owe you my life and I want to have this baby with you. I can't do it on my own.'

My grip grows tighter on him.

'You don't have to,' he whispers. 'I'm yours, forever.'

Epilogue

Who am I?

I called Lawrence Franklin as Albert told me to. I told him about how I knew Albert. He laughed when I told him this was Albert cashing in his favour, and when he asked how he was, I told him what had happened. After that, I knew I had his attention. As though helping me is now personal to him. It will make his job easier since he already has Bryce in custody, I hope.

He's agreed to visit me at Olivia's house. Getting out and about with a full leg plaster cast isn't the easiest of tasks. It's a mission to even go to the bathroom, and also a little embarrassing too.

Noah's upstairs, which puts me at some ease, Ava is out shopping with Olivia, baby shopping I believe. A bit early for all that for me, I'm only ten weeks.

I wonder how they will feel when I tell them I would like to name the baby Billy, regardless of boy or girl?

My palms are sweating; my fingers stick together as I fidget and make a fist over and over. FBI Agent Lawrence Franklin is very intimidating. Tall, exceptionally well built, and if he weren't here as a friend, then I'd be terrified. I'm not terrified, but I still push myself further back into the sofa, hoping it will swallow me up.

Why am I getting so nervous? I need to get a grip, he's here to help me, and this is the right thing to do. It's what Albert wanted me to do. It's the only thing I can do now.

We chat, he asks questions, as though I'm the one being investigated.

'I don't know how much I can do from my end with no solid evidence. If that ledger was destroyed in the fire, then we're at a dead-end, I'm afraid,' he explains in his solid American accent, stronger than Noah's.

'And if it wasn't destroyed?'

He leans forward and rests his hands on the worn coffee table, intrigued at my question.

'Do you know why I owe Bertie a favour? How we met? Years ago, when Bertie and Alice were here on vacation for New Year, my wife and I were attacked by three men walking home one night after having a meal in town. One of the men held me, whilst the other knocked me unconscious. The third man pushed my wife into the harbour after striking her in the face, and they all ran off. When I came to in the hospital, I found out a strange Englishman saved my wife and my unborn son. He dived right under the ice and pulled her out. If it weren't for Bertie, I would've lost them both that night. I owe him everything. It's how we met, and I've held him a close friend since. So, is there something you want to tell me? If that ledger wasn't destroyed, then I can bring Bertie's killers to justice a lot faster. It would give me great pleasure in doing so.'

I don't answer right away. I don't know this man, but I need to put every bit of trust I have left in him like Albert asked me to.

'If we're going to help each other, I need you to be honest with me. Please?' his eyes plead with me, and I see the hurt in them for Albert.

After everything I've told him, surely, he can understand why I'm so cautious. I try to keep an open mind.

'The ledger wasn't destroyed in the fire,' I say, gazing at him, taking in his reaction.

'How can you be certain of that?' his voice low, stunned.

'Because I have it.'

ABOUT THE AUTHOR

K T Lyon

KT Lyon is the girl who loves being lost in an excellent book, oblivious to surroundings and satisfied with a break from reality. That break being a psychological thriller, the more morbid the better, she says. She's a sucker for a soppy romance too, though.

Writing a novel has been a lifelong dream of hers, now a reality with her debut novel Newborn Deceit complete.

She loves to take part in creative writing courses and her cure for writer's block is writing anything random that fills her thoughts, turning them into mini anecdotes. She doesn't like to waste creativity.

KT loves to travel with her husband and two daughters and suffers from withdrawals if some form of holiday isn't being planned. When she isn't travelling, she's at home in Stirling, Scotland.

Printed in Great Britain
by Amazon